BLACK SHEEP

For the former DJ Carbon
and all others who dared to rewrite the script

JANETTA OTTER-BARRY BOOKS

Black Sheep copyright © Frances Lincoln Limited 2013
Text copyright © Na'ima B Robert 2013
Extract from *Monarchy* copyright © Indigo Williams
reproduced by kind permission of the author

First published in Great Britain in 2013 by
Frances Lincoln Children's Books, 3 Torriano Mews,
Torriano Avenue, London NW5 2RZ
www.franceslincoln.com

A catalogue record for this book is available from the British Library.

ISBN 978-1-84780-235-4

Printed and bound by CPI Group (UK) Ltd, Croydon, CR0 4YY

1 3 5 7 9 8 6 4 2

BLACK SHEEP

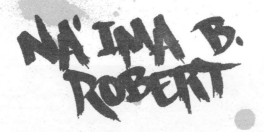

NA'IMA B. ROBERT

F

FRANCES LINCOLN
CHILDREN'S BOOKS

Just so long as you know
That these roads
Are our roads,
So we will fight for these streets,
Yes, we will die for these streets
Because they are the only thing
That have ever given us a place
In this monarchy,
The closest thing I have to an identity
So yes, I will die to be me –
I may have been born a pauper
But ya dun know I'ma die a king.

Extract from *Monarchy* by Indigo Williams

Black Sheep

DWAYNE

"Yuh wort'less, Dwayne!" Mum's shrill voice cut through my sleep. I rubbed my eyes, all confused. What was with the harsh wake-up call? "Yuh wort'less, just like yuh father!"

Then I remembered. Mr Douglas from the school had called the night before: just a short, hurried phone call to tell my mum, Alicia Kingston, that I was failing at school and that, at this rate, I wouldn't even get enough GCSEs to drive a dump truck. Mr Douglas had said that they would be entering me for the lower-tier exams in as many subjects as possible but even then I would be lucky to pass. Screw him. Who cared anyway?

Mum was vex' and refused to speak to me all evening, making sure she scraped the pot out before she went to bed so that I'd have to eat peanut-butter sandwiches for dinner. Please! Hadn't she ever heard of ordering pizza? But I guess as far as she was concerned, I didn't have money for take-away. Which was fine by me. The less she knew about my finances, the better, y'get me.

Mum kicked the pizza boxes to the side and glared down at me, her hands on her hips. But as I looked across at her, I caught sight of my new kicks. They hadn't come easy but, damn, they looked good. I was gonna wear them on stage at the club on the weekend – they were the fiercest piece of footwear I'd seen in a long time.

"And take yuh shoes off me sofa, y' hear me, boy?" Mum sure knew how to pull an angry face. Frowning, her light-brown eyes blazing, she glared at me, her black, black son, lying on her sofa, her hard-won, highly prized leather sofa that she had bought in instalments from DFS. I didn't move.

"Dwayne!" she barked. "Yuh no hear good? I said get yuh blasted trainers down from me sofa!"

I rolled my eyes and let out a loud sigh and cussed – but only under my breath. I wasn't in the mood for a slap so early in the morning. I took my feet down from the sofa and looked up at her, trying to look like

I didn't care, one eyebrow raised. That was the most I dared.

"There," I said. "Happy now?"

But Mum just kissed her teeth and stomped out of the room, muttering, "Only God knows where he got the money to buy dem tings..."

Mum? Happy? Of course she wasn't happy. She was never happy with me. As far as she was concerned, I couldn't do anything right. I was wort'less, as she said, just like my father.

And true say, I was just like my father in so many ways. For a start, I was just too fly, y'get me, the hottest thing to hit the streets in 2005. I turned 16 that year and I just knew it was going to be a good year for me. I was a sweet boy like my dad, with the silky smooth tongue, all the lyrics, all the lines. But that was probably why Mum hated me so much. My looks, my dark skin, my street style all reminded her of him. When she looked at me, it was as if she didn't see me, Dwayne. She saw someone who was gonna break hearts, just like my dad broke hers.

Even sixteen years later, she hadn't forgotten how he made her pregnant at seventeen, then left her standing at the altar. Ruined her life. Left her with me, growing inside her, making the white dress that she borrowed from Nan too tight around the middle. All the neighbours could see, she says, and they talked about her for ages.

Allow them, man, why should you care if people ain't got nothin' better to do than chat yuh business? Free that. I didn't know my dad. Didn't business about him, where he was, what he was doing. I had my life, he had his, y'get me. It's just that Mum's cusses always brought him back up in my face: they were like a soundtrack, as regular as her going to church on a Sunday.

But my soundtrack was way, way more than the beef between my mum and me. My soundtrack had rhythm. My soundtrack had rhyme. My soundtrack had *beats*. Man, when the beats got inside me, I didn't think about Mum, or the bruck-down council estate we called home, or my mad teachers, or the Larkside mandem from the estate across the way. All I thought of was the beats and the rhymes and the way they came together to create something lyrical, powerful, *magical*. I would spit anywhere: in the school playground, on the estate, at raves, house parties, MC battles, anywhere where they would pass me the mic. I wanted to make my mark, y'get me. I was Boy Wonder, future star.

Oh, yeah. Then there was Misha, that piece of

chocolate-fudge-coloured, sun-kissed sweetness: my girl. She was part of my soundtrack too, for sure.

I had met her at a rave six months before, in West London. In a crowded room full of man flashing cash, sweating in their silk suits, and gold-diggers trying to score a play, Misha stood out as a class act. I don't know if it was the way her smile lit up the room or the way she turned away from big players like my main man, Tony, to talk to me. Whatever it was, I couldn't keep my eyes off her. I felt myself being pulled towards her, magnetised, mesmerised, *hypnotised*, like the whole party was nothing but a mixtape of bodies and movement, noisy, unreal, making no sense. It was like we were the only two people in the world, that we were all there was. I know it sounds crazy, but that's how it felt, for real.

That was the beginning.

✧ ✧ ✧

She gave me her number.

"I don't normally do this sort of thing," she said, scribbling the mobile number on the back of a taxi-cab card.

I could feel myself getting well into her, man – she was just so different. The way she spoke – all posh and proper, but a bit naughty at the same time; the way she looked straight into my eyes, not all shifty; the way she asked me about myself as if she really wanted to know.

Down my sides, girls don't talk much sense, not the ones I know anyway. Chirpsing them is like playing a soundtrack on a loop: you say the same tired chat-up lines and they respond with the same tired responses, loving themselves too much, trying to play hard to get. But you can always get them in the end, if you still want to after listening to their foolishness for most of the night.

Girls can be divided into two groups: skets and neeks. The skets are just plain nasty – and I *don't* do nasty – and the neeks aren't worth bothering about. But Misha? She confused me; I just couldn't place her. She was like a girl from another world.

"So why're you breaking your own rules?" I had to ask, with a cheeky grin.

You know what she did? She looked me in the eye and smiled. "You seem like a nice guy," she said – just like that! Then her friends pulled her away, out to the cab that was waiting to take them back to where they were staying.

I was in shock, for real. Almost one hundred per

cent sure that no one, no girl, had ever called me a 'nice guy' before. I shook my head and smiled.

'This one's going to be interesting, blud.'

'Ya dun know!'

Then I felt a heavy arm across my back and caught a whiff of *Paco Rabanne:* it was my mate, Jukkie.

"Oooh!" he growled. "Get a load of that t'ickness, bwoi! Man'd like to mash dat, one time!" Jukkie was proper drooling as he watched Misha and her friends get into the cab.

"I beg you shut up, man!" I sneered, shaking his arm off. I was proper vex'; I didn't want Jukkie and his nasty self getting in my way. And I didn't like the way he was eyeing Misha up either. "No girl in her right mind would want you and you know it, man. So fall back!"

"What you sayin', blud?" Jukkie's eyes were bloodshot and the whisky on his breath was so strong that it made my eyes water. Not the best time to pick a fight.

Then Tony, Jukkie's older brother, stepped to us and put a hand on each of our shoulders. "Easy, man, easy! No point getting into a fight about it. They've gone now, anyway."

That was Tony, man, always there to take the edge

off things, to calm things down. Tony was a don, a proper don. I had bare respect for him. I'd lost count of the number of times I had wished he was my brother as well as Jukkie's. But then, being in RDS meant that he *was* my big brother, still. And it helped that he took my side against Jukkie, at least some of the time.

"And where's your girl, anyway?" Tony asked Jukkie. "How come you're stepping on Dwayne's toes, entering his *territory*?"

Jukkie grunted and took a drink from his plastic cup. "Allow her, man. She's been takin' bare liberties lately. Had to slap her up, teach her a lesson, y'get me."

Jukkie was the kind of guy who got mad angry when he was drunk: it was time to get him home. "Come we get out of here, man," I said, taking Jukkie by the arm. "Tony, you got your keys?"

Sweetness

DWAYNE

I thought about Misha all the way home in the car. As soon as I got into my room, my palm started to itch. I needed to call her, to make sure she hadn't given me a fake number or something. I dialled the number she had written on the card.

"Hello?"

"Misha?"

"Yes, who's this?"

"It's Dwayne... we met at the party?"

"Oh my God," she laughed. "You're supposed to wait at least twenty-four hours before calling me, you know, to make me get all worried that you aren't going to call!"

I was embarrassed but I laughed, still. "I just wanted to check your number, innit."

"Right..." I just knew she could tell I was bluffing. Then she said, "Call me tomorrow, OK?"

"OK, yeah... yeah, sure..."

"You sure you can wait that long?" Her voice was teasing and I could hear her friends laughing in the background.

"Now you're takin' liberties, man," I growled and came off the phone.

That wasn't my usual style, letting the girl know that I was eager and that. But she had told me to call and, to tell you the truth, I was almost going crazy waiting until the next afternoon. And when I rang, she laughed and told me, "Congratulations," saying I had waited "a respectable amount of time" before phoning. I felt stupid, but kinda proud in a silly way. I could tell that she liked me. Man can just tell these things, y'get me.

MISHA

Dwayne was not my type, not by any stretch of the imagination. And yet, there was something about him.... He was so funny, so different. I began to feel quite giddy whenever I saw his name flash up – but I had to remind myself: I am Misha Reynolds and

I don't do 'lovesick teenager'. I will play hard to get. I will not let him charm me. If he puts one foot wrong, he's out. Simple. I've got things to do – no sixteen-year-old 'sweetboy' is getting in the way of that.

At first I actually refused to meet him. I told him I wasn't sure that we were compatible, that I didn't go out with random guys. But after a couple of weeks I decided to give it a try. To be honest, I didn't expect much: a movie, a meal at Pizza Hut, maybe. But Dwayne surprised me.

"Let's go Battersea Park," he said on the phone.

"Yeah?" I smiled, thinking, 'this is different.'

"Yeah, the weather's nice, innit? I thought we could chill there... unless you wanna catch a movie." I heard him catch his breath then – maybe he was worried that he had read me wrong, thinking maybe I would have preferred to do something ordinary, safe. Not knowing that Battersea Park was one of my favourite places.

"No, no!" I protested. "Battersea Park sounds perfect."

We met at the gate, shy and hesitant, as if we were seeing each other for the first time.

"You look nice," he nodded, smiling the smile I remembered so well.

I giggled then and turned away.

"Hey, don't go all shy on me now, girl, you know you look criss! Come here, are we gonna do this or what?"

And he took me by the hand and we walked in through the tall wrought-iron gates. I expected him to pull his hand away after a while but he didn't. And I didn't pull mine away either. It just felt like the most natural thing to do. We walked like that, hand in hand, through Battersea Park; past the miniature zoo, lingering by the lake, watching the families in paddle boats, buying ice-cream from the kiosk. While we walked we talked, of a million and one things and of nothing: school, family, friends, music, the latest TV shows, who was better, Chelsea or Man U.

"Can you ride a bike, Misha?" he asked me.

"Yes, of course I can! Can you?"

"Yeah... let's grab some bikes and go for a ride then, innit."

"Are you serious?"

"'Course I'm serious – don't go all stoosh on me now, yeah, all girly and ting. If you know how to ride a bike, let's see you ride one, innit!"

I tried to punch him but he blocked my fist and made a face at me. "Not bad, not bad – for a girl...."

"Right," I shouted, laughing, "that's it – you're finished!" And I swung my other fist at him (Dad would have been proud). But he dodged and began to run, over the grass, under the enormous oak trees whose leaves whispered in the breeze, while I chased him, determined to teach him a lesson in gender equality – with my fists.

DWAYNE

True say, I don't know what got into me that day at Battersea Park. I felt free, like a kid again, living for the moment, not caring what anyone thought. Usually, I would never act like that – let my guard down – with any girl, but especially not one I'd just met. Mans got a reputation to think about, y'get me. But Misha, Misha was different. She wasn't part of all that, you know? I felt like I could relax with her – and I could tell that she felt the same. What did it mean? I didn't know at the time; I was having too much fun...

When I got tired of running, I slowed down enough for her to catch me and jump on my back. But then I thought, 'Nah, man, that was too easy!' and I grabbed hold of her legs and began running again. Now she was shouting, laughing, pounding me on the back.

"You're crazy!" she screamed. "Put me down, you nutter!"

"Ha!" I laughed. "Make me! I ain't lettin' you go, girl, you're stuck with me!"

But then she stopped hitting me and held me, just for a moment.

Something inside me shifted. I let go of her. It was all getting too heavy. I turned round and, when I looked into her face, something passed between us, a spark. I could tell that she felt what I felt: this – whatever it was that was happening between us – was something special.

It was a moment.

But I couldn't handle it in the end. What can you do with a girl who looks you in the eye so that you can see exactly what she's thinking, what she's feeling? You either do the same or you fall back, innit. Instead of looking in her eyes again, I took her hand and said, "Let's get those bikes, yeah?" But my voice was softer than before.

We spent the rest of the afternoon chilling, riding around the park, going all the way up to the promenade along the River Thames.

After we'd returned the bikes, we bought sandwiches and sat down on the grass to eat.

"What you got in your bag?" I asked. You can tell a lot about a girl by what she carries round with her.

She shrugged. "Not much. Some make-up, a bit of cash, a book..."

"What book you readin'?"

"*Lord of the Flies*, we're studying it at school." She passed me her copy, full of tiny scribbles in the margins, thick lines under some of the sentences.

"Yeah, I know it – it was pretty good... I thought the language was kinda tired, though."

"Oh my God, are you serious?" Misha's hand was on her heart. "I love the language Golding uses! It's so poetic!"

"Poetry? That ain't poetry! That's just a long ting – this is poetry..." And then I did my thing: I spat a little freestyle, a freestyle rhyme about a girl with sweet chocolate fudge-coloured skin, with three gold earrings and a weakness for raspberry ripple ice-cream; a girl with a supermodel smile and a mean left hook.

A poem about her.

Have you ever seen a black girl blush? It's the prettiest thing. I could tell from the way her eyes opened wide and the way she bit her lip that she was blown away. I knew I had her then, so I decided to deliver the death blow.

"Read some to me then, innit," I said, handing her the book. "Let's see if this Golding bredder can spit as good as you say..."

So she read to me from her copy of *Lord of the Flies*. And that book that had made me die from boredom in English class came alive. I lay down next to her on the grass and closed my eyes, listening to her reading in that pretty, posh voice of hers while the bees buzzed above us, the afternoon sun warm on my skin.

MISHA

It was the thrill of it, really, the thrill of the unknown, the unknowable, that first got me interested. That and his devastating smile. And he had soulful eyes. They weren't dead like so many of the others I had seen. His eyes spoke of a depth, a richness, a life within, waiting to be uncovered.

When he looked at me, looked deep into my eyes, I felt as if he was drinking in every word I said, that everything I said mattered, not because it was perfect, but because I had said it.

There were teething problems, of course. His street talk perplexed me – so many double negatives!

So many grammatical inconsistencies. But once I learned to listen, to tune into the essence of his words, I fell under their spell. He was a poet: a street poet, a poet with no respect for Wordsworth, but a poet nonetheless. He wove a spell with his words, making them dance and jive and shimmy – just for me.

I guess you could say he captured my heart with a poem about chocolate fudge-coloured sweetness, spitting it on a two-step breakbeat.

Thug 4 Life

DWAYNE

"I'm out, man," said Tony, looking down at the playground in front of the estate. "Last weekend was my last rave. I'm done."

We were all sitting on the balcony at Jukkie and Tony's mum's house, smoking. Misha and I had been seeing each other for a few weeks and I was sending her a text message, the kind I knew made her melt. When Tony mentioned being 'out', I stopped thumb-typing and stared at him.

"What are you talking about, man?" I couldn't believe what I was hearing. Tony? Quit raving? "But why, man? What's up?"

"You know I took my *shahadah*, innit, a few months ago now. I became a Muslim. And I've just been playing around. But now it's time to quit messing about and do this *deen* ting. Do it properly. No more raving, no more drugs, I'm out of the game."

Jukkie kissed his teeth and got up. "Sounds like some lame-arse ting you're on, Tony. What d'you mean, you're out? When you're in the street life, there ain't no getting out. As for me, I know what I am: a thug for life." And he went inside.

This thing was blowing my mind. "You mean you're really gonna take this Islam ting serious, bruv? Are you sure?" I tried to imagine Tony living a clean life: no more guns, no more drugs, no more raving... no more money. "Yo, how the hell are you gonna pay for that new ride and the watches and champagne and ting without food? What you gonna do, sign on?"

I laughed at the thought of Tony, Mr Big Stuff himself, going into the Job Seekers' office to apply for a job as a driver.

But Tony didn't laugh, y'know. Instead, he chewed at the skin under his thumbnail. "I don't know, man. I don't know. But I can't die like this, y'get me. Imagine we out raving tonight, bunnin' weed, drinkin', and we crash the car and – pop – that's it! Done! I ain't goin' out like that..."

"Easy on the drama, man! No one ain't gonna die, not any time soon. There's plenty of time for that

Muslim stuff later, innit? We're young now, we're making money – life is good. Don't go mashing tings up by getting too serious... now turn up the volume, man, I love this track." And soon my head was nodding to the sick beats.

I didn't care what Tony said: there was no way he was going straight. Not while it was all going so well for us in RDS. Man would have to be a fool to turn his back on the streets when we were running tings.

❖ ❖ ❖

RDS had been my crew since I was 11. Only we never called it that back then. We were just a group of friends who all lived on the Saints Town estate. Our mums all knew each other and we all went to the same school. Trevor, Simon, Leroy, Nicholas, Ali, Ross, Baba, Tony and Marvin.

Tony and Marvin Johnson were brothers – same mum, different dads – and I'd known them forever. Tony was six years older than Marvin and me and I looked up to him big time.

Tony was always smooth, man, always on top of his game. From way back, I could remember seeing him waiting in the stairwell at the bottom of our estate, shotting, waiting for the junkies with their wild eyes to come for their fix.

In those days, we used to think it was good fun to shout out and warn the older boys if we saw or heard the 5-0 coming. We didn't know that, one day, we'd be the ones standing in the stairwell, listening out for the sound of a siren.

But Tony didn't stay on the street corners for long. Nah, Tony had bigger plans, bigger dreams. He was into fraud, Tony was. It came easy for him because he was a smooth talker and knew how to con people. Plus he was good with computers and that. So, when Tony began to roll in a Jeep and flash a gold Rolex about, we youngers knew what was up: Mr BigStuff Tony was scoring big-time.

Tony became a proper legend on the Saints Town estate. People told nuff stories about him: some said that he had a huge stash of coke hidden in his girl's ground-floor flat. Others said he had shot a policeman in New York and got away with it. Some said the police had even made a deal with him to keep the 'hood under control and keep the drugs on the estates and stop it leaking out into the suburbs, where the posh people lived.

But those were all rumours at the end of the day. What I knew for sure was that Tony had a lot of money for watches, gold chains and diamond rings. And cars, of course, a new one each month. Sometimes it was a Porsche Cayenne, or a Bentley convertible or a black Range Rover Sport with blacked-out windows and matching black rims. I learned to drive in that car.

Tony was a natural leader: he knew how to get respect from people – and he knew how to keep us youngers in line. We all knew that Tony had our backs – we *trusted* him – and that's what made the RDS such a safe crew: mans were *loyal* to each other. Tony was the one who had made us that way. He was the big brother I never had.

Then there was his little brother, Marvin, who we started to call Jukkie. He had been my mate since nursery school. I'll never forget how one of the older kids had pushed me off my tricycle after I had been at nursery for about a week. Marvin jumped that kid, pushed him to the ground, and beat him down with his fists, as if he was the senior and the older boy was just a snivelling newbie.

"That's my friend!" he shouted, just before the nursery teacher came to haul him away. "Don't you disrespect him, yeah?"

As Tony's younger brother, Marvin knew

all about respect: who had it, how to get it and what to do if people didn't give it to you. While the teacher told his mum what had happened he bounced past them both and put his arm round me.

"Don't worry, Dee," he said, his voice full of confidence. "You and me, we're cool. I'll look after you, yeah? Safe."

He was the same height as me, the same age, but to me, he looked six feet tall. He was Tony's little brother and he had my back. What more could I ask for?

But that was all back in the day when we could spend the whole time riding bikes, cussing each other, nicking stuff from shops, getting told off by each other's mums. That was back in the day, when we walked without fear wherever we wanted, when we went to play basketball down Larkside because my cousin lived there. That was back in the day, before my cousin killed a man and had to fly to Jamaica to avoid getting arrested.

Those were the days of innocence.

Then Trevor Dennison, who was about two years older than us, came on to the scene. Me and Marvin were only 11 when Trevor, who everyone started calling Trigger, invited us to start 'juggling' for him and Tony. Back then, Tony had felt that we were too young to play the game – but after Trigger gave us our first taste, even he realised that we were just as hungry, just as primed, as any of the older boys. Then he let us get a piece of the action.

"So, d'you boys wanna make y'selves some dough?" Trigger had asked after letting us try a bit of his joint.

The smoke burned the back of my throat and I struggled not to cough. Marvin just took it in, nice and easy. The idea of making money sounded good, especially as Mum had been bugging about buying me the new trainers I really wanted.

"Yeah!" we said, our heads feeling light.

"Here, take this." Trigger pushed a couple of packets into our hands. "This stuff is worth at least £500, yeah? You can pay us back when you sell it."

"Sell it to who?" I wanted to know.

"Eediat!" Trigger spat on the floor beside my worn black trainers. "To the mandem at school, innit! Go for the Year 11s first, yeah? I'll come check you later, see how you got on."

To tell you the truth, I wasn't sure about selling at school. I knew that others did it, but I just wasn't sure. And Mum would bare kill me if she found out.

"Stop dreaming, fool, and put the stuff away before someone sees you!" That was Marvin, always the practical one. "We're gonna be rollin' soon, blud!" he crowed. "No more tired trainers for you! No more Primark T-shirts! We're gonna be big men, just like Tony! And no one ain't gonna be able to tell us *nuffin'*!"

That's how it started: a few bags of weed.

Soon we were all into it. It was safe making our own money, coz none of our parents could afford to buy us the designer kicks, the crisp garmz, the stuff that made us look and feel good. And of course, no one's mum was gonna hand over money for cigarettes, a bottle of Jack Daniels, a spliff or something harder.

A few years later, we all knew how to make money. We became experts, innit, with mad money-making skills. A little dope here; a nice watch stolen there, while out in the West End; a delivery, a favour. Me and my crew had arrived. And we had a name now: RDS, short for Run Da Streetz and Tony was The Main Nigga in Charge.

Those years changed us, man, I tell you. We became boys who 'ran tings': we wore red bandannas under our hoodies, and we didn't give a damn about school or our parents or even the police. Our parents couldn't tell us nothin'. And we would take the fall for each other, standard.

I think that's when Mum really gave up on me, y'know. Before, she had always called after me as I left the house, bopping like a badman, 'Dwayne! Come back here, boy!' She had stayed up late to wait for me, scared every time she heard a police siren. She couldn't sleep when I didn't come home.

But then she just stopped.

"His father was the same," she began to say all the time. "Wort'less, nuttin' but trouble since the day he was born."

Rising Star

MISHA

"Well done, darling, I knew you could do it." I could hear the pride in Mum's voice as she hugged me, the letter from Oak Hill still crisp in her hand.

I smiled up at her. I still couldn't quite believe it myself but the letter said it quite plainly: *On the strength of her mock exams and her predicted results, Oak Hill School for Girls is pleased to offer Misha Reynolds a provisional place in its prestigious Sixth Form to study Mathematics, Physics, Biology and Chemistry. The offer will be confirmed once the final exam results have been published.*

Mum kissed my forehead and squeezed me again. I felt a bubbling inside me then, a surge of pride and satisfaction. This was what Mum had been preparing me for: greatness. And with 13 GCSEs to sit and at least 10 predicted A and A* grades, I was well on my way.

Don't get me wrong: I'm not big-headed or anything – that's just how Mum taught me to express myself. It's hard to shake that kind of habit.

But although I was pleased, a tiny part of me felt bruised. I had really wanted to take my 'A' Levels at my current school, a well-respected private school in Dulwich, but Mum insisted that I apply to Oak Hill. She also insisted that I drop my favourite subjects – French and Spanish – and apply to do Sciences and Mathematics.

"Oak Hill is far more prestigious than your school," Mum had said. "And they have a much higher number of students getting into Oxford and Cambridge. You're better off there, Misha, where the top students are."

"I suppose so, Mum," I nodded. It was easy to agree with Mum. I had been doing it all my life. "It's just that I really like my teachers – and the Sciences aren't my forte."

"You can do anything you put your mind to, Misha," Mum had said firmly. "I don't have to tell you how complex this society is, darling. The whole system is riddled with racism. Black people need to work twice as hard to succeed and as a black woman, it's not enough for you to be good, or even very good: you have to be the best."

It was a sort of mantra, a regular part of our life together as single working mother and only daughter: *be the best, work hard, never use your race as an excuse.* I knew that was why, when Mum finally started earning enough money to be able to get a mortgage, she bought a house near the best independent girls' school in south London, far from Brixton where I was born, where she grew up.

At the time, I couldn't understand how Mum could bear to be so far from Gran, so far from the familiarity of Brixton and the Caribbean community there, and live in such a white suburb but, as I got older, I began to figure it out. Mum didn't want to be near other black people, especially black people on estates, 'low class' black people: 'ghetto people'. As far as Mum was concerned, we were better than them. We were upwardly mobile: educated, cultured, refined and as far away from state benefits as you could get.

"If black people are going to get ahead," Mum would say, "we're going to have to stop segregating ourselves. We need to get rid of our ghetto mentality. We need to aim higher, to be the best. That is what I want for you, Misha."

Mum hugged me again, looked at her watch and said briskly, "I've got to go, darling, I've got a meeting with the mayor in less than 45 minutes... on a Saturday, would you believe?" She drained her coffee cup before pulling on her grey wool coat. Then she reapplied her lipstick and smoothed her hair. "There," she said, knotting a purple silk scarf around her neck and throwing her shoulders back. "How do I look?"

"Fantastic, Mum." I wondered why she still had to ask. People regularly mistook us for sisters. With her smooth nut-brown skin and dazzling smile, Counsellor Dina Reynolds – Mum – was one of those many black women who just did not seem to age. I hoped I would inherit that from her side just as I hoped I wouldn't inherit early greying from Dad's.

Just then, my mobile vibrated. A text. I picked it up and read the message:

Hey sweetness. I wanna c u 2nite. I'll cum 4 u @ 8. D.

My heart fluttered ever so slightly. I had to look away to hide my smile from Mum. Thankfully, Mum's Blackberry vibrated too, giving three sharp rings. She turned towards it to look at the screen.

"Oh, Lord!" she exclaimed. "I completely forgot: Auntie Loretta got us tickets for the Alvin Ailey performance at the Royal Albert Hall tonight!

And it's the last show! How could I have forgotten?" She chewed her bottom lip briefly, then her face brightened. "Right, I'll have to meet you after work. Have you got your travelcard or do you need a new one? And do you have anything to wear or do you need to pick something up? I can't believe I forgot..."

I bit my lip. I had seen the great African American dance group perform before and had been blown away by the power and grace of their performance. Mum had sent me to ballet and African Dance lessons until I was thirteen – so I could totally appreciate the Alvin Ailey dancers' expertise. I would have loved to see them again, had it not been for Dwayne... I had to think fast.

"Er, Mum," I said, trying to sound casual, "do you really think I should? I've still got loads of work to do on my course-work ... I might have to give it a miss this time, what do you think?"

Mum thought for a few moments, then sighed. "Well, I suppose you're right. Your studies do come first." She glanced at her watch again. "Now I *really* have to go or I'll be late for this meeting. Help yourself to fish from the freezer for your lunch and have the lasagne for dinner – and make sure you make yourself a salad!"

"All right, Mum, enough! Off you go!" I laughed as she finally got out of the door. Then I leaned back against it and reread Dwayne's text message.

Hey sweetness. I wanna c u 2nite. I'll cum 4 u @ 8. D.

All of a sudden I felt light-headed, and a thousand butterflies fluttered in the pit of my stomach. I simply loved the way he did that, made it sound as if he needed me, as if seeing me was as vital as air.

Of course I'd had other boys tell me they fancied me, but I'd never listened to their ridiculous chat-up lines, never fallen for their charms. One of the unspoken lessons I had learned from eavesdropping on Mum's conversations with her friends was this: never trust a man.

But although I still knew hardly anything about Dwayne, I knew there was something different about him. I felt it in my bones.

Cutting Up Mandem

DWAYNE

Marvin was known as 'Jukkie' because he had a way with knives. But because he knew how to put on the baby face, he was the only one of my friends Mum could stand. Mum always smiled when she opened the door and found him standing on the mat outside the door, his hood off, cap in his hand.

"Good morning, Mrs Kingston," he would say in his most proper voice. "How are you today?"

"Well, Marvin," Mum would reply, smiling like crazy, "I've seen better days but I can't complain. How's your mum?"

"She's good, y'know, Mrs Kingston, really good. She asked me to remind you about that carrot juice you promised to make for her. 'The best carrot juice she's ever tasted,' she says!"

Then Mum would laugh and open the door to let Marvin in. "You tell your mother I'll bring it on Sunday – when she invites me round for her roast chicken and macaroni pie!" She would laugh again and Marvin would laugh too, leaning towards her, touching her arm with his long fingers.

Then I would see him turn to walk away and roll his eyes. Mum didn't know about how Jukkie got mad when he drank whisky, how he loved to carve man up, just for the hell of it. She thought he was still the polite boy she used to teach at Sunday School. Parents are such chiefs. They only see what they wanna see.

Once he had sweet-talked Mum and was in my room, Marvin was Jukkie again, screw-face as always.

That Saturday morning was no different. "Yo, Dwayne!" he barked as he pulled my covers off. "Get up! What's wrong with you, man?"

For the second time that day, I was getting a wack wake-up call. I rubbed my eyes, then looked over at my mobile. Three missed calls. One text message.

Where the hell are you? T.

It was Trigger. Then I knew what Jukkie was on about.

"Dwayne, man, Trigger's been waiting for you for twenty minutes and he is not happy! After what went down last night, I suggest you get your lazy arse up and out of here before he comes to get you – personally!"

I didn't need telling twice. While Jukkie pulled out his latest toy, a switch-blade that glinted when it caught the light through a gap in the curtains, I yanked on my tracksuit pants and black hooded top. Damn, I couldn't even remember where I had put my red bandanna, I was so out of it. Jukkie reached into his pocket and pulled out a spare and threw it at me.

"Thanks, man," I muttered as I tied the bandanna over my forehead. "Where d'you get this from, then?"

Jukkie's frown disappeared and he flashed a brilliant smile and touched the tip of the switch-blade to his gold tooth. "You know what they say," he said. "Always be prepared."

The two of us practically ran over my younger brother, Jerome, on our way out. My man, Jay, the best little brother in the world – and the mouthiest too.

"Where you lot off to?" he called after us.

"Got some errands to run, bro," I called back.

"But you promised to take me bowling, man!"

"Later, yeah?"

Trigger was waiting in his bright yellow Lexus Jeep with the tinted windows and alloy wheels, vex'. As much as I would have preferred to go bowling with Jay, he would have to wait.

Trigger didn't even look at me when I climbed into the car. I mumbled something about being sorry, having overslept. The others all looked at me, screw-face, and Trigger kissed his teeth before reversing out of the estate car park, leaving black tyre marks on the asphalt.

No one spoke for a long time. I looked around the car and noticed that Kofi, the little runner we all called Lightning, wasn't in the car. I frowned. Kofi was always with us, standard. Even when his crazy mum locked their front door and threatened to burn his clothes if he tried to go out, Lightning would find a way out, even if it meant jumping from his window on the second floor.

I got a weird feeling then, when I saw that Lightning wasn't there. I was sensing a vibe, a bad vibe. After a long time, Trigger spoke. "So," he growled, looking at me in the rear view mirror, "what the hell happened to you last night?"

"Last night?"

"Yeah, fool, last night! We was meant to go see dem man on the other side of the Oval estate, down Larkside. Remember?"

Damn. Only the weekend before, Larkside mans had caused some trouble with Flinthead and Spoonz, two of the youngers in RDS. The story went that one of their boys had grabbed Flinthead's new bike and when Flinty challenged him, five or six of them jumped him and started laying into him. Spoonz had stepped in to help Flinty and ended up with a bottle in his face. Friday night, RDS was meant to have gone over to Larkside, rolling ten man deep, to take care of them.

Trigger had asked Jukkie to bring his collector's set of knives. Different lengths, different strengths, multi-purpose knives. "I'm in the mood for carving up mandem," he said.

I remember my insides starting to cramp up when I heard him say that. And I knew straight away that I wasn't going to be with them.

I hate knives. I've always hated them, y'get me. And from when Trigger said he wanted to carve up those Larkside boys, I knew I wasn't going to reach, no way. It was just convenient that Mum and me got into a fight over that dumb phone call and ting.

Don't get me wrong, I can fight. I can proper take man down, take down three, four of them at once. I ain't scared of that. But I proper hate knives.

Then Trigger spoke again. "Some mans think that dis is a pick'n'choose ting, yeah. But what they don't understand is that you're either in or you're out. When I say that RDS gonna roll up in a place, I expect everyone to be there." He was looking right at me. "Or there'll be consequences."

"Ya dun know!" Jukkie glared at me and kissed his teeth. That was Jukkie these days. Ever since Tony had stepped back from the gang life, Jukkie had been trying to get in with Trigger. It was like he was looking to replace his big brother or something. Either that or he hoped to be first in line when Trigger started sharing some of the food.

I looked out of the window. I missed Tony. He'd always been great for a laugh; we'd had some fun times. But he'd been keeping a low profile lately. Nuff man had been going on dark about his decision to go straight – I wasn't even sure it was safe for him on the estate. Although Tony hadn't been the type to make enemies on purpose, you can't live the gang life and keep every man as your friend. It just isn't possible.

Now, with Trigger in charge, RDS had changed: things had become a lot more serious, darker. It wasn't about rolling and making money and having a good time any more. It was about keeping control, making sure others respected us: beef.

Trigger was the kind of black boy people crossed the street to avoid. He had a whole heap of marks on his face from acne when he was younger and he was permanently screw-face. His eyes were usually red from all the weed he smoked and when he looked at you, proper staring you down, you felt real fear. He was cold, man, stone cold.

I decided to ignore Jukkie's foolishness, just to keep the peace. "What happened to Lightning, man? Where is he?"

Jukkie looked up from the knife he had been using to clean his fingernails. "He got beat down, man, badly. Police came and everything, called the ambulance. He's in Bay Street Hospital, proper bruck-up." He shook his head. "Dem Larkside mans are proper psycho."

Run Da Streetz

DWAYNE

The work we had to do was soon over: just a few packages to deliver, some money to hide in a safe house, nothing too difficult. Trigger parked the Lexus and we went to pick up chicken and chips and some drinks from our favourite shop in Camberwell.

As we crossed the street, I saw a girl wearing denim shorts with a small red leather backpack, standing waiting for the bus. She was facing away from me and I did a double-take. That was Misha's bag. And Misha's hair, no doubt about it! What was she doing up these sides? But instead of going up to her, I pulled my hood up over my head, hunched my shoulders and began walking in the opposite direction, behind Jukkie.

I didn't want her to see me, not with my RDS boys.

The less she knew about that, the better.

We all bought drinks, making so much noise in the off-licence that the Indian man behind the counter told us to get out. But we ignored him, of course. When we finally got out of the shop, Trigger reached out and snatched a new-looking Burberry cap off a white boy's head. The boy swore and swung round, ready to fight. Then he saw Trigger's bloodshot eyes and bared teeth and went red. He quickly got the message and moved on.

When we reached the strip of grass where we had been planning to cotch, we found it covered with dog mess.

"There's just nowhere to go in this hellhole," snapped Trigger. His fuse was short today, I could see that.

There were six of us, spread out across the pavement, spilling off the curb and on to the street. We bust some jokes, we spit some rhymes, we hassled some girls who were standing across the road. We shared a blunt and I felt the buzz start to take effect.

Everyone who saw us, mums on their way home from the hairdresser, kids on their way to football, little girls in plastic sandals with handfuls of sweets, crossed the road to avoid us, we were that intimidating.

But one woman, tall and slim, with an expensive-looking double buggy and a designer handbag, kept walking on the pavement towards us. I don't know what got into that chick , why she didn't just go round like everybody else.

We were all listening to one of Jukkie's wild stories and I was the only one who noticed her at first.

"Excuse me," she said, all posh-sounding. "Could you move out of the way, please?" Something in her voice reminded me of Misha but I pushed it away. Not now. Not here.

The woman's face was red – it was turning into a hot day – and her babies were asleep with their mouths open. The curb was high and her buggy was massive. No wonder she wanted us to move. I looked over at Trigger to see if he had heard the woman. He was staring intently at Jukkie, pulling on his rollup, but I could tell that he had heard her.

The woman raised her voice. "Excuse me, could we get past please?"

Jukkie stopped talking, surprised at her tone, but still Trigger did not look her way. I recognised that look, the slow burn in his eyes and I felt a chill work its way right through me.

'Move on, man,' I said inside. 'Just move on. Go round.'

But the woman didn't move on. Instead, she leaned forward and shouted, "Do you mind? You don't own the pavement, you know! I'd like to get past, please!"

"*What*?" Trigger's voice was thick and rough, but still he did not look at her. Instead, he pointed at her with his thumb and rasped, "Did you hear what that white bitch said to me?"

'It's on now,' I thought, and I looked away as Trigger turned to the woman, his face all twisted. He shouted, "What did you say to me, bitch?"

The woman's face turned pale and she started to stutter, trying to get her buggy to move backwards, but Trigger grabbed at her buggy and ripped it out of her hands, shoving it towards the others. She let out a sharp scream and Trigger slapped her, full in her face.

"Shut up, bitch!" he snapped. "Tell me what you said again! Go on!" Slap, slap. The woman was crying now, blubbering about her babies, reaching out to them. But Jukkie and the other boys had got hold of the buggy and were shaking it, shaking it, laughing at the terror in the babies' eyes and their little cries.

Trigger was pushing the woman again and again, shouting at her.

Spoonz bounced over to her and tore her bag from her shoulder, emptying it out on to the ground. He picked out a nice-looking pair of sunglasses, a set of keys and her wallet, checking to see how much cash she was carrying, how many cards.

My mind was fuzzy from the alcohol and the spliff, and everything in front of me started swaying and shimmering with light and shadow. I could hear myself laughing, could see myself pointing at the older baby who was trying to twist around in his chair, trying to find his mum, snot running into his open mouth. But it was as if I was outside myself looking on, staring at this strange boy I didn't recognise.

I felt sick, to tell you the truth. When I looked at the woman, I was stunned by the terror in her eyes, and the mad crescendo that grew out of her pleas for help, her babies' yells and the jeering and crowing of boys I called my friends. And the fact that no one dared step in.

Then, just as Trigger grabbed the woman by the hair, we heard the sound of sirens. My stomach lurched. 5-0.

Trigger swore and looked around wildly, his hands

still holding the woman's hair. Then he turned back to the woman, drew her face close to his and spat at her. His spit landed on her cheek and slid down. She cowered and whimpered, shrinking away from him.

"You don't know this face, y'understand?" he hissed. "You ain't never seen me. Ever."

He pushed her to the ground and she crawled along the pavement towards the buggy, blubbing, wiping her nose on her sleeve. Then she looked up at me and our eyes met for a sliver of a second. But I blinked and looked away. I didn't feel high any more.

True say, I wanted to help her up. I wanted to say I was sorry for what had happened to her, sorry for her babies.

But I didn't.

Instead, I turned and ran down the street with the others, jumping the wall to avoid the police car that pulled up next to the woman and her two babies. I just wanted to get out of there.

"Were you in Camberwell today?" Misha asked me at her house later. "I thought I saw someone wearing a bandanna and top like yours..."

"Nah, man," I replied, as smooth as silk. "Must have been someone else, innit."

Of course I didn't tell Misha about the woman with

51

the double buggy. But I washed my face and hands again and again in her downstairs bathroom, using the lemon-scented soap, trying to get rid of the smell of the greasy chicken and chips, trying to wash the stain of the afternoon from my mind.

Maybe, a few months ago, the same thing could have happened and I would have shrugged it off. Who cared about some posh bitch and her pickney, right? But something had changed. *I* had changed. And I was feeling something I hadn't felt in a long time: shame.

Bad Boys

MISHA

I woke up late on Sunday morning and stretched luxuriously. Sunlight was flooding in through the net curtains in my room and I could hear the birds singing in the chestnut tree outside my bedroom window. This was why I slept with my curtains and window open: this exquisite morning symphony, this glorious performance of polyphonic sound and scattered light, filtered through chestnut leaves. Enough to make me want to write poetry!

I caught the scent of lemons and my thoughts turned to the night before. I smiled and hugged myself. It had been another great evening, full of laughter and interesting conversation, among other things. That was what was special about Dwayne, unlike some of the halfwits out there. Not to say I always agreed with all his opinions: I definitely didn't. But it made him different from other boys I knew. He had a completely different take on life. And he wasn't afraid to make his views known.

The night before, we had argued again about his use of the 'n' word.

"Chill out, man, Misha!" he laughed when I objected for the third time. "It's just a name, innit. I call my boys all sorts of names: boys, man, niggaz..."

"No, Dwayne, I'm sorry," I interrupted, cutting him off with a sweep of my hand. "Using the 'n' word is totally unacceptable! That name has been used to insult black people for centuries. Haven't you read *Roots*? Don't you know about slavery and civil rights? I don't see how anyone can justify using a word that is so steeped in violence and hatred – unless you actually hate yourself as a black person..."

"Ah, come on!" Dwayne laughed, like he always did when I got serious with him. "You're making it into a big deal. It's just a word, baby, just a word!"

Then it occurred to me that perhaps he hadn't read *Roots* or even watched it. Well, if he didn't know better, it was my job to educate him.

"There's no such thing as 'just a word'. Language is

power, Dee. As a poet, you should know that!" I sat up on the sofa and looked straight at him. I wanted him to take me seriously, to let what I was saying really sink in. "It affects the way you think, the way you act. Look at all those gangsta rappers, talking about bitches and hos, carrying guns, boasting about shooting *other black men*!"

But Dwayne grinned again and looked at me like I was crazy. "Those are just tunes, man! That's just what kids wanna listen to these days, innit!"

I raised my eyebrows and crossed my arms. "Maybe that's why black people are so messed-up. How you can justify violent and misogynist lyrics is beyond me. Have you ever heard any other people in the world describing themselves in such awful terms? Huh?"

He was quiet then, not grinning any more.

"Exactly. If you don't have pride in yourself, how are you ever going to rewrite the script?"

But he did that thing, that infuriating thing of dodging my question. "So what's a posh girl like you doing with a nigga like me, then, eh?" His voice was teasing and his smile tugged at that part of me, the weak part, that found him so impossible to resist.

Suddenly I didn't want to talk about black pride and gangsta rap any more. I allowed myself to smile at him and gave him a look."Coz you're my bad-boy lover, that's why."

"That's right, baby," he murmured, leaning over. "That's right."

Back in my Sunday morning bedroom, I smiled to myself again and shook my head.

Mum still didn't know anything about Dwayne – but I was starting to feel that maybe, just maybe, it was the right time to tell her. After all, we had been seeing each other for a few weeks and it didn't look like things were going to cool down any time soon. Plus, it felt strange to keep such a major thing from Mum.

We had always been very close, she and I, sharing everything ever since she and Dad split up when I was five. Mum knew practically everything about me – mainly because I had always told her everything. Things began to change, though, when I turned 11, around the time we left Brixton.

"You've become so secretive all of a sudden," she used to say. I started voicing my opinion less, mainly because I knew by then that when Mum had made her mind up about something, it was useless to try to convince her otherwise. It was easier to keep your opinion to yourself and agree with her.

Just then, she knocked on the door and poked her head round. "Morning, darling," she smiled, blowing me a kiss. "Did you sleep well?"

"Like a baby," I replied. "What time did you get back?"

"Oh, about midnight. Auntie Loretta said she felt like dancing after the show so we went to a wine bar, a really nice place, great band. Didn't you get my message?"

I turned away guiltily. I had heard the message come through but I'd been a bit preoccupied at the time. "Text?" I mumbled vaguely. "Oh, yeah..."

"Silly girl," Mum laughed. "You were probably so into your chemistry books, eh? Or was it physics?"

'Something like that,' I thought to myself, ducking under my duvet.

"Anyway, darling, I'm going to get ready for church, OK? Grandma needs me to pick her up and Sylvia's singing a solo with the choir. Wear your cream trouser-suit – I like that one on you. And wear your hair in a low bun – that suits your face the best."

I nodded. I had almost forgotten all about church.

Prodigal Sons

MISHA

The pavement outside Gran's church in Brixton was packed and the crowd heaved with greetings, laughter and the click of high heels on tarmac. The pavement was covered with immaculately turned-out African-Caribbean men and women – no one spared any effort in getting dressed for church. It was one of those occasions women still wore hats. They shimmered in gorgeous maxi-dresses, pencil skirts and smart trouser-suits.

I mentally assigned points for the different outfits, something I always did at the Brixton church. Our church in Dulwich was a more sedate affair – most of the people there were white, so everything was much more toned down.

As a little girl, I could remember standing outside

the church building and being fascinated by the women's gorgeous skin tones: deepest ebony, walnut brown and amber – and their hair – the smooth, synthetic weaves, bouncing braids and sleek up-dos. The church ladies were always styled to perfection, their make-up flawless.

This Sunday, I couldn't help noticing that several of the younger members of the congregation wore tank tops, skinny jeans and the latest style gladiator platform heels. Hadn't Pastor James spoken about that just last weekend?

Grandma took my arm and walked painfully towards the entrance. She kissed her teeth and muttered, "These young people have no shame – coming to the house of God dressed for the dance hall."

I helped Gran climb the steps and settle herself in one of the front rows. I was so pleased to see her, I just sat next to her, my hand in hers, stroking the sleeve of her turquoise silk suit jacket. It had been three weeks since Mum had last agreed to attend church in Brixton and Gran wouldn't come to the church in our area. I had missed her. And I had missed the church that I'd grown up in too.

Pastor James, his bald patch shining under the

neon lights, was on fire that day. He gave a sermon based on the story of the prodigal son, from Luke, Chapter 15. His deep voice rumbled through the hall as he retold the story of the son who asked for his inheritance early, only to waste it on fast living, ending up humiliated and abased, feeding pigs while wishing for their food.

Then the pastor's voice lightened, his words rippling and flowing over our raised heads, like water over pebbles in a stream, as he spoke of the father's joy at seeing his prodigal son return home and the feast he prepared in his honour.

"But, my brothers and sisters," he continued, his eyes bright, "the man's elder son was not pleased, not at all! And he questioned his father. He said, 'Look, these many years I have served you, and I never disobeyed your command, yet you never gave me so much as a young goat that I might celebrate with my friends.' Imagine his bitterness, brothers and sisters! And he continued, saying, 'But when this son of yours came, he who has devoured your property with prostitutes, you killed the fattened calf for him!' And what did the father say, brothers and sisters? What did he *say*? That father said, 'Son, you are always with me, and all that is mine is yours. It was fitting to celebrate and be glad, for this your brother was dead, and is alive; he was lost, and is found.' What did the father say, my brothers and sisters? He was lost and is now *found*, Amen!"

It was an emotional moment and I felt my heart beating along with the cries of *Amen* and *Hallelujah!* that came from the congregation. The choir broke into a hymn, one of Grandma's favourites, and people rose to their feet, swaying to the music, clapping their hands. When the refrain had been sung for the third time, Pastor James lifted up his hands and everyone settled back into their seats.

The pastor's face was serious now and he scanned the crowd before crying out, "Now, where are all *our* prodigal sons?"

Silence settled in the church and Pastor James cried out once more, his voice echoing through the hall, driving right through me. "Brothers and sisters, I ask you again: *where* are all our prodigal *sons*?"

Pastor walked down from the podium, his microphone in hand. "I'll tell you where our prodigal sons are: they are out on the *streets*! They're out there, robbing, stealing, doing drugs, selling drugs, *fornicating*! Shooting innocent *people*! They are languishing in *jails*! They are rotting in *crack houses*! They are in every evil place, doing every evil thing! They are living a life of *wickedness*, just like in the parable!"

He stopped for a moment to mop the sweat that dotted his forehead, breathing hard, looking around him, his eyes blazing. As usual, during a sermon, I searched my heart to see if, somehow, the message applied to me. No, thank God, I was no prodigal daughter. Mum didn't have to worry about me, not at all. But a small voice inside my head taunted me: 'What about last night?'

"Some of you don't know where your sons were last night. Some of you don't know where your sons are *right now*! You don't even ask any more! Why? Because we have come to *fear* our own children, brothers and sisters. We have come to fear our own flesh and blood!"

I heard the sound of sobbing a few rows behind me and I turned to see an older Ghanaian woman, her wrapped head bowed, crying into her handkerchief. There were others too. The pastor's words had touched a raw nerve.

I looked over at Mum to gauge her reaction and saw that she was looking straight ahead, her face betraying no emotion. But her hand was holding on to mine so tightly that it hurt.

Pastor continued. "I would like to say to all those prodigal sons: come back, my children! Come back to the house of your Father! Come back to the body of the Church! Leave your evil ways and be welcome! This is what we must tell our wayward children, brothers and sisters: that they are always welcome in God's house."

Ms Braithwaite, the piano player, played the first bars of the hymn and Sylvia stood up. Her pure, sweet voice rang out into the rafters of the building and I honestly felt like crying, it was so beautiful. As she sang of forgiveness and being washed clean of sin, we all rose to join in and sing the hymn together. I soon found tears running down my cheeks. And I knew that it wasn't due to Sylvia's singing alone.

When the service was over, Pastor James congratulated Sylvia on her singing, asked Grandma about her arthritis, and then went to speak to the woman who had been crying. It turned out that her son had been badly beaten by a gang of thugs late on Friday night. He had been knifed in the leg and was in hospital. He was twelve. I was shocked. Twelve? My step-brother, Mark, was twelve! Why would anyone stab a twelve-year-old?

"How could this happen?" The Ghanaian woman wailed, clutching her hands together in front of her chest. "I tried so hard... so hard..." She wept into the pastor's shoulder. "I didn't even know he had gone out. When I checked his bed, I saw that he had stuffed it with his clothes to make it look like he was still asleep... I didn't even know he had left the house."

The pastor shook his head as he patted her back. "Indeed, this is a trial, sister," he crooned. "We must all pray for these sons of ours... there is no doubt that they are in need of strong prayer."

"We should go," said Mum.

"Come on, Gran." I took my grandmother's arm. "Let me help you..."

In the car on the way home, Mum said, "You know what? Every day I thank God Misha was born a girl. I don't know what I would do if I had a son to worry about. Especially with the way things are these days."

"Yes, it's true," Gran agreed. "In my day, you worried about the girls more. Now, it seems the boys are getting into worse trouble. Lawd a'mercy, what a time we are living in."

"And I thank Him that I was able to move us out of this terrible place – Brixton!" Mum pretty much spat out the word. "Can you believe that? A child from a good, church-going family, sneaking out and getting into fights – at twelve years of age? I tell you, this area is toxic for our children."

I shifted awkwardly in my seat when I saw Gran press her lips together. 'Not now, Mum,' I thought, 'please don't go on one of your anti-Brixton rants...'

But Mum acted like she didn't feel the frosty vibe that Gran was giving off. "Mummy," she began after a pause, "have you given any more thought to what we spoke about last month? About you moving in with us?"

Gran huffed impatiently and kissed her teeth. "I've told you before, Dina, I'm quite happy where I am now, in the house where you children grew up! Your father would have wanted me to look after it, to keep it in the family."

"But, Mum, that house backs on to that gigantic estate – and terrible things are happening there now. It's even worse than it was when we lived there! You hear all sorts of horror stories: gangs, drugs, delinquent kids. It's just not safe any more."

"I feel perfectly safe," replied Gran indignantly. "Besides, everybody knows me here. We're a community. I go to the Caribbean Centre to meet my friends from the old days; I can walk down the road to get my *akee* and saltfish, my hard dough bread. Where you live? No, darlin', it's not for me."

"Oh, Mummy," Mum sighed in exasperation. "It's really not that bad! It's a very diverse area, really."

Gran made a clucking noise and frowned. "Is that what you call it? Diverse? How come me can walk to the shop three times a day for a week and not see another black person? No, darlin', your place is not for me." And she clamped her mouth shut and looked straight out of the window, clutching the handbag on her lap.

I looked outside. We had reached Coldharbour Lane. The market was already buzzing with life. Fruit'n'veg sellers shouted out their special deals of the day, "Four for a pound!" Loud reggae music vibrated under the walkway and everywhere I could see the rich mix of Brixton.

There were the Rastas with their bulging knitted hats; the African women, still dressed up for church in stiff wax-print head-wraps and two-piece skirt suits, carefully coordinated with bags and shoes; the black Muslim men in their white robes and thick beards, standing behind stalls selling incense and giving out pamphlets. It occurred to me that I hadn't seen anyone from the Nation of Islam around for a long time. They had always been easy to spot with their upright bearing and smart suits and bow-ties.

Dotted here and there, weaving in and out of the market stalls, I could see the new kids on the block: the scruffy-looking white people who flocked to experience the Brixton vibe. I chuckled to myself. Only a few years before, few white people would have dared set foot in Brixton. But now the vintage clothing shops and the impossibly trendy bars and organic restaurants along Coldharbour Lane catered specifically for them.

I felt a surge of homesickness.. This was where I had spent the first eleven years of my life. My old primary school was round the corner. My best friend from primary school, Rachel, lived on the Saints Town estate.

'I wonder if she is still there...' I mused, thinking of the gulf that would be so obvious between us now. I spoke differently, of course, I knew that. You don't go to private school and keep your Eliza Doolittle accent, that's for sure. My old friends would definitely tease me for 'talking posh'. But there were other things too: the way I dressed, the labels I chose, the way I styled my hair, the jewellery I wore, the books I read, the films I watched. I was studying Latin at school, for Goodness' sake.

What would Rachel and I have to talk about? Where was she now? Was she at school? Still playing football? Or had she dropped out to have a baby? Or maybe she was one of those girls who hung around with gangs of boys, looking hard and unreachable.

The thought of Rachel leaning against a car, surrounded by boys in hoodies and bandannas, made me think of the conversation I'd had with my schoolfriend, Aalia.

✿ ✿ ✿

"Dwayne sounds like a really nice guy, Misha," Aalia had said. "But I think you should find out more about those gangs on his estate. It's highly likely that he's either a member of one or affiliated to one. All the boys are these days."

"How would you know, Aalia?"

Aalia was the quintessential quiet Muslim girl who, although she didn't wear a scarf, always wore a pair of straight trousers instead of the pleated skirts that most of us wore. Her hair was pulled back in a neat ponytail and the only hint of exoticism was her tiny gold nose stud, something a lot of Pakistani girls had.

"I live in South-East London, Misha," Aalia replied. "I pass those estates every day. Plus... my brother's been getting into some trouble lately. Gang trouble."

"What do you mean 'gang trouble'?"

Aalia's voice was pained. "Some of those gangs are really bad, Misha. They sell drugs, they rob and stab people and destroy property. Haven't you seen some of the shops in the really rough areas? They're all boarded up to stop the thugs from smashing the windows and robbing the store.

"All I'm saying is you want to be sure that Dwayne's not involved in that stuff. I'd hate to see you sucked into that life. I know you live in leafy Dulwich and all that, but you need to open your eyes more. Not everything is as green and serene as it is on this side of the school gates."

✿ ✿ ✿

As I sat in the back of the car, watching the buildings flash past, my stomach began tying itself in knots. I thought once again about the pastor's sermon and whether it was relevant to my own life. And I closed my eyes and recalled an image of a tall black boy, with the same hooded top as Dwayne – looking *exactly* like Dwayne – crossing a busy street in Camberwell, surrounded by a group of rough-looking black boys in hoodies, bandannas around their foreheads. I had to rub my arms hard to get rid of the goose-bumps.

Succession

DWAYNE

I was proper mash-up on Monday morning when I went to school. I couldn't stop thinking about Trigger and Jukkie. That madness with the woman and her babies had been playing on my mind all weekend – and then there was Lightning. We'd all gone to see him in hospital on Sunday morning and he was proper bruck-up, his eyes swollen shut, one side of his face dark with bruises. His arm was in a sling and his leg was bandaged up. Dem man didn't even care that he was just a little kid, a younger who didn't know any better. They bruck him up, same way.

His mum went mad when she saw us at the hospital. We all went, even Tony. It wouldn't have been right otherwise. Tony looked different, though, with less bling and a different look in his eyes. I could tell that his time with the 'brothers' at the mosque was having an effect on him.

"What are you doing here?" Lightning's mum shouted, proper loud so that all the patients and nurses turned to look at us.

"I'm so sorry, Mrs Appiah," Tony said, all humble. "I don't know how this happened... you know we've always looked after little Kofi." That was Lightning's real name.

"Looked after him?" Her voice was hoarse. "You're the reason my son is lying there now! You and all these boys let him hang around with you even though you knew I didn't want him to!"

"We tried our best to protect him, Mrs Appiah," repeated Tony, looking down at Lightning. "This should never have happened." Then I saw him cut his eye at Trigger. Trigger shifted his eyes, quick-time. I didn't understand what it was all about but I could see that Tony was vex'.

"Well, you didn't try hard enough." Mrs Appiah's words came out like bullets from a gun, hitting all of us where it hurt most. Lightning was one of us, a Younger. He was our responsibility and we'd let him down, big time.

When we got outside the hospital, Tony turned on Trigger. "What the hell are you *thinking*, blud?" he yelled, pushing Trigger against the wall.

"*What*?" Trigger screwed up his face and tried to push Tony off but Tony pushed him further up the wall.

"You *know* what, blud! Don't act stupid!" The spit from Tony's mouth landed on Trigger's face as we all watched, tense, wondering what was going to happen next. I was totally confused – what was Tony on about?

"You! You and your foolishness with the Larkside man is what caused this!"

Then I understood.

"I'm not the one who beat Lightning, so get *off* me!"

"You started this beef ting with Lockjaw and you knew that dem man wasn't gonna walk away! You knew they wouldn't back down but you went for them anyway! What you tryin' to prove?"

"Don't try and boy me, yeah!" Trigger kicked out at Tony and his new trainer hit Tony in the knee. Tony staggered backwards and Trigger rushed at him, grabbed him by the collar and pushed him up against one of the parked cars. I looked round quickly and saw one of the security guards coming towards us.

"Allow this, man!" I said, pulling Jukkie by the arm. "We need to duck out of here."

But Jukkie stood still, as if he was in a video game stuck on pause. He was just staring at Trigger and Tony as they struggled between the parked cars. A vein in his forehead throbbed and he was chewing his lip like crazy. I guess it must be hard to watch your elder brother being beaten up by your new mentor.

"All right, you lot, break it up!" Two security guards stepped up to Tony and Trigger and pulled them apart. They struggled and cussed but the two guards didn't let go. "You boys better move along. If you carry on like this, we'll have no choice but to call the police."

That was enough to cool their blood. Both of them stopped struggling and stood there, breathing hard, wiping their mouths, eyeing each other up. The guards pushed them to get them moving and barked, "Clear off, the lot of you!"

We stumbled towards the two cars, Tony's and Trigger's, all of us a bit dazed by everything that had just happened.

When we got to where the two cars were parked, Tony turned to face Trigger, who pulled himself up and scowled at him. "Trig, I'm warning you, blud. Be careful with dem Larkside mans. You've got to take care of RDS now – protect what we've built – and that ain't gonna happen if you get involved in a mad turf war with dem man."

Trigger twisted his face and snarled, "I ain't afraid of no one, y'get me. Anyway, you ain't part of the RDS no more, innit? So what you worrying about? Go back to your mosque and leave man to take care of business, yeah?"

Tony looked at Trigger for a long minute, then shook his head and sighed. "Juks, let's go." He turned to leave.

"Nah, man," said Jukkie, all quiet-like. "I'm gonna roll with da mans."

Tony looked at him, kinda hurt and surprised-looking. Then he shrugged and walked off to his car. He didn't look back once.

Heavy. Jukkie told me later that Tony had gone home and packed a bag, telling his mum that he was going to the Midlands to stay with 'the brothers', to 'clear his head and decide what's what'. I think he couldn't stand to see everything he had built being jeopardised by Trigger. Or maybe he just needed to get himself into the zone so that he could 'do' his Muslim ting properly, as he kept saying. All I knew was I was going to miss him, no doubt. I tried to write some rhymes when I got home but, true say, I wasn't feeling it. I felt mad jumpy, as if I could hear a timer ticking somewhere, the bomb about to explode any minute.

❖ ❖ ❖

Walking into school that day, my mind was working overtime. What happened between Tony and Trigger was major, y'get me. We RDS boys had always respected Tony, always trusted him. Even if you didn't like something Tony did or a decision he made, you'd go with it out of respect. Coz you knew that, any time anything went down, Tony had your back. But now that Trigger was top dog, things were changing in RDS. Trig wanted to prove himself, innit. I knew one thing for sure: Tony would never have let things get this bad with Larkside. He wasn't about beef, no way. He just wanted to live good: make money and have girls.

But Trigger? He was on a different flex. It was as if he wanted to prove to everyone how bad he was. Trigger wasn't interested in partying. For him, it was all about control and respect, making man fear him, know what he was capable of. The garmz and the cars were a side thing. What really got him off was the power. And I could see Jukkie becoming the same. Or maybe he had always been that way but just couldn't express it too tough with Tony in charge....

I was so busy thinking, I didn't watch where I was going. Suddenly I felt something bang into me.

"Are you *blind*, rudeboy?"

I staggered backwards, my bag weighing me down. When I looked round to see where the voice had come from, I saw Leon Mackay glaring at me. Though he was short, Leon was a champion boxer with the biceps and six-pack to prove it. He was in Year 11 too, but in a different class from me. I didn't really know him too tough but I knew better than to get into a fight with him. He was standing with his boys, some of them from our school, others in hoodies and green bandannas.

Green bandannas.

Larkside boys.

Leon looked me in the eye and snarled, "You're Jukkie's best mate, ain't ya?"

I nodded, not saying anything, trying to figure out what they wanted with me, what they wanted with Jukkie.

But then Leon was up in my face and I stepped back

until I could feel the school wall behind me. It was hard and rough, and I thought to myself, 'Anyhow this damages my leather jacket...' But before I could tell Leon to take it easy on the garmz, he grabbed my jacket and hoisted me higher up against the wall. "He's goin' down for what he did to my cousin," he hissed, and his breath stank like he hadn't brushed his teeth in at least two weeks.

"Your cousin? Who's your cousin, man? I don't know what you're talking about!"

"He knows." Leon clenched his jaw and brought his face so close to mine that I could see the blackheads on his nose. "You tell your mandem," he growled, "that we're coming for them. They picked the wrong crew to mess with." Then I felt something cold and sharp press into my cheek. I couldn't stop myself shuddering as I realised what it was. It was a tiny switch-blade. "Do I need to give you a little reminder, blud?"

I shook my head, trying not to show how scared I was. "Nah, man, it's safe," I said hoarsely. "I...I'll pass the message... I'll pass the message!" Gathering up my strength, I shoved Leon off me and the boys all shifted, ready for Leon's signal. But Leon just smirked and put his knife into his pocket.

"Yeah," he sneered. "I know you will. Coz you's

a batty man like that best mate of yours, Jukkie."
The other boys all sniggered as I scrambled for my
bag. "Go on, run, run like a bitch!"

Boy, I wasn't about to stick around! I grabbed my
bag and legged it, in through the school gates and all
the way to the toilets, where I spent a few minutes
heaving. Knives, man. Knives and I just were not
meant to be together. If I didn't know better, I would
think I was allergic to them.

As I washed my face and looked in the mirror at the
water dripping down on to my school shirt, I heard
Leon's voice: 'You's a batty man, like your best mate,
Jukkie.'

I shook my head and wiped a tissue over my face.
This beef with Larkside was getting proper ugly.

Circles

DWAYNE

Third lesson was Maths with Mr Dawson, my worst teacher. I actually wasn't too bad at Maths but I couldn't stick that Mr Dawson. I'd started off the year all right, but there was just something about him that put me right off. By the third week, I was like everyone else in the class: sending text messages, throwing spit balls, drawing tags in their Maths books or bustin' joke behind Dawson's back.

But that day, I just wasn't in the mood for the madness. I was thinking about Misha and what she would think if she saw this crappy classroom with its busted chairs and graffiti carved into the desks. Misha's school sounded proper posh. I imagined it all big and stately-home-looking, with green lawns all around it. All the girls would be wearing them old-fashioned blazers and be able to speak at least three languages.

Misha was always asking me about school – what could I tell her? That I hated it and couldn't wait for the year to be over so that I could hit the road and make some serious Ps? Nah, that would be a disaster. Misha *believed* in school. She believed them when they told her that all she had to do was study hard, go university, get a good job and buy a house. And maybe it was true – for her and people like her. As for me, I knew that it was all a big lie.

"School's just a holding cell for us black boys," Tony used to say. "Just a place for them to keep us until we're old enough to go jail. But not us, eh, guys? We're smarter than that. We ain't never gonna get so cocky that we let the 5-0 take us down."

But what was it Misha had said? 'Rewrite the script, Dee. If you don't, who will?'

I looked up to see Mr Dawson handing out sheets of paper for a pop quiz.

I cracked up when Mr Beanpole himself, Greg Tiller, screwed up the piece of paper and threw it into the bin. "Oh, look, sir!" he called out. "Pop goes the quiz!"

Mr Dawson shook the hair out of his eyes.

"Any more of your nonsense, Tiller, and you'll be going to see Ms Walker, d'you understand? Now go and retrieve your quiz and get yourself back to your seat!"

I looked at the paper in front of me: circle geometry. I smiled. Circle geometry made total sense to me. While I looked over the questions, it was as if I could feel my brain getting to work, connecting things, making sense of things – I got it.

'Rewrite the script. Ace the test.'

'What?'

'Don't act dumb, man, you heard me: ace the test.'

So I did. I answered every question, double-checked, found a couple of careless mistakes, corrected them, and then sat back, grinning.

'You did it, blud. Nice one.'

'Thanks.'

'Shut up.'

Silence.

'That's better.'

Mr Dawson told everyone to stop writing. The time for the quiz was up. Then he asked Stuart 'Swottie' Henderson to read out the answers. I could feel my heart start to beat fast as I reached the end of the paper and looked back at the row of ticks along the side.

I had aced the test. I really had!

Mr Dawson called out, "OK, who got full marks?" I swear, he sounded so bored, I wondered why he had given us the quiz in the first place. He was looking towards Swottie and the other kids in the front row, Azad, Miranda, Kwesi and Suad. They all raised their hands, like they always did.

Then I did something crazy, something I would never have done before: I raised my hand, from all the way at the back of the class. Mr Dawson looked up and saw me – and his mouth just kinda fell open. Then he pulled himself together and frowned.

"Mr Kingston," he whined, as if he was talking to a retard, "is there a problem? Did you not complete the test?"

I forced myself to speak even though I was regretting ever having raised my hand. "I...I did, sir."

Rashad was looking at me, all screw-face, as if to say, 'What you doing, bro, raising your hand in class? Are you out of your mind?'

Mr Dawson flipped his hair out of his eyes and sighed loudly, saying, "Mr Kingston, we shall all have the opportunity to ask questions later. Right now, we are trying to see who passed and who failed!"

"But that's why my hand is up, sir."

"What?"

"I passed, sir. I got full marks. Remember? You told the people who got full marks to raise their hands..."

Mr Dawson's jaw dropped for the second time and he shook his head a couple of times, looking from the swots sitting in front of him to me, the tall black boy with the expensive trainers in the back row. Then he narrowed his eyes and marched over to where I was sitting. He snatched up my paper and looked over it. Then he looked down at me and his lip curled.

"You didn't do this, Mr Kingston," he said, just like that. "This is not your work."

"What?"

"You don't expect me to believe that you actually understand anything about circle geometry, do you? I mean, let's face it, Mr Kingston, you're no whizz kid!"

Oh, then I started to feel the rage build up inside me and my face began feeling hot.

Mr Dawson continued, "I suppose it's to be expected, a desperate attempt to get some passing grades so near the end of term but the trouble is, it's too late. Do you understand? *It's too late.* Anyway, I know your lot; you'll never amount to anything..."

"What d'you mean '*your lot*'?" I asked. I was

proper bubbling now.

"Yeah, man!" said Rashad. "What the hell is *that* supposed to mean?"

"Racist!" someone shouted at the back. Everyone started talking at once.

"Can you believe he said that, though?"

"He's out of order, mate!"

"Bang the teacher! Bang the teacher!" The other kids starting banging on the desks and drumming their feet on the floor.

Mr Dawson stepped back, anxious now, his eyes flicking about the room. "All right, everyone, calm down! I didn't mean it like that, there's no need to make a big deal out of it!"

After a while everyone calmed down, but they were still grumbling.

"Now, Kingston, the sooner you confess to *cheating* on the pop quiz, you sooner we can get on with the lesson." And he turned to walk back to his desk.

"But, sir, I didn't cheat!" That was when I pushed my chair back from my desk. "I didn't cheat!"

Mr Dawson didn't even turn to look at me. "Save it, Mr Kingston, you can either admit to cheating on the test, in which case I will award you an 'F' grade, or you can continue to deny it and be awarded an 'F' grade *and* a visit to Ms Walker."

I felt the pressure build up inside me and I heard the whistling, whistling in my head, like the sound of a really fast train on a massive collision course. Just then, it was more important to me than anything that the teacher admit that I had passed, that I wasn't a waste of space, a loser.

I stood right up and my chair went flying, clattering to the floor. I was so mad, I was shaking, my nostrils flaring like crazy. I held my paper out towards Mr Dawson. "Sir!" I called out. "Test me again if you don't believe me. Go on, test me!"

The others backed me up: "That's right, Sir! Just test him, innit."

Mr Dawson turned slowly to look at the class. "I'm afraid that would be a waste of class time. Now, kindly take your seat, Mr Kingston, or you will leave me no alternative but to issue you an official warning."

"Allow this, man!" I shouted. I could feel my eyes start to burn. I tore the test paper in half, threw it on the floor, grabbed my coat and bag, and charged out of the room. *What a waste of time, man!*

"Mr Kingston! Mr Kingston, I'm warning you!" But the slamming door cut off Mr Dawson's voice.

✿ ✿ ✿

Outside the school building, I stood in the car park, my shoulders heaving, the heat pounding in my head. I was proper vex'– what was the point of trying if they never gave you a chance?

I looked out into the car park, trying to find Mr Dawson's dark blue Fiat. It was right at the end, near the fence. I didn't have to think twice.

'Don't do it, blud!'

'Shut up!'

'Don't do it, man, he ain't worth it!'

'I said SHUT UP! No one disrespects me like that, yeah? No one!'

'It ain't worth it, blud.'

'Yes it IS!'

My house keys jingled in the silent car park as I pulled them out of my bag. Then, slowly and carefully, I pulled one of the keys along the side of Mr Dawson's car, again and again. The sickening screech of metal on metal hurt my ears but I didn't stop until I had left a whole heap of silver lines in the dark-blue paint work.

Then I heard a voice shout out, 'Kingston! What the hell d'you think you're doing?'

That's when I ran.

Ms Walker

DWAYNE

"Dwayne, Dwayne Kingston, isn't it?" Ms Walker, the new head-teacher who struck fear into even the baddest students, was glaring down at me.

"Yes, Miss," I mumbled. I looked down into my lap and hunched my shoulders. This was the last place I wanted to be, sitting in the head's cluttered office with my mum huffing and puffing next to me.

Mum poked me, hard. "Speak up and sit up *straight*, boy!" she hissed. She was vex' that she had had to take the morning off work to come and speak to Ms Walker about her wort'less son.

"This is just a waste of my time," she had grumbled, as we got on the bus.

I glanced up and saw Ms Walker looking at Mum. Then she pursed her lips and sat down, turning to me. I looked down straight away.

"Mr Dawson says you were rude and disruptive in his class yesterday," she said quietly. I was surprised – I was expecting her to yell at me, go crazy and that. But she didn't. She just kept on talking. "He says you caused a scene. And another member of staff said that they saw you vandalising Mr Dawson's car. What do you say?"

'Tell her!'

'What?'

'Tell her exactly what happened!'

'Nah, man, I ain't telling her nothin'!'

'You'd better tell her, mate, or your chances of getting out of this will be even less than they are now. You're already on a losing streak. Speak up now, before it's too late.'

Silence.

'OK, suit y'self. But don't say I didn't warn you.'

Then Mum spoke up. "Ms Walker, I don't mean to be rude but this really is a waste of time. Dwayne doesn't care about school. He doesn't care about exams or teachers or any of that. So you might as well just give him whatever punishment you like and send him back to class – and let me get back to my job. I don't get paid for taking time off to talk about Dwayne's bad school record – can't you tell a hopeless case when you see one?"

"Jeez, thanks for the vote of confidence, Mum." I felt a lump in my throat and I turned away from her. She really had given up on me; I could hear it in her voice. I don't know why I cared but, right then, I did.

Then Ms Walker turned to Mum. "Well, Mrs Kingston, although it might seem the sensible thing to do, I am not ready to write your son off just yet. I would still like to hear his version of what happened with Mr Dawson." She looked over at me, obviously expecting me to come up with my side of the story.

So I told her about the test, about getting everything right, about Mr Dawson refusing to believe me, accusing me of cheating, refusing to let me take the test again.

"I was vex', Miss, proper vex'. It's not fair to accuse someone and not even give them a chance to defend themselves. Do you know what he said to me, Miss? He said that my lot – boys like me – will never amount to anything! But how can we if even our teachers don't believe in us?"

Ms Walker nodded. "You have a valid point there, young man. Black boys in this society face many obstacles as it is and low expectations from teaching staff just add to the problem. Don't you agree, Mrs Kingston?"

"To tell you the truth," replied Mum with a sour look on her face, "it all sounds like excuses to me."

Ms Walker raised an eyebrow and gave me a look. "Well," she said, "there can be no excuse for damaging a teacher's property, no matter how angry you are. That was a stupid thing to do – Mr Dawson could choose to press charges. It is vandalism, as I'm sure you know..."

"Press charges, Miss?"

"Yes, Mr Kingston! The man's car is a mess! You didn't seriously think you would get away with it, did you?"

I scratched my head and looked down. Coz I hadn't been thinking at all, y'get me.

Mum spoke up then. "But Ms Walker, why can't these boys just show some respect? Why can't they just put their heads down and work hard? We did it! But all they want is easy money; all they want is to look like badman out on the street. Then they get involved in all sorts of things: stealing, gangs, drugs, knives, guns, all that madness! Who taught them all that? Not me! Not their parents! They went out there and looked for it, that's what I say! That's why I give up, Ms Walker. There's only so many times your heart can break, yuh see. This boy here, he done broke my heart a hundred times. Whatever yuh want to do to him, it's fine by me. Maybe you'll succeed where I failed." And she sniffed and wiped a tear from her eye.

'You made your mum cry.'

'Shut up, man!'

'But you did.'

Silence.

'How do you feel?'

Silence.

'Like crap, innit?'

Silence.

'Yeah, I thought so.'

"Well, Dwayne," Ms Walker continued, "I don't expect you to tell me the ins and outs of your life outside school. What concerns me is your performance in school." She looked right at me as she leaned back in her big leather chair. "Where do you see yourself in ten years' time? Have you thought that far ahead?"

I looked at her, my face blank. How was I meant to answer that question?

"Perhaps you'll have your own car, a 'phat ride', and a wardrobe full of designer clothes? You might even have your own business, hustling, selling drugs, dealing in stolen merchandise. Does that sound about right?"

Mum glared at me and I kept quiet. I wasn't about to get caught out by that one.

"But then again, maybe you'll be in jail by then, rotting away with thousands of other black boys that society has tossed to the side. Maybe you stabbed somebody, or shot someone's son, or got caught during a robbery? Maybe you'll be an addict yourself. What will it be? Heroin, cocaine? Or something less glamorous, perhaps, crack maybe?"

A crackhead? *Me*?

"Nah, Miss, I ain't going out like that, no way!"

She raised her eyebrow again, her arms folded in front of her. "OK, then, maybe you won't become a criminal at all, just an unemployed bum, signing on, drinking his Jobseekers' Allowance on the street corner. Just another statistic. What will it be, Dwayne? What will it be?"

I said nothing. I just knew she wasn't finished. She didn't know that she was asking me all the questions I had been asking myself ever since I met Misha.

"Are you intending to continue your studies after GCSE?"

That was the biggie: the one that had been wrecking my head. Misha thought it was possible, said she knew

I could do it... but who else from my sides was going down that road? No one, that's who. But maybe... just maybe... I could be the one.... Maybe?

"Well," I answered, choosing my words carefully, "I might want to get a piece of paper, just in case. But I don't think I'll be able to do the whole 'A' Level, uni ting. My marks ain't been great so far, plus I don't think I'm cut out for all that..."

I heard Mum take a deep breath next to me. "No one in our family has ever been to university," she explained to Ms Walker. "I try to teach my boys to be realistic and practical. What are the chances of my children getting into university – with all those posh people? It's better they keep their feet on the ground and not get carried away with wild dreams." But the way she was looking at me was different from the way she normally did. Like she was seeing me for the first time.

Now it was Mum's turn to get the raised eyebrow treatment. "If you truly believe that, Mrs Kingston, it's no wonder Dwayne is underperforming at school." Then she turned to me, flipping through the folder on the desk in front of her. "You may need to retake some GCSEs next year, Mr Kingston, judging by your current performance. Are you prepared to do that?"

"I think so." I couldn't believe that I said it, but I did.

"Well, you need to be absolutely sure that this is what you want, Dwayne. It's not going to come running towards you. You're going to have to be hungry. Stand up."

I was proper embarrassed then, but I stood up anyway, looking everywhere but at this lady in front of me with the fierce eyes and the straight talk.

"What I see before me is unfulfilled promise. Do you have what it takes to rise above your circumstances and fulfil your potential? Do you?"

I kinda nodded. What did she expect me to say?

"Hmph," said Mum. "This I have to see." But there was a smile forcing its way through her scowl and I thought, 'That's it, she's chuffed. I'm not the wort'less Dwayne now, am I?'

Then Ms Walker clapped her hands together and marched round the side of the desk to stand in front of me. "So, you, Dwayne Kingston, will be entered in the higher-tier exams for Maths. You will take extra lessons with Mr Patel as well as helping the Year 8 children after school. I suggest you start serious work on your coursework, although it may be too late to get the kind of marks you need. But getting serious with your books will keep you occupied and, hopefully, out of trouble. You will also have to pay for the repairs to Mr Dawson's car. And," she added, wagging her finger at me, "if there is any more trouble, you will have me to answer to – and I may not be so optimistic next time, understood?"

I nodded. I understood perfectly. Crystal clear.

Ms Walker put her hand on Mum's shoulder as she stood up. "Try to give him another chance, Mrs Kingston. He may surprise you. In fact, I am almost certain he will."

Mum gave me a look and sniffed. "We'll see, Ms Walker." But she waved at Ms Walker as she left the office.

"Mum..." I wanted to apologise, to tell her I would do better, that I wouldn't let her down.

She turned to face me. "What is it now, Dwayne?"

I could hear that irritation rising again and I fell back. I couldn't say sorry. I just couldn't. Plus, I didn't want to disappoint her again. "Have a nice day, yeah?"

"Thank you, son," she said, before opening her umbrella and stepping out into the rain.

I stood and watched her go.

'You made her day now, innit.'

'Yeah.'

'Didn't I tell you?'

'Yeah, you did.'

'That's coz I look out for you, blud, standard.'

'Yeah, I know.'

'So, we cool?'

'Yeah, we cool.'

'And don't even get me **started** on how pleased Misha is gonna be with you!'

'Shut up now, man. Enough!'

'A' right.'

Silence.

Crazy In Love

MISHA

Dwayne had entered my bloodstream.

Without me even knowing how, that boy had worked his way into my head in such a way that, every time I closed my eyes, I saw his face. Every time I caught a whiff of peppermint gum, I thought of him. When he told me he would call later, I was jittery with nerves, literally jumping every time my phone rang. I was constantly on high alert, waiting for a text, for a phone call. And when it came it was like food to a starving woman: I just couldn't get enough.

Suffice to say, I had it bad.

But I still hadn't plucked up the courage to tell Mum. Ordinarily, I would tell her as soon as I met a guy. She had always encouraged me to be upfront about boys, anyway.

"I prefer to know what I'm dealing with," she liked to say.

"How come you haven't told your mum about Dwayne?" Aalia wanted to know.

I rolled my eyes. "Well, the fact that I met him at a party Mum didn't even know about is a pretty big factor."

"You snuck out to go to that party?" Aalia's eyes were wide. Of course, she would never dream of doing such a thing, I thought. Her father would probably skin her alive if he caught her.

"I wouldn't exactly call it sneaking out," I replied. "We stayed over at Victoria's house and her mum knew where we were going..."

Aalia gave me a look and put her hand on her hip. "*Victoria's mum* knew where you were going?"

"Yeah, we told her we were going to a party in South London!"

"And was she actually awake at the time?"

I grinned sheepishly and shrugged my shoulders. "Hey, we told her, OK?"

Aalia flicked her ponytail. "Whatever you say, babe."

I knew what Aalia was thinking. We both knew the real story about Victoria Adebayo, she of the Naomi

Campbell looks, silky straight weave and fabulous house in Ladbroke Grove, next door to Richard Branson.

Several times a year Victoria's dad, who was the latest in a line of wealthy chiefs, would visit his other wives and children back home in Nigeria in his private plane, often returning with one or two kids who were ready to start boarding school in England.

But every time he flew back to Nigeria, Victoria's mum sank into depression and spent several weeks stoned on Prozac.

So I knew full well that Mrs Adebayo would not have had any clue about what party we had been to, or where. Which led to the problem I was now facing: Dwayne was becoming a huge part of my life and it was becoming impossible to pretend otherwise. For a start, Mum had started giving me very funny looks every time my text message alert sounded. Must have been the way I leapt to the phone as if my life depended on it, while trying to act casual.

"But I'm not sure what my mum will think of him," I confided in Effie, my mentor in all matters of the heart. "He's not exactly the kind of boy she encourages me to date: polite, well spoken and well brought-up, from a good family, a boy with 'prospects'..."

"You mean boring as hell?" Although Effie was the daughter of two Ghanaian professors – Dr and Dr Mensah – she was probably the wildest girl in the school.

Amongst the other black girls at our school, Effie was most definitely the Queen Bee. Now that she had passed her GCSEs and was doing her 'A' Levels, she had cemented her reputation as a good-time girl – she lived hard and fast, although her parents had no idea.

"As far as I'm concerned," she would say, "life would be unbearable without two things: hot guys and a healthy dose of excitement."

"Don't you mean living dangerously?" I was constantly in awe of Effie's double life – and the risks she was prepared to take.

"Yup, I'll own up to that. You only live once, right? What's the point if everything is boring and predictable? In my book, there is no such thing as 'safe sex'. It's either maximum excitement or a cold shower, sweetheart, so deal with it!"

Effie remembered Dwayne from the party in South London so she had been impressed when I told her that we had been talking on the phone and that I was considering going out with him.

"Oooh," she crowed, "baby Misha is finally growing up, huh? A roughneck boyfriend, eh? Congratulations, darling!"

I ignored her patronising tone.

"Not quite as rough as your latest, I see," I said, eyeing the two purple lovebites on her neck. Her shirt collar wasn't quite high enough to hide them.

"I've been wearing a lot of scarves at home," she smirked. "Anyway, don't change the subject! I want to know if you've asked your mum's permission. You know what a total control freak she is..."

"I prefer the term 'caring parent' myself," I remarked, shooting her a look. "And anyway, I don't even know whether anything will come of it so I'm not going to mention anything yet."

My initial plan was to keep Dwayne a secret for a while, just to see how things turned out. But the way things were developing, I was going to have to come clean. So, two months after I started seeing Dwayne, I told Mum about him, and how I felt about him.

"Mum," I began while we were having our regular Saturday morning coffee at Starbucks, "I've met this guy."

"Really?" said Mum, taking a sip of her latte.

"Tell me about him..."

"Well, his name's Dwayne, Dwayne Kingston and, oooh, he's *wonderful*!" I practically shivered with delight, causing Mum to raise an eyebrow. "I swear, Mum, this is it, I know it! He is 'the one'!"

"Oh, really?" Mum smiled, amused by all the giggles and girly emotion. "So when do I get to meet this young Romeo?"

"Whenever you like, Mum," I responded breathlessly. I was so high on Dwayne-love that I was sure Mum would be as taken with Dwayne as I was, that she would see what I saw: a diamond in the rough.

Closing In

DWAYNE

After weeks of bugging me, my little brother Jay finally cornered me as I was coming out of the shower on Saturday morning.

"You've *got* to take me bowling today, bro," he said, his arms folded across his puny little chest. "No excuses."

I mentally checked my diary: all good until six. There was a jam happening up in Tottenham and I wanted to go down and spit some bars. I preferred to leave my endz to do my music: mans around here were hard to please and every local jam I'd ever done had ended with man cussing each other and someone throwing a fist, a bottle or both. Jukkie loved the excitement and went out of his way to start a fight, but for me it was about the beats, not the beef.

"OK, little brother," I said, punching him lightly on the shoulder. "You're on."

"Jerome!" Mum called from the kitchen. "Come and eat your breakfast, boy!"

"What about me, Mum?" I cocked my head and listened, then smiled when I heard Mum kiss her teeth. I knew that she wasn't going to cook breakfast for me. She had stopped doing that long ago. "Thanks, Mum," I called back. "You sure know how to make a man feel special."

Then I saw Jay look away and I felt bad. He hated it when Mum and I argued. "Sorry, little man," I said softly. "Don't watch me, yeah? Me and Mum are cool."

Jay looked up at me, his face all doubtful. "Are you gonna get chucked out of school, Dee?"

"Nah, man, nah! Nothing like that, man. Nothing like that."

Jay shrugged. "It don't make no difference anyway, does it? Spaz told me that he's gonna make mad loot when he joins RDS for real. Then he won't need school and he can do what he likes."

"Oh, yeah?" I squatted down in front of Jay, my back against the wall. "What else did little Spazzie say?"

"He says mans like be makin' about a grand a week, running errands for Trigger. A grand, y'know! Can you imagine how many kicks you could get for that money?" Jay's eyes glazed over and I could see him imagining himself in a phat ride, maybe a red Lamborghini, gold chains swinging, diamond rings twinkling, driving round the estate, a big man.

"With that kind of money, who needs a job, man?" Jay continued. "I say school's for losers who ain't got no sense." And he walked off down the corridor, all hard now, bopping in the exact same way as his best friend, Spaz.

I looked at my kid brother's back, ten years old and already wise to the ways of the street. Had I been so clued-up at that age? I couldn't help thinking of what Ms Walker had said, earlier in the week. I wondered what she would make of little Jay, a street-life apprentice before he even knew his times tables.

Then I kissed my teeth. Enough of this crap. I had a day to get through.

❖ ❖ ❖

On the way to the bowling alley in Streatham, Jay was in hyper mode, chatting about everything and nothing. Poor guy was stoked because I had agreed to take him out. I definitely needed to be there for him more. Streatham seemed a safe enough area, I thought to myself. No risk of running into any beef there. At first, I tried to keep track of all his stories but after a while, I zoned out and began to think of other things, trying to sort through the crap that was clogging up my brain.

'Dwayne, man, what're you doing?'

'What do you mean, 'what am I doing'? Ain't it obvious? I'm taking my kid brother to the bowling alley.'

'Nah, man, I ain't talking about that. I mean what're you doing with your life?'

Silence.

'Well?'

'I don't know.'

'But why don't you know, tho?'

'I don't know, I'm confused, innit!'

'What are the choices?'

'What d'you mean?'

'Don't act dumb, man, you ain't in school! What are your choices, Dwayne?'

'Well...'

'Yes..?'

'I ain't good at a lot of stuff, y'know.'

'Spare me the sob story, yeah, I've heard it all before.

We've been hearing it since forever! It's time to flip the script. Tell me what you **can** do.'

'Well...'

'Yes...?'

'Well, I'm good at Maths, innit. I can take a set of numbers and spin it on its head and make it come alive and start dancing like it's on fire or something... I can do that.'

'OK, that's a start. That's a good start.'

'I can spit too, like a maestro.'

'True dat...'

'Thanks.'

'Shut up.'

'OK.'

'I said, 'Shut up'!'

Silence.

'Good. Right, what about these GCSEs, man, what's up with them?'

'Nah, man, I can't be dealing with those exams! Ms Walker may think she's got it all figured out but she don't know my reality.'

'What about Misha? She definitely seems to know what she's doing...'

'Dem people's different, man, we ain't the same.'

'Why not?'

'I don't know, they're just different. Kinda like white

people... I can't explain it. All I know is, yeah, there ain't
no teachers at my school who believe that any of us are even
gonna pass our exams, let alone go to college or university.
It just ain't gonna happen, blud.'

'Says who?'

'Everyone knows that.'

'Everyone?'

'Yeah... no.'

Silence.

'Not everyone.'

*'So what do **you** know?'*

'I know you need to get the hell out of my head, that's
what I know!'

Silence.

'So that's it?'

Silence.

'Really?'

'I'll say one last thing...'

'Ha, I knew you was still there!'

'I'm out, mate, I'm just gonna say one last thing: you
need to check this beef with Trigger and Larkside mans.
Before it's too late.'

'That's it?'

Silence.

'OK.'

We had reached the bowling alley. We bounced off the bus and on to the curb but, as we walked towards the large yellow building I slowed down, my heart hammering in my chest. I caught sight of a green bandanna under a hood and, as if in slow motion, the boy wearing the hood turned towards me and I saw the scowling face and the scar running like a silver ribbon across his forehead.

My heart stopped dead in my chest.

It was Lockjaw, head of the Larkside Crew.

Straight away, I looked around and saw four, five, six of them, bopping towards the bowling alley. And I knew then that there would be no bowling for me and Jay that day. I didn't know what Larkside mans were doing down Streatham sides, but I wasn't about to hang around and find out. With all the beef that was going on, I couldn't risk it, not after what had happened to Lightning and Spoonz.

I flipped up my hood.

"Come on, bro," I muttered, my hands like steel on Jay's shoulders. "Let's get out of here." Ignoring his squeals, I pushed him on to the bus that had just pulled up and marched him up the stairs to sit at the back. I looked out of the window to see whether they had followed us but I could see that the last of them were going into the bowling alley.

But I didn't see Lockjaw. Had he seen me? Had he followed us on to the bus?

Seconds dragged like nails on a blackboard as I kept looking towards the bus stairs, expecting Lockjaw to come bounding up. But then the bus began to move and I sat back in the chair, relieved.

But I had to look out of the window one last time – and that was when I saw Lockjaw standing at the bus stop, staring right up at me, a hard, cold look in his eye, like he wanted to smoke me right then and there. He reached towards his back pocket and pulled something from it.

Instinctively I ducked down, pulling Jay with me.

But when I looked again through the back window, when the bus was a safe distance away, I saw Lockjaw's empty hands swinging free.

"Sorry about that, Jay," I muttered, closing my eyes. "Let's go get some McDonald's down our sides."

I could feel everything closing in on me. How the hell was this beef with Larkside ever going to end?

Wrong Side Of The Tracks

MISHA

"Why don't you invite your boyfriend Dwayne to a barbecue this weekend?" asked Mum, watching the weather forecast. "We could invite Auntie Loretta... oh, and Auntie Dionne – and Uncle Sam – I owe them an invitation actually."

I groaned, audibly for once. "Do we have to invite Uncle Sam, Mum? It's just that he's so... difficult."

"Hey, young lady, watch it. That's family you're talking about." She thought for a minute, then said, "Why don't you ask Effie to come too? That way Dwayne won't feel like he's being put on the spot."

I thought about that: Effie might be a good choice. She had met Dwayne before and liked him (well, she thought he was hot, anyway). And she knew how to charm adults, no doubt about that. Maybe her being there *would* make it easier for Dwayne....

But Dwayne wasn't too keen on the idea of coming to my house and actually meeting my mum.

"What if she doesn't like me?" he fretted. "I don't get along with adults too tough, y'know. Anyway, how come your mum wants to meet me? Does she have to approve your boyfriends or something?"

I said nothing. How could I explain to Dwayne how my mum saw things? My business was her business. It wasn't that Mum was a control freak, not exactly. Just that she had very specific ideas about what was best for me. She had had the same ideas ever since she had moved us out of Brixton. I was her only daughter and I was going to be a success, a high flyer. Everything – even my clothes, my hair, my school, my choice of friends – had to be in line with that vision. Everything had to be up to Mum's standard. That's how it had always been.

"Dwayne, this is something important to me and I want my mum to know about it. She trusts me and I wouldn't like to betray that trust, you know? I feel bad enough that I've kept it quiet for this long."

Dwayne shook his head, chuckling. "You lot are different, man. My mum doesn't care about what I do – as long as I don't come home with no baby.

Down my sides, if you get with a girl, you get with her, not her and her grandad's cousin. It ain't none of their business, y'get me. But if this is important to you, babe, I'll do it. You need me to be there, I'll be there."

I thought about the relief of not having to sneak around and hide any more and smiled. "My mum has good taste," I said. "She's going to love you, you'll see."

✿ ✿ ✿

The week flew by and, before I knew it, it was Saturday, the Big Day.

I was so excited that I didn't know what to do with myself: I tried my hair in four different styles, tried on three different outfits, reapplied my make-up twice. I looked at my reflection in the mirror – I was glowing. And looking kinda gorgeous too.

Finally, Mum became exasperated and called up the stairs. "Are we going to get any help around here or are you going to spend the whole day getting dolled up for your boyfriend?"

Then I calmed down and the enormity of what was about to happen hit me: I was about to introduce Mum to the first boy I really cared about – and if it didn't go well, it would be curtains for Dwayne and me. If Dwayne failed to impress Mum and my aunties, I knew exactly what would happen: Mum would forbid me from seeing him and I'd be on lock-down.

When I heard Uncle Sam's voice downstairs I started to feel sick. This visit was make or break. I only wished I had given Dwayne more warning or prepped him better. But it was too late now. He would have to sink or swim.

'Oh, God,' I prayed silently. 'Don't let him let me down.'

❖ ❖ ❖

Effie arrived first, full of smiles and smelling delicious.

"Is that a new perfume?" I asked as I hugged her. It smelled grown-up and sophisticated – and expensive.

"Yes," she beamed. "A gift... think of it as taking the rough with the smooth." She turned away mysteriously, leaving me to wonder which guy she had her hooks into this time.

"Hi, Councillor Reynolds," she called as she walked into the kitchen where Mum was tossing the salad. She always called Mum by her title, for no other reason than that she liked the way it sounded.

Mum grinned at her and kissed the air next to her cheek. "Gorgeous perfume, Effie," she remarked as she looked her up and down. I could see that she approved of Effie's cutting edge military-style jacket, skinny jeans and embroidered ballet pumps. Just the right mix of trendy and classy.

Auntie Dionne had met Effie before and was eager to introduce her to Uncle Sam.

"Effie's father is a professor of African Studies at SOAS," she said, holding Effie by the arm. "And her mother works as a consultant to the Runnymede Trust, isn't that right?"

"Yes," replied Effie, "she gained her doctorate last year, so now they are Dr and *Dr* Mensah – very confusing!"

They all laughed and Uncle Sam nodded his head approvingly. "So, you attend the same school as Misha – that fancy school in Dulwich?"

"Yes, I've been there since Year Eight."

"I hear it's a fantastic school," enthused Uncle Sam. "Nothing but the best for you girls, eh?"

"Well," said Auntie Loretta archly, "with the money my sister pays in school fees, it had better be nothing but the best!"

"Oh, Loretta," sighed Auntie Dionne, "not

everything is about money, you know."

I flinched for my favourite aunt. She was so different to Mum and Auntie Dionne. For a start, she had never married and she still lived in Brixton, near my grandma. But there were other differences too, ones I couldn't easily put my finger on.

Was it that Auntie Loretta was more down-to-earth than her sisters, more connected to her roots? I wasn't sure – all I knew was I was banking on her support that afternoon. I knew that she would warm to Dwayne and, to be honest, listening to the conversation about expensive schools and doctorates, I realised that Dwayne was going to need all the friends he could get.

"He's a bit late, isn't he?" murmured Auntie Dionne.

"Not a good start, eh?" chuckled Uncle Sam. My dislike for him grew just a little more.

The conversation turned to the new television show Auntie Dionne was hosting on Sky One. I was proud of my aunt, of course, but my stomach was tying itself in knots and I just couldn't relax.

At last the doorbell rang and I leapt out of my chair. Everyone turned to look at me and I felt my face grow hot. Talk about pressure.

"Shall I come with you?" Effie asked, getting up.

"No, no," I waved, "I'll be fine."

I peeped through the spy hole. It was Dwayne. He looked so good that I felt my insides ache. In that moment, I wanted to just take him by the hand and run away with him down the street, away from Mum and Auntie Dionne and Uncle Sam. We were all right when it was just the two of us. But here? My feelings of optimism had trickled away to nothing.

I just didn't believe Dwayne would survive the Reynolds Inquisition.

Dwayne, on the other hand, was super-chilled. He smiled at me when I opened the door and leaned in to kiss me. On my doorstep, with my mum right inside? He had to be joking! I turned my head to the side and gave him a brief hug.

"Why you trippin', girl?" He was too mellow, too laid-back. It made me even more nervous.

"You're late, Dee," I hissed, closing the door behind him. "Everyone's been waiting for you..."

Dwayne took his cap off and rubbed his new haircut. "Boy..." he breathed. "I must be crazy..."

Then Mum appeared in the doorway, a bright smile on her face.

"You must be Dwayne!" she beamed, reaching

out to shake Dwayne's hand. "We've heard so much about you!"

"Hi, Mrs Reynolds," Dwayne mumbled, ducking his head. "It's nice to meet you."

"Come in, Dwayne, come and meet my sisters..."

I watched as Mum led Dwayne into the living room. All of sudden, he looked so out of place. I could see that he had made an effort: he wore his newest kicks, designer jeans and a leather jacket. But I saw Mum take in the tight fade, gold rings and diamond earrings and I knew just what she was thinking: typical ghetto style.

By the time I plucked up the courage to go out into the garden, the Inquisition was well underway.

"So, Dwayne," Auntie Dionne was saying, as if she was setting up a television interview for her morning show, "where did you say you lived?"

"Saints Town Estate, up in Brixton."

"Oh, that's right near Mum's house, isn't it?" said Auntie Loretta, her face lighting up. "My shop's not far from there."

That's right, Auntie Loretta, I thought, *I knew you'd be in our corner!*

But Auntie Dionne wrinkled up her nose and said, "Brixton? I see... and who do you live with?"

"My mum and my kid brother."

Uncle Sam joined the interrogation: "No dad around, huh?"

"Nah," replied Dwayne, totally unaware of the trap he was walking into, "my dad ain't around. I don't really know him, to tell you the truth."

Uncle Sam sniffed and murmured, "So far, so typical," before lifting a forkful of M&S rocket salad with cherry tomatoes and balsamic vinegar to his mouth. When he had finished chewing, he said, "Did you know that 60% of Caribbean children are raised in single-parent households? Shocking, isn't it?"

"And then you have wonderful, stable couples like you and my sister who decide not to have children at all," Auntie Loretta said brightly. "Ironic, isn't it?"

Uncle Sam almost choked on his salad and Auntie Dionne shot her sister a look. I was glad. Someone needed to put that man in his place!

Mum came out from the kitchen with some grilled salmon and a couscous salad and sat down at the table. "So, Dwayne," she said brightly, obviously unaware that the questioning had started without her, "I hear you go to a comprehensive school, is that right?"

"Yeah, that's right, I go Saints Hill, just down the road from my estate."

I saw the look on Mum's face and felt the will to live slowly draining out of me.

Saints Hill was a notorious school, well known for failed OFSTED inspections, a revolving door of teachers and a serious drug problem, from Year 7 up. As a civil servant in local government, Mum knew all the gory details. And to make things worse, Saints Hill Primary School was *my* old school, the very school Mum had worked so hard to get me away from.

I had to try and salvage the conversation: "But he's really good at Maths, aren't you, Dwayne?"

Dwayne nodded, frowning slightly. "I get by, innit..."

Mum tried to recover from the shock and smiled a big fake smile. But her next question was the nail in the coffin: "So, which college are you looking at for 'A' Level?"

"Umm, not sure about 'A' Levels, y'know. Might have to retake some exams. School's never been my strong point, y'get me. Not sure if I'm up to 'A' Levels, still..."

Mum sucked in her breath and said nothing more. Auntie Dionne raised an eyebrow and glanced over at Uncle Sam. Auntie Loretta looked over at me feelingly. Effie just concentrated on the pile of rocket leaves in front of her.

The conversation moved on to other things and Dwayne found himself ignored by everyone but me and Auntie Loretta, who asked him about his family and someone called Ms Walker, the headteacher at his school.

"We went to school together – she's one of my best customers. A fantastic woman, really caring."

Effie tried to lighten the mood but I wasn't up to humouring her.

I squeezed Dwayne's knee under the table and tried to smile encouragingly at him but he didn't respond, preferring to concentrate on his barbecue chicken.

Not long after we had eaten, Dwayne excused himself, saying that he had some errands to run for his mum.

I saw Mum and Auntie Dionne exchange a look before Mum smiled up at him and trilled, "Lovely to meet you, Dwayne. Thanks for coming."

"Thanks, Mrs Reynolds," he replied, looking around at everyone. "It was nice to meet you all too." But his voice was flat and his eyes had a hard, closed look. He practically pushed past me in an effort to get out of the door.

"Dwayne?" I began, unsure of his mood. "Speak later..?"

"Yeah, of course," he shrugged and, with that, he was gone. No hug, no kiss, no backward glance.

I shivered as I watched him walk away from me. And as I turned to go back inside, it occurred to me that this could possibly be the last time I would ever see him.

Disrespect

DWAYNE

I ain't gonna lie: I was bubbling when I left Misha's house. I was so vex', my head hurt from having to hold it down for so long. Of course I wasn't about to lose it in front of Misha's family, but damn! They sure knew how to make man feel small.

'What was you expecting, blud?'

'Some respect, man, at least. Man comes into your house, the least you can do is give him a chance, y'get me. It was like they had already made up their minds about me from time. Like I care what they think!'

'They weren't feeling you, blud, that's for sure...'

'But why, though? Because I live on an estate and don't go to a posh school and speak all proper, like them? That's just shallow, man. I don't know what the hell Misha was thinking. She should have known what her people were like...'

That was when my phone rang. It was Misha. I bit my lip. I really didn't want to speak to her too tough – but I knew how she felt about me not picking up her calls. I took a deep breath and counted to ten. I didn't want her to know just how vex' I was. When the phone rang off, I rang her right back.

"Hey, babe," her voice was all soft on the other end of the line. "You all right?"

"Yeah, Misha, I'm fine..." I wanted to let her know how I was feeling, not keep it all inside – but I couldn't find the words. "About today, Misha..."

"Yeah, Dee, about today..."

"I'm sorry, man, but..."

"I'm sorry too, it was awful..."

"What your mum and them did was wrong, putting mans on the spot like that. I could tell they didn't like me the moment they saw me. Like they'd judged me already. I don't like that kind of thing, man, it's not right. You have to give people a chance, y'get me?"

"I know, Dwayne, I know."

But I was in full flow now. "They don't know nothin' about me, nothin' about my life, but they wanna come judge me. Screw them, man! I don't need that crap, y'get me!"

Then Misha was quiet and I wondered whether

I had been too blunt. I knew that Misha wasn't used to people telling it straight. In her world, that was considered rude. But that was me, innit: a rudeboy, through and through. And that wasn't going to change, no matter how many times Auntie Dionne looked down her nose at me.

"Dwayne." Misha's voice was all small and I could hear that she was trying to choose her words really carefully. "It'll better next time, OK? They just need a chance to get to know you, that's all. It's a new experience for them too. Maybe if you could just..."

But I didn't want to hear any more. I didn't want to hear her making excuses for them. "Look, I need to clear my head, OK? It's best we don't talk now."

"Yeah, you're right..."

"Catch you later, yeah?" And I hung up.

Free that.

I got into the Tube wound up like a spring. It was Saturday night and the train was full of people on their way to the West End, ready to party. Some of them had already been to the pub and were making bare noise in the carriage. It hurt my head. I pulled my hoodie over my head and sank down lower in my seat.

Right across from me, this tall white guy with a stubbly chin was staring at me, his eyes red, his lips all wet and slack. Nastiness. I scowled at him and turned away, expecting him to do the same. But he kept looking at me, this little glint in his eye saying, 'What you gonna do about it, sonny?'

"Do you know me, blud?" I barked, loud enough for the other passengers to hear me and stop their chatting.

But the fool just kept eyeing me up as if he hadn't heard a word I said. I could feel the anger pulsing behind my eyes, all the stress of the past week building up like a volcano inside me. This guy was messing with the wrong one tonight.

"Are you deaf or something? What you staring at me for?"

"Take it easy, man," said the guy who was sitting next to me. "Can't you see he's drunk?" And he put his hand on me.

What?

"Don't touch me, blud!" I roared, turning to grab him by the collar. I pushed him up against the train window and held him there. His girl was crying, hanging on to my arm.

"Please," she was screaming, "he didn't even do anything to you!"

"Shut up, man!" I shrugged her off and she fell

to the floor as the train lurched through the tunnel.

The sound of the train and the pounding in my ears was deafening. I felt the man's Adam's apple bobbing against my fists and I felt choked by the need to beat him down, to hear his nose crack, to feel his blood, hot and slippery, on my knuckles. I just had to get this anger out somehow. I drew my fist back and got ready to rearrange this feisty boy's face.

But I couldn't move my arm. All of a sudden, someone with a vice-like grip had grabbed hold of it and twisted it behind my back. I was too surprised to struggle.

"Stop, Mr Kingston," a familiar woman's voice rasped in my ear. "Stop before you do something you will regret."

I'd know that voice anywhere. It was Ms Walker.

The next thing I knew, we were at the station and the doors were sliding open and Ms Walker was pushing me out through the doors, still holding me in a man-sized bear hug.

'Mind the gap.'

The other passengers hurried to get away from us and, in a few moments, we were alone on the platform.

Only then did Ms Walker let me go.

I spun away from her, breathing hard. "What d'you do that for?" I shouted. "Are you crazy or something?"

"Dwayne Kingston, I was trying to save your backside from a night in a jail cell! What do you think would have happened if you had assaulted that boy and the police had turned up? Who do you think they would have taken away? Huh?"

I struggled to get my breath back. I knew she was right. If the police had turned up, I would have been screwed, for real. My pride was wounded, still. I'd been taken down by the headteacher, man, in front of a whole carriage-load of strangers!

"You ain't my mum, y'get me. What makes you think you can save me – or any of us?"

Ms Walker's chest was heaving and she looked straight at me. I could see the tears shining behind her glasses. "Because my son was your age when he died," she said, her voice all hoarse.

Ms Walker had a son once?

She answered my question before I could ask it. "He was stabbed by another boy. A stupid argument, really, over nothing. But it cost him his life..." Ms Walker took out a piece of tissue and blew her nose loudly. "You boys don't realise it, but the choices

129

you make – whether you retaliate or walk away, forgive or seek revenge – have lasting consequences, for you and everyone else. I don't want to see you make the same mistake..."

I felt proper bad then. Ms Walker had been through a lot and she still cared so much. It made me feel like a real scumbag. I kept quiet. Ms Walker started walking towards the exit. I followed her. When I spoke again, my voice was softer. "Did they ever find out who did it, Miss?"

Ms Walker took off her glasses and cleaned them with a piece of tissue. When she looked up, her eyes were tired. I had never seen them like that before. "The police couldn't prosecute due to lack of evidence. No one in the community would come forward."

I was silent. No one ever gave the police information about beef on the estate, not if they wanted to keep living there.

But as we got to the top of the elevator and walked out onto Brixton High Road, Ms Walker started talking again, quieter this time, sounding less like a fierce headteacher and more like one of the mums on the estate, mine, Jukkie's, little Lightning's.

"The house felt so quiet without him. Even with all the relatives and neighbours coming in to talk to me, to offer support, comfort, I could still feel his absence. It felt like I had lost my right arm." Ms Walker breathed in deeply and her voice shook.

I knew she wasn't talking to me any more, not really. I just happened to be there. Part of me was proper embarrassed. Part of me felt sorry for her, guilt running through every vein. Mans like me had caused this.

She kept talking. "My youngest was only eight at the time. He wanted life to go on as normal, to go out to play with his friends down the street. But I wouldn't let him. I had already lost one son; I wasn't about to lose another." She looked me straight in the eye. "These streets are the killing fields for young black boys like you, Dwayne."

Then she walked away quickly, holding her bag close to her side, her high heels tapping on the concrete.

I ran my fingers over my fade – freshly cut for my visit to Misha's family – and thought to myself, 'What a mess, man. What a rhated mess.'

The Verdict

MISHA

"Well... that was interesting... I haven't spoken to one of those in a while." Auntie Dionne's voice reached me in the hallway.

Then Mum: "Don't, Dionne. It may be amusing to you but it isn't to me. This is my daughter we're talking about."

"Oh, don't be so anxious!" said Auntie Dionne, chuckling. "She'll be over him in no time, once she sees what a loser he is."

"And in the meantime, what am I supposed to do, stand by and watch her mess up her life? You know what happens when girls hang around with boys like that! That lifestyle is dangerous – she could get involved in any number of crazy things, things she would never even have reason to *think* about

132

if it were not for him!"

"Why so over-dramatic?" laughed Auntie Loretta. "You were sixteen once; we all were. We all did crazy things. I thought he was quite sweet – reminded me of my first crush. Misha is no different to how we were, no different from any other sixteen-year-old out there."

"That's where you're wrong, Loretta. Misha *is* different. She is made for better things..."

"OK," sighed Auntie Loretta. "Just don't say I didn't warn you: you make a big deal out of this, you'll only fan the flames. Ignore it and it will all go away, I'm telling you."

"Oh, you mean like what happened with Keisha?" Mum's voice turned harsh. Keisha, my cousin who had fallen pregnant at 17: Mum's poster girl for Brixton parenting gone wrong. "You ignored that, didn't you, and look where it got you!"

I heard Auntie Loretta suck in her breath. "I might have known you would bring that up, Dina. You never could let anything go, could you? Thanks for reminding me why I never bother disagreeing with you. You just can't take anyone telling you that you're wrong. You couldn't handle it with Mum and Dad and you couldn't handle it with Isaiah..."

My heart leapt when she mentioned my father's name.

"Don't you dare bring him into this!" Mum spat out. "No one wants as much for Misha as I do, no one, not even her father! I have given her everything she needs to succeed – and I won't allow anything to get in the way of that!"

Auntie Loretta: "Oh Lord, Dina, does it always have to be about you? What about what she wants – have you even thought about that? Have you?"

"I know what is best for my own daughter, thank you very much!"

Their voices rose and rose, and I blinked back tears as I turned away. I was careful not to make a sound as I went upstairs to my room and closed the door softly. My fingers were trembling. I dreaded hearing Mum call my name. I knew just what she was going to say. There was no doubt about it now.

I changed into my pyjamas quickly. I needed to get into bed, to pull the duvet over my head and sink into sleep, to forget everything. But as I got under the covers, I heard a knock at my door. It was Mum.

"Misha?" She poked her head round the door. "Are you still awake?"

As my light was on, there was no way I could

pretend that I was sleeping. I nodded and she stepped into the room.

"I want to talk to you." Her voice was hoarse.

I sat up against my pillows and crossed my arms, trying to keep my expression neutral even though I knew what Mum was going to say, even though I knew that I would not be able to change her mind, and that I was going to cry.

"Misha," Mum began, "you know how much I love you, don't you?"

The tears had already started to sting my eyes. I nodded, blinking.

"And that I only want what's best for you?"

I nodded again.

"Well, as your mother, I am telling you that I don't want you to see this boy, Dwayne, again. I want you to end it with him."

I opened my mouth to protest but Mum continued, her voice rising slightly. "I know his type, darling, and believe me, he is not the kind of boy you want to be having anything to do with." Mum shook her head and looked away, blinking several times. "Not you, Misha. Not now."

I finally found words. "So you won't even give him a chance, then? I mean, you only met him for the first time today!"

"Not at the risk of you getting hurt, Misha, no." Then Mum looked me straight in the eye. "That kind of boy is trouble, believe me. I don't want you mixed up with all that ghetto stuff, d'you hear? I mean, what could you possibly want with a sixteen-year-old ghetto badboy? Why do you think we moved out of Brixton? You're worth more than that, Misha, much more! We're not going back to that life, not after we've worked so hard to get out. That boy is bad news. I want you to end it, OK?"

I didn't say anything; I *couldn't* say anything. I always agreed with Mum. She knew best, right? This time was no different. I nodded.

Mum smiled, sighing with relief. "I knew you'd understand," she said, patting my hand. "Don't be upset, honey. It's for the best; one day, you'll thank me for this..."

I only pretended to listen. My heart felt small and tight inside my chest. This was the first time, the first time I had really wanted something, something that made me sing inside, something that made me look in the mirror and see a gorgeous being, full of light and love – and Mum had just shut it down. End of discussion.

136

Later that night, after Mum had gone, I cried bitter tears, thinking of all the things, all the people that I had given up because Mum said they weren't good enough for me. My heart ached for afternoons with Gran at her house in Brixton, for my best friend from primary school, Rachel, for our old house with the blackberry bush in the garden. And my heart ached for Dwayne, of course.

I would have to tell him.

Romeo and Juliet

DWAYNE

Misha rang me the next morning. "I need to see you. Meet me at Battersea Park after school."

I said yes straight away. I felt really bad for hanging up on her the day before. She didn't deserve that.

But when I saw her, she looked different somehow, small and closed, not her usual smiling self.

"What's up, girl?" I asked.

She felt different when I held her, brittle, like she might just break if I hugged her too hard.

Misha looked away, into the park. "Can we walk?" she asked. "I don't have long; I've got to get back home."

"Sure, babes, whatever you want." We started walking, neither of us saying a word. I was blown away by how different it was from the first time we had been there. I bit my thumbnail, jiggling my keys in my jean pocket. In the end, I cracked: I just couldn't take it any more. "Yo, Misha, what's up with you, man? This is killing me."

"Look, Dwayne, my mum said that I can't see you again." She came out with it, just like that. Then she shrugged, biting her lip. "Yeah, so..."

I should have known her mum would pull a stunt like that. "Yeah, so what? That don't mean we have to stop seeing each other. We just have to be more careful, innit, on the down low and ting."

Misha looked at me. I could see that she really didn't believe that it was that easy, that she could just do what she liked, no matter what her mum said.

I stopped walking and took her face in my hands. I wanted her to know that I was for real. "Misha, I don't business that your mum don't like me. What matters is that you like me. What matters is that we're tight. The rest of the world ain't got nothing to do with it. You know we've got something special. Ain't no one coming in the way of that." Then I kissed her like I really meant it.

"Yes," she murmured, "yes, I'm going to do this. I'm going to do this for me."

I didn't know what she was going on about.

All I knew was that she was with me, in my arms, and it felt right. The rest of the world could go to hell for all I cared.

❖ ❖ ❖

"So, who's this new gyal den?"

"Just some girl, innit," I mumbled.

I didn't feel like getting all conversational with Jukkie – I was still vex' with him. It pissed me off, the way Jukkie kept sucking up to Trigger, trying to get on his good side. It was obvious that he just wanted a bigger piece of the action.

Jukkie was changing, there was no doubt about it. But maybe I was changing too, just like he said.

"So what, are you bangin' her?"

"What?" I scowled and turned to him. "Why you in my business, blud?"

"It ain't no fing," replied Jukkie, lazily twirling one of his knives in the air. "I just asked if you were mashin' her, innit."

"Shut up, man."

"Nah, you shut up, you know you ain't mashin' no one!"

"Shut up, man, you know I done mashed nuff girl, y'get me. Just come out my business, blud. I don't check for that kind of thing."

I could feel Jukkie watching me, could hear him laughing quietly to himself as he cleaned his nails with the knife. Then he jumped up and grabbed my phone, flicking until he got to the text messages. He was the last person I wanted reading my messages to Misha and I grappled with him for the phone but he managed to hold me off long enough to read my last conversation with Misha. He started creasing up then and threw the phone at me.

"Oh my days!" he hooted, ducking away from me. "That is some pure gay business! What's this? Date? Battersea Park? What the ...?"

"Ah, shut up, man!" I said, whacking him on the head. He turned and hooked his arm around my neck and tried to hold me down. But I kneed him and landed a sweet left hook on his jaw. Then he smacked me in the eye.

We weren't fighting, not really. It was more like wrestling, kidding around, like we used to do when we were younger. But I could feel some of the anger that I felt towards him welling up and coming out. I wanted to show him that I wasn't a chief, that he couldn't disrespect me and get away with it.

In the end, Jukkie managed to get hold of my arms

and pin them behind my back. I struggled against him and we stayed locked together like that for a few moments, our feet trampling the grass.

"You're going soft, blud," he hissed in my ear. "Just don't go forgetting your boy over some gyal, yeah?" Then he pushed me away, letting go of my arms. I swung around to punch him and he laughed, dodging my fist. "Not bad, Mr Loverman, give me your best shot, go on!"

So I did. And so did he.

By the time we were ready to go home, we were both dusty, with cut lips, leaning on each other. The fight had settled things between us. We were buddies again.

❖ ❖ ❖

We went past Jukkie's on the way home. He had the latest edition of GTA – and he wanted to take me on.

"Where's Tony, man?" I asked as we walked along the corridor towards Jukkie's door. "I ain't seen him for time. Is he still up in Birmingham?"

Jukkie kissed his teeth. "He's on a long ting, man," he sneered. "He got back last night and he's gone mad religious now – you can't even talk sense to him." He shook his head. "He used to be a playa, man, a don. Now he's just a chief..."

But when Jukkie pushed his door open, there was Tony, larger than life. His face went all bright when he saw me. Jukkie grunted and pushed past him into the flat but Tony just stepped to the side.

"Hey, what's happening, bruv? Long time no see!" We shook hands and hugged, just like old times. It felt good to see him, man, real good. Like everything would be all right now that Tony was back. Even though I knew that it wasn't like that any more, not really.

"Safe, man, I've been around, innit. Where've *you* been, blud?" I was proper pleased to see him again.

Jukkie shouted back from the kitchen. "At the mosque, innit, where else?"

Tony rolled his eyes and jerked his thumb at Jukkie's back. "He's got issues, man." But he didn't seem too upset by Jukkie's stink attitude. "I've been in Birmingham, y'know, keeping a low profile." He smiled and his fingers went up to scratch his jaw through his beard. I noticed that, although he was wearing a thick silver ring, he didn't have any other jewellery: no chains, no earrings, nothing.

"Seen, seen. But you look different, man. What's up with the facial hair? Is it part of your Muslim ting?"

Tony tugged at the beard again. "Yeah, it is."

The beard looked good – although I would have shaped it up a bit, gone for a goatee instead.

"So how's it going, the Muslim ting? You ain't been partying... and you ain't on the game..."

"Yeah, I had to come off that stuff, innit. Too much badness around these days – I ain't in all that no more. Being away from everything really helped. The brothers in Birmingham helped me get myself straight: y'know I needed to come off the weed and cut some of my old ties, learn how to pray and that. They helped me through it all. Oh yeah, and I was giving *da'wah* to my girl – you remember Lorraine?" Tony's face lit up as he mentioned the long-term girlfriend he had been cheating on for the last year.

"You were 'giving her *da'wah*'?" I asked. "What's that, then?"

"It's when you tell someone about Islam and invite them to become Muslim."

"And..?"

"Yeah, man, she accepted Islam, bro! I was so happy, man, it was like God – Allah – just answered my prayers. Lorraine's a good woman, y'get me. She didn't deserve all that crap I put her through."

"So now...?"

"Well, we got married, innit..."

I did a double-take. "You *married* her, bruv?" I couldn't believe it. Marriage just wasn't something young guys like Tony did. I mean, you could have kids with your baby mother and maybe even live together – but marry her? Nah, that just wasn't something that mans did.

"Yeah, we're both Muslims now, innit? Can't be fornicating and that. Got to make things legal, y'get me, make it *halal* and ting... anyway, what you been up to?"

I didn't answer Tony's question. I was still shocked by the change in him. He had been a real playa back in the day, with a different girl every week; he had taught me some of my best chat-up lines! And now here he was, all married and ting. Talking about *fornicating*!

That was some deep church talk, right there. Mum would have been impressed. But then Tony wasn't going to church, was he? He was a Muslim... *a Muslim*. Images of the Twin Towers crashing down flashed through my head.

"So what, are you on some Al Qa'eeda ting, bruv, blowing up planes and stuff?"

Tony laughed and said, "Nah, blud, don't watch that stuff, man. That's just the media hype, y'get me.

145

'Nuff man are becoming Muslim nowadays – we had about five young brothers from the endz come and take *shahadah* just this last Friday."

"I thought that only happened in jail, man."

"That's coz when you're inside, you got 'nuff time to reflect, to think about your life, where you're going, what it's all about. And Islam? Islam is just the truth, bruv, plain and simple. It just makes sense..."

"Woah, getting heavy now, talking about truth and ting. You do your ting, innit, if it's working for you. That's safe..."

"Yeah, it is, *alhamdulillah*. I mean, don't get me wrong; it ain't easy. But it's good, still. It's made me change my life around, get cleaned up. I'm off the weed now, clean, and I'm on a course at Brixton College. They told me take a plumbing course but I said, nah, I wanna study business, y'get me. Make some food the legit way..."

I almost laughed out loud: Tony, the big man playa and hustler, a *plumber*?

But I had to respect him still. He was doing something different, rewriting the script, as Misha would say. How many man could say that? "You know what, bruv? Gwan – you're taking care of business. I respect that. Your girl... wife... must be pleased too, right?" It still sounded so mad to talk to Tony about his 'wife'.

"That's right, bro," replied Tony feelingly, "mans got to come correct. In Islam, that's the man's role, y'get me, to provide and ting. So I know I need to get straight!"

We laughed but I could hear Jukkie grumbling in the background.

"How long you gonna listen to this foolishness? Are you here to play X-Box or what?"

Before I left Jukkie's crib, Tony gave me a book: *The Autobiography of Malcolm X.*

"Try and read it, bruv," he said. "It's a wicked book." Then he shook his head and laughed. "Man, I never thought I would hear myself say that!"

True dat!

Revelation

MISHA

Effie opened her front door, her face lit up with a mega-watt smile.

"Misha!" she squealed, pulling me in. "What took you so long? I've been ready for ages!" We hugged briefly and she pulled me through the hallway towards the living room. "Come and say hi to Mum and Dad before we go. I told them about Oak Hill so you can imagine how pleased they are..."

I smiled, half-pleased, half-embarrassed, as I allowed Effie to lead me into the living room where her parents were sitting, reading. Dr Mensah took off his glasses when he saw me.

"Ahh, Misha," he exclaimed, beaming. "Our shining star!"

"Hello, Dr Mensah," I said, smiling, "how are you?"

"I'm very well, thank you," he said, "and how are you? How is your mother?"

"We heard about your good news, Misha," said Effie's mum in her soft voice. "Congratulations, my dear."

I turned to her. "Thank you, Dr Mensah, but I haven't been fully accepted yet."

"They're waiting till after the exam results are published," Effie explained. "But that won't be a problem, will it, Misha?"

"Oh, I am sure it won't be a problem," Effie's dad said, an approving look on his face. "Now, if you can only influence Efua here to become more studious..."

"Ohhh-kay, Dad," Effie said, pulling me towards the door, "we have to go. Misha's dad is expecting us."

"OK then, girls," called Effie's mum, "have a nice time. And Efua, don't be late home. You girls have school tomorrow."

"All right, Mum!" Effie called back before we bounded up the stairs.

Once in her room, Effie looked in the mirror, eyeing her reflection critically.

"Do you think I'm too short to wear these jeans?" she said, turning to look at the way her skinny jeans fit.

"Not necessarily," I murmured. My main question was how she hoped to be able to sit down in them.

"Well, not with these shoes on, anyway!" laughed Effie, picking up a pair of high-heeled ankle boots and waving them in front of me.

I gasped, my eyes open wide. "Effie!" I shrieked. "Where did you get these? They cost, like, a grand from Selfridges! I saw them in the weekend paper!"

Effie smirked and started putting the boots on. "They were a gift..."

"Another gift?" I said, incredulous. "Who from? "

"Lawrence."

"Is he your latest honey, then?"

"Uh-huh." Effie picked up her favourite tube of red lipstick.

"Hey, Effie, easy on the lipstick; we're going to Selfridges, not a party."

Effie looked at her heavily made-up face in the mirror and wrinkled her nose. "D'you think it's too much?"

"Yeah, just a bit. I'd stick with the lipgloss." I shook my head. "Anyway, why is this Lawrence character buying you one-thousand-pound boots?"

Effie turned to me, her eyebrow raised, a sardonic smile on her face. "Why d'you think, Misha Baby?"

My eyes were wide. "You mean you..?"

"Yes..." Effie smiled patiently.

"With *him*?"

"Yeah, and what's wrong with that?"

"How old is he anyway?"

"Oh, about 21..."

I stared at her, incredulous. I couldn't believe she could be so nonchalant about this. "Effie, what 21-year-old do you know who can afford 'gifts' like these? Aren't you worried about where he might be getting all this money? He could be a drug dealer, for all you know!"

"Well, we can't all have sweet Romeo and Juliet romances with little sixteen-year-olds, can we?" Effie teased.

"Effie!" I couldn't keep the concern out of my voice. For once, I wanted her to take me seriously, not make a joke out of everything. "Are you sure you know what you're getting yourself into?"

Effie smiled and said, "You know I can't resist guys like that. They've just got such a mysterious air about them!"

"Hmm, mysterious or dangerous?"

"Ooh, preferably both! And it's flattering! He could have any girl he wants and he chose me. Plus, there's the excitement and the fun times. Guys our age don't know how to treat a girl – they think that taking you

151

out for a box of chicken and chips means they've scored! With older guys, it's different: they give you more, they're experienced; it's just totally different!"

"Do your parents know?"

Effie burst out laughing. "Oh, please! Can you see Dr and Dr Mensah agreeing to their daughter going out with a guy like Lawrence? No, as far as they are concerned, I am studying hard at school and will soon be on my way to uni like Ama..."

"So, what, you're not planning on going to uni any more?"

"I didn't say that, did I? God, don't be so dramatic! I just want to have a bit of fun first, that's all."

"Well," I murmured, "I hope you know what you're doing..."

"Don't worry, Misha, as you know, I can handle this. I'm a big girl; I know how to take care of myself. If I were you, I'd be worrying about my own business. After all, you're not quite Little Miss Upfront and Honest any more, are you?" She knew that I was still seeing Dwayne even though Mum had told me to end it. "Does your mum suspect anything?"

"We're being really careful. He only calls me while she's out at work or after she's gone to bed. And no text messages, in case she checks my phone."

"Would she do that?" Effie was incredulous.

"She's done it before – and if I give her a reason to think something is up, I know she'll do it again."

Effie whistled. "West Indian Psycho..."

"Don't," I pleaded. "Come on, we'd better get going – we're already late."

"BMT – black man time, innit?"

And the heavy mood lifted as we laughed and left the room.

✪ ✪ ✪

Aalia was less than impressed by my plans to continue seeing Dwayne behind my mum's back.

"I don't know, Misha, it seems like a big risk to take." Her brow was furrowed as she picked the onions out of her salad. "How do you know he's even worth the stress if your mum does find out?"

I sighed and tugged at my fringe. I didn't really expect Aalia to understand – but a bit of faith in me would have been nice. "I just know, OK?"

But Aalia was persistent. "I mean, aside from the fact that he's a hottie and he makes you laugh, what do you really know about him? You didn't even know which school he went to until he dropped it at your house. You don't know where he lives, what his family is like... what if it turned out he lived in a crackhouse?"

I stared at her. That was impossible – wasn't it?

Aalia laughed at my expression. "OK, maybe not a crackhouse but you see my point, don't you?" She put her hand on my shoulder. "Look, Misha, I'm not judging him but I think you need to be more careful. Your mum trusts you. You've taken years to build that trust; don't throw it away over some guy who will be here today and gone tomorrow."

I smiled ruefully at her. "You are such an old auntie, do you know that?"

She giggled. "Hey, I don't have this moustache for nothing, you know. It's my job to keep you on the straight and narrow. So I suggest you do a little bit of research about Mr Dwayne Kingston before this goes any further. Any gang activity? Prior convictions? *Baby mother*? Better find out everything now than get a nasty surprise further down the road. Does that make sense to you?"

I gave her a hug. "Yes, Auntie. It makes perfect sense."

To be honest, I hadn't even considered the possibility that Dwayne had been less than 100% straight with me. The thought that he might have been lying

154

to me – or at the very least keeping things from me – scared me to death.

I had come to trust him.

I wasn't ready to face a betrayal just yet.

DWAYNE

I'd never been a book reader. I learned to read at school, of course, and I remember liking it for a while. But then it seemed that most of the books they expected us to read were chatting about people who were nothing like me, going on about stuff I couldn't relate to. The world of books was nothing like my world.

Aside from the ones they forced us to read at school – and most of the time, I just skimmed through anyway – the last time I read a book on my own was when I was, like, 10 years old. After that, books totally disappeared from my life. Anyway, who needed them when life was so much more exciting? And it was real, in your face, not some made-up fairy story.

So the early days in RDS, the days we were shotting for the elders, nicking stuff from shops, smoking our first blunts, those things took over. The music took over. I didn't have room in my life for book stuff:

I wanted the real deal, the knowledge you can only learn by going out and doing time on the streets.

But I took that book from Tony anyway. I reckoned if Tony thought it was good, there must be something to it.

And there was.

I started reading about Malcolm X's life when I got home that night – and I couldn't put that book down. I was proper hooked! I mean, it was long and sometimes he used words I didn't know, but the story he told was off the chain. It was like he was speaking to me, to my own story, to the reality I was facing. He knew what it was like to be a black boy surrounded by madness and badness – and to believe that the only way to survive was to jump right in and fight your way to the top.

But Malcolm survived it. He managed to come out of the madness and choose a new life for himself. He became someone people listened to, someone people admired. He got respect. And wasn't that what I had been fighting for all my life?

While reading the book, I found myself asking questions I had never asked before. Does God exist? What does 'manning up' really mean? Why were we black boys rapping about, dreaming about and going about killing other black boys? Were white men devils? What were our original names before the slave masters gave us theirs?

That book opened my eyes.

All of a sudden, I started noticing things around me, things I hadn't paid attention to before. I saw how many black women wore weaves and straightened their hair: Malcolm spoke about that, said it was because we as black people had been taught to hate ourselves and want to be white. I saw how many off-licences there were around my endz – Malcolm preached against alcohol too. I took note of the lyrics in my rap tunes – Mos Def, Q-Tip from A Tribe Called Quest, all Muslims, rapping about Allah and prophets and Islam.

And I wasn't the only one.

Around that time, I started to see Muslim youth everywhere, all around South London. But these weren't Asians or Somalis: they were West Indian boys, English girls, some of them as young as 14, all high on this new Muslim vibe. I even heard that some of the guys from PDC, the Peel Dem Crew from Angell Town, had become Muslim in prison. Islam was the hottest thing to hit the streets since hiphop. It seemed like every next man was wearing a *keffiyeh*, a Palestinian scarf, or a skull cap, a *kufi*. Everywhere I went, man would be shouting out, '*Salaam alaikum*, ackee! What's good?"

I grew up going to church, innit, but by the time I was ten, I didn't have the patience to sit through those dry sermons in a suit. My feet itched to be on road with my boys, causing mayhem. I gave Mum so much grief that, in the end, she had to start going without me, dragging Jay behind her by the collar of his too-big suit. Of course, all he wanted to do was stay behind and hang with me.

I talked to Tony about the book. I told him that a lot of what Brother Malcolm said made sense to me – although some bits were a bit mad, still.

"Yeah, Brother Malcolm was on the Nation of Islam for a long time, innit. So he believed that white men were devils and that black men were superior..."

"Until he went on Hajj... right?"

"Right! That was the first time he understood that the colour of your skin isn't the most important thing in life, that it is possible for different races to treat each other like brothers – to *be* brothers." Tony looked at me carefully then. "But if you really want to understand what Islam is about, you have to read the Qur'an."

"What, is that like the Muslim Bible?"

Tony smiled. "Yeah, kind of..." And he gave me a book with a hard green cover with nuff gold patterns all over it. "Let me know how that moves you, bro."

So, for the second time in a month, I started reading another mad long book. I struggled with it at first. It was nothing like Brother Malcolm's book which was more like a movie, all exciting and ting. The Qur'an was serious, man, proper deep: all about God – Allah – and worship, Paradise and Hellfire, rules about how to live a good, upright life. And it talked about prophets too. I had read the Bible, innit, so I knew all the stories and that. I was surprised to read similar versions in the Qur'an, like they were part of the same message. I felt myself being drawn deeper and deeper into this strange new way of looking at the world.

Da Endz

MISHA

Wrapped in my pink terry dressing gown, hair pressed straight, I looked through my wardrobe again, mentally discarding anything that looked too middle class, too posh, too expensive in an understated kind of way. In the end, I settled for jeans and a fitted white t-shirt and my only pair of trainers. Where I was going, I needed to blend in. I looked in the mirror as I brushed my hair back into a high ponytail, a style I never usually wore because Mum said it wasn't classy. A bit of mascara, lip gloss and some silver hoop earrings and I was ready to go.

The bus ride up to Brixton was uneventful. I read a book while sitting downstairs, looking up briefly whenever the bus stopped to let more people on. A Muslim woman with a huge black scarf and double

160

buggy got on, struggling to manoeuvre past the other passengers. Her children were young and they looked close in age. The father was obviously black. The woman looked tired and her face was pale, the colour of skimmed milk, as if she hadn't been getting enough sleep. I noticed that she avoided eye contact with the other passengers, preferring to concentrate on the adverts that lined the upper wall of the bus.

"Excuse me," I called out, "would you like to sit down?"

The woman turned to me, clearly surprised. Then she smiled and I noticed her tiny diamond nose stud and how blue her eyes were. "Yes, thanks," she said quietly. "I'd love to." Her strong South London accent took me by surprise. I had expected her to speak with a foreign accent, Eastern European, maybe – Bosnian or Kosovan.

I stood up and held on to one of the poles while the Muslim woman moved her big double buggy closer to the seat. Some of the other passengers grumbled but the lady just smiled apologetically at them.

When at last she had sat down, she looked over at me and mouthed 'Thank you', before taking a little book out of her bag. When she opened it, I saw that it was full of Arabic letters, a Qur'an. Aalia had one just like it. The woman's lips moved silently as she read, her head bent low, biting the fingernail of her right thumb.

The next stop was mine: this was Saints Hill, my childhood home. Up ahead, the tower blocks of Saints Hill Estate loomed.

Dwayne's 'endz'.

I paused and looked around me when I got off the bus. I was a long way from leafy Dulwich, that was for sure. I gazed up at the uniform groups of concrete tower blocks, with their rows and rows of front doors and their rows and rows of kitchen windows, and I shuddered. They reminded me of that old film, *Candyman*, the one I had watched with my cousins, where a black serial killer stalked children in the inner city projects in the US. This was definitely *Candyman* territory. It hadn't looked like this when I was eleven. I took a deep breath and began walking.

As I approached St Peter's, Dwayne's building, I saw a large group of boys grouped around a car that was pumping loud, throbbing music. One of them was free-styling, spitting to the beat. The others listened to him; some stood around, some sat in the car, others on the car bonnet, moving their heads with the music, joining in from time to time, cheering whenever he came up with a tight rhyme. One of them filmed it all on a mobile phone while another patted the bull terrier at his side.

I was intrigued. I slowed down so that I could hear what the boy was saying. Just to compare his rhymes with Dwayne's. But his lyrics were quite different; he had a different style entirely. His spitting was much edgier, more staccato, laced with expletives, dissing 'next man' and 'next man's crew'. The other boys fell about laughing, pumping the air, making faces and posing, badman style, for the camera.

They were having a good time.

One of them, a light-skinned boy with long braids and a gold ring in his ear who was lounging against the car bonnet, saw me watching and winked at me. He nodded at me, full of confidence, and gestured for me to come over. That was when I looked away, stuck my hands in my pockets and began to walk on.

In seconds, he had bounced off the hood of the car and was walking beside me.

"Hey, girl, wassup? Why you actin' all stoosh? Come and chill with de mandem, innit?"

"No, it's OK," I replied, turning and giving him a polite smile while trying to walk faster. "I'm going to see someone."

The boy laughed and touched his hand to his mouth when he heard me speak. "Raah," he exclaimed. "You're one of dem posh girls, innit! What you doin' down here den?"

"My friend – my boyfriend – lives here." Still trying to outwalk him.

"Ahh, safe, safe." Then he stopped and pulled me lightly by the arm. "Teach me how to talk posh like you, den."

"I've got to go," I said as loudly as I could, even though my voice shook slightly, and I was aware of the other boys all watching, excited, amused, wondering what was going to happen. "Sorry."

"Ah, don't be like that! Come on, maybe you can teach me how to talk 'French', eh?" And he stuck his tongue out and grabbed at his crotch. The others all burst out laughing and the boy acknowledged the applause of the crowd, nodding his head. "Why not? I'm a fast learner..."

My face burned and my heart thumped in my chest, sweat prickling my armpits. How was I going to get out of this? How could I get away from here without making them angry? What if they did become angry? Would they hurt me? Tales of gang rapes and 'happy slapping' echoed in my head, fed by a dozen news reports. Where was the boy with the camera? Was he on standby to film me being humiliated?

"Yo, Dez!" I heard a rough voice shout out. "Leave her alone, man, that's Dwayne's girl." I looked over the boy's shoulder to see the one who had been petting the bull terrier sauntering towards us. He pushed the boy's shoulder and he stepped back, his face apologetic.

"OK, safe. Go to your man, innit." He turned away and bounced back to the others, grabbing their attention with a furiously paced freestyle. The guy with the phone lifted it again and all eyes were on the boy with the cornrows.

It took me a moment to gather my thoughts and realise that the boys weren't even looking at me any more. But the dog owner was still standing in front of me, eyeing me coldly. I tried to smile up at him. His dog growled, deep and menacing.

"I don't think we've met..?"

"You're Misha, innit?" he almost snarled. "Dwayne's piece..."

I balked at being referred to as a 'piece' but I could

tell that he meant to make me feel uncomfortable. I wasn't welcome.

"And you are..?" I tried again.

"Jukkie, Dwayne's bredren. What you doing down these sides, anyway?"

"I came to see him."

"Yeah? Well, watch your back, yeah. We ain't keen on strangers round here. A posh girl like you could get hurt..."

It was only then that I realised that he was playing with a small Swiss Army knife, turning it over and over between his fingers.

"Err, thanks for the warning..." I whispered and backed away, struggling to take my eyes off the knife. "I'll tell Dwayne you said hi, shall I?"

"I don't need you to tell him nuffin', y'get me?" And he kissed his teeth, turned on his heel and strode back to the group of boys beside the car. His dog looked back at me one last time and bared its teeth.

I couldn't get into that St Peter's lift fast enough.

Home Turf

MISHA

Dwayne lived on the fifteenth floor. It was a long way up and the lift stank of urine; graffiti tags and swear-words scarred its walls. I held my breath for as long as I could and was relieved when the bell sounded and the doors opened, just as I ran out of air. 'Dwayne comes home to this every day,' I thought. He really was from the other side of the tracks.

I was still shaken by my encounter with Jukkie, Dwayne's friend. Why had he been so hostile towards me, his best friend's girlfriend? Why the veiled threats? I shook my head, trying to block out the sight of that knife turning over and over.

I didn't dare look over the edge of the railings that lined the corridor. I didn't think I could handle the view, fifteen floors up. And I certainly didn't want to see Jukkie and the other boys again, even at this distance.

Dwayne's house was 15F – 15 for the floor, F for the flat. I got to the door and hesitated, suddenly unsure. Was I doing the right thing? What was I hoping to find out? Was I really ready for whatever the truth turned out to be? Was I ready to see Dwayne in his own environment, no matter how awful it turned out to be? I shivered. But 'Auntie' Aalia's voice was still ringing in my ears and I knew that I was doing the right thing.

I rang the doorbell and waited.

After a few moments, I heard a young boy's voice on the other side of the door. "Who is it?"

"Umm, it's Misha," I called out. "I'm here to see Dwayne..."

And the door opened immediately.

I looked down at the toffee-coloured boy with light eyes and beautifully braided hair who stood in the doorway, a look of curiosity on his face. "Are you Jerome?" I smiled tentatively.

"Yeah, that's me," he replied, full of confidence. "You're Misha, Dwayne's girl, innit?"

"Umm, yeah, I am. Is he here?"

"Yeah, he is. Come in. My mum's gone to church."

"OK, then. Thanks." This was it. I stepped on to the dark brown carpet of the hallway as Jerome ran off into the living room. "Yo, Dwayne!" I heard him call out. "Someone's here to see you."

"Sorry," he said when he came back to find me standing in the dim corridor, "could you take your shoes off, please? My mum doesn't like shoes on her carpets."

I bent to untie my laces. "Of course, sorry..."

Jerome stood watching me, his head to one side. "My brother said you were nice..."

I got up and raised an eyebrow at him. "So what else did he tell you about me?"

Jerome grinned. "He said he really checks for you, innit."

I ducked my chin, my cheeks warm. 'He told his little brother about me,' I thought to myself with a flutter in my belly. I followed Jerome into the living room, fearing the worst. But there was no squalor here, only sunlight shining through the muslin curtains on to the neat and orderly living room. The room was decorated in shades of deep yellow and terracotta, with dark brown accents.

I was suddenly ashamed of myself. Why had I expected mess and mayhem? I guess my ideas about how people lived on council estates had been shaped by Mum. Even when we lived in Brixton, I had never been allowed into any of my friends' houses if they lived on an estate.

So I didn't expect the matching three-piece suite, the mirrors on the walls, the dried flowers displayed in tall wooden vases that sat on the floor to either side of the disused fireplace.

Jerome noticed my surprise and chuckled. "Mum likes things a certain way, y'get me? She's a bit of a neat freak, really..."

"It looks great," I assured him.

That was when Dwayne came into the room, still dazed and confused with sleep, wearing rumpled tracksuit bottoms, in the process of pulling a white t-shirt over his head. "Jukkie, wassup, man? Where've you been...?"

I coughed.

Dwayne stopped dead in his tracks, and poked his head out of the top of his t-shirt at last. "Misha?" He seemed stunned to see me there. "Hey, girl, what you doin' here?"

"I came to see you," I replied, feeling shy all of a sudden.

Jerome perched on the edge of the sofa, looking on,

unimpressed. "Yo, Dwayne, ain't you gonna kiss her or somethin'?" He ducked as Dwayne swung his fist at him playfully.

"Shut it, you! Come on, Misha, let's go to my room – where we can have some *privacy*..."

"Woooh!" hooted Jerome, ducking again as Dwayne passed him and pushed him on to the sofa.

I giggled. Jerome reminded me so much of Mark, my stepbrother. The same impish grin, the same careless charm. Jerome made me miss him.

'I've got to call him when I get home,' I thought.

✿ ✿ ✿

Dwayne looked around self-consciously, then flipped his duvet cover over the sheets and went to pull back the curtains and open the window. It was funny to see him look so vulnerable, so unsure of himself.

"Sit down, babe." He gestured towards the small sofa that faced the bed. "You OK? You need anything? A drink or something to eat?"

"Just hold me, Dee," I said. "I need you to hold me." And he did. In his arms, I forgot all about the stinking lift and the graffiti and the tower blocks outside. I forgot all about Jukkie and the boy downstairs. Of course Dwayne was nothing like them. He didn't belong here, not really. He was better than all of this. And I felt the tightness in my heart begin to ease.

"I just can't believe you're here, man," he murmured, a soppy smile all over his face. "It's so good to see you, girl... Let me go get you a drink."

Alone in his room, I was able to look around. Dwayne's room wasn't anything like what I expected a 16-year-old boy's room to look like. Aside from a few clothes scattered over the grey carpet, the room was pristine, almost military in its neatness. The dove-grey walls were covered with posters of various hip-hop artists and a dart board; a bench press and ironing board stood to one side.

Nothing suspicious. On the floor next to his bed lay a book, face down on the floor. Dwayne had been reading in bed? Curious, I picked it up to see what had cured him of his allergy to books and reading. It was *The Autobiography of Malcolm X* . I sat back on my heels, totally taken aback. Where had he got this from? It looked like he had almost finished it too.

As soon as Dwayne was back in the room, I blurted out, "How's the *Malcolm X* book going?" I took a sip of my drink, hiding my expression. "Is it any good?"

Dwayne's face lit up. "Listen, yeah, that book is off da chain! Mans going to sleep late and ting, just to get to the next chapter and find out what happens!"

"Really? I don't think I've read it..."

"Oh, Misha, you should, y'know, you really should. It's funny, a lot of what he describes in the book, I can relate to: the total wildness of his life before he joined the Nation of Islam, the hustling, the drugs..."

He paused then, glancing up at me, trying to understand my expression. I kept it neutral.

He continued: "I can understand why man would want to be on that Nation of Islam ting, y'get me. For the first time, you feel good about yourself, about being black. You've got a community that's trying to better itself, build something for the next generation. That's powerful, man." His eyes were bright and I looked at him curiously.

"Dwayne? Are you actually convinced by the Nation of Islam's ideas?"

"Some of it sure makes sense to me!"

"What, about white people being devils and the Qur'an being the book of God?"

Dwayne shrugged. "The way I see it, white men been acting devilish for a long time, y'get me. Brother Malcolm just calling them out on their badness." He laughed then. "But nah, I don't believe that all white men are devils just like I don't believe that all black

173

men are angels. There's good and evil in all of us, y'get me. That's how God made us."

I did another double-take. Dwayne, talking about God?

"I see... and just what else have you been thinking about since you read this book?"

"Well, I ain't just reading that book – I'm reading this one too." And he picked up a green hardback book from the coffee table behind him. It looked just like the one I had seen the Muslim woman on the bus reading.

"Is... is that a Qur'an?" I asked, somehow dreading the answer.

"Yeah, it is," Dwayne replied, his face glowing with a shy pride. "It's been giving me 'nuff to think about, y'get me. I've started thinking about life and what it means. Which is the true path and that. And... I've been thinking about what it would be like to be a Muslim."

I sat up abruptly. "*What*?" I could hardly believe my ears. Here was Dwayne, non-religious and aware of little outside the bubble of his own life, talking about black consciousness – and thinking of becoming a Muslim! "Why on *earth* would you think about becoming a Muslim, Dee?"

He leaned forward, his eyes bright. "I've been reading, Misha, reading the Qur'an and 'nuff tings about Islam. At first, it didn't make much sense but then, as I started to read more, I started to get it. Right here." He pointed to his head. "And here." He pointed to his heart. "You remember I told you about Jukkie's brother, right, the one who became Muslim?"

I felt a shiver run through me at the mention of Jukkie's name. But I swallowed hard and nodded.

"Well, I've been spending 'nuff time with him for the past two weeks, asking him questions, debating, reading books and ting. I've been going there every day after school... and I've been praying too. Not like how Muslims pray, but in my own way, y'get me."

"How come you never told me about all this then?" So, Dwayne had been keeping secrets from me, just not the kind I had been expecting. "How come I'm only finding out about this now?" In truth, it felt strange to see Dwayne light up over something I didn't understand. I had become so used to teaching him, having him defer to me, that it felt strange to listen to him talk with such passion about something I knew nothing about. If I'm honest, I felt almost... *jealous*.

"I've just been on a bit of a solo ting, Misha," Dwayne replied seriously. "Everything that's happened over the past six months has made me really think about my life and where I'm going. It's like there's this mad chain of events and it's leading somewhere. I can't be sure that I know the destination but I've got an idea. Check it: first I meet you and you make me see a whole other side to life. And then Ms Walker pulls me up at school and puts me on this advanced maths programme, kinda saving me from totally flunking out. Then Tony, the big brother I never had, starts to do what I'm trying to do: turning his life around, getting an education, settling down, and I'm thinking that there's more to life than this madness we're on – it's like God is preparing me to make a change..."

"I always knew you had it in you, Dee," I said, admiring the passion in his voice, the light in his eyes. "But that doesn't mean you have to become a Muslim! That's a bit drastic, isn't it?"

"Don't you see, Misha? Nothing is ever random; everything happens for a reason. So there's a reason that I'm reading the Qur'an and feeling what it's saying. There's a reason I'm chatting to you about this now... I know there is."

I didn't say any more, I just sat there and watched him. He was talking, telling me more about the

Qur'an, but all I could hear was a ringing in my ears. He looked like the Dwayne I knew but he sounded different: serious, passionate, inspired. I had never seen him like this before.

It was wonderful – and terrifying.

A New Lens

DWAYNE

How can I describe the way I felt when I saw Misha standing in my living room that day? Of course she looked hot, so that was great, but then I was like, man, what's she doing here? She wasn't meant to come down my sides. I didn't want her getting involved in my life at that level. What had she seen on her way up? Did any of the mans see her? And did I leave anything in my room that would make her start asking questions?

Good thing the book was there. That totally distracted her. Otherwise she may have noticed other things and started asking difficult questions, questions I wasn't about to answer, y'get me.

So I was jumpy as hell as we left the house. Misha had told her mum that she was going up North London to see her dad, so she couldn't stay long. She had to get to her dad's quick, before her mum rang and checked up on her. I wasn't gonna argue. The sooner Misha got off my estate, the sooner I would be able to relax.

Lately, Jukkie had been acting proper off-key about Misha and I didn't get it. He'd never had anything to say about my girlfriends before. I mean, what did it have to do with him, right?

Just the other day at the gym, he'd started on it again. "You know what, blud? Since you've been seeing that posh girl, you've changed. You ain't the same as you used to be."

"What do you mean, man?" I tried to ignore him and concentrate on the bench press that was just about ready to mash me up.

"Where was you last Friday night? Out with Posh Spice while the mans were at a rave in Camberwell. You didn't even bring her down! That's lame, man."

"She ain't into that scene, Jukkie, you know that. Why am I gonna bring someone to a rave who doesn't wanna be there?"

"So who's the man then, you or her? If I tell my girl to reach , she better reach, y'get me? She's got to know how it goes: it's bros before hos, y'undertand?"

I ground my teeth and didn't say anything.

What was the point? Jukkie would never understand. To him, girls were there to be used and abused. As long as he gave them stuff, he expected them to put up and shut up. And most girls did. It was a status thing to be known as Jukkie's girl, even if it was only for a few weeks.

Boy, it used to be like that for me too, until Misha came along. Back in the day, I could have had my pick of any girl on the estate, young ones, older ones, they were hungry for me. But I wasn't on that now. I didn't need all those girls chasing me. I had Misha. And I wanted it to stay that way, which is why I wanted to keep her as far away from my estate and the RDS boys as possible.

I only relaxed when I remembered that there was a dog fight happening that day – for sure Jukkie, Trigger and the others would be there. The estate was safe – for now.

Once I had chilled out, I could enjoy showing Misha around. Mr Davis on the ground floor had set up a barbecue in his front garden and was blasting old school reggae tunes through a set of mash-up speakers. The music echoed through the courtyard, reminding me of the old days when we used to ride through the estate on our bikes. Some little girls were skipping, singing the lyrics of Beyonce's latest hit; baby mothers were out with their Nike and D&G babies, blowing bubbles while they pushed them on the swings.

'Nuff people called out to me as I walked past with Misha, asking after my mum and Jay.

"That your new girlfriend, Dwayne?" asked Auntie Biba, who was sitting on a folding chair outside her front door, squeezed into a vest top and jogging bottoms. "Watch him, love," she chuckled, shaking her head, "he's a heartbreaker!" When she grinned, her gold teeth caught the sun.

Misha smiled over at her, all shy. "Does everyone know you around here?" she asked, as if it was something strange.

"This is home, innit," I shrugged, stopping to wave to Old Man Des, who was sitting stooped over a battered old guitar, strumming the strings with his long, bony fingers, crooning to himself. "That's Des. He tried to teach me how to play the guitar when I was a little kid."

"What happened?" asked Misha, smiling over at the old man. When he grinned back, his lips stretched to show all the teeth he was missing.

"I guess I was more interested in hanging out with

my boys – never went back after a couple of months. I could have taken it further..." Misha looked up at me, like she was surprised by the way I said it. But true say, I missed those days with Des, jamming on that beat-up old guitar.

When we reached the main road, we saw a small, battered minivan driving into the estate. It was full of boys, most of them Jay's age, some a bit older, laughing, singing and banging on the windows.

"OK, brothers, that's enough, quiet down!" It was Damon, the local youth worker, his voice all hoarse. Obviously they had given him a hard time, wherever they'd been. He jumped down from the front seat of the minivan and banged on the door. "Keep it down now, or you'll shatter every window on the estate with your terrible singing!"

The boys all creased up and then started singing again, properly this time, a little kid with braces taking the main part.

"Oh my God," breathed Misha, "he can really sing!"

"Yeah, that's Brother Damon from the local youth group. Yo, Damon! Wha' gwan, blud?"

Damon looked harassed as he glanced over at us, squinting. When he recognised me, he smiled and waved. "How's it going, man?"

"It's all good, Damon. What you doing with this lot?"

"We just came back from camp, actually. Took the boys out on an excursion to Devon. Why didn't your little brother come? He'd have enjoyed it."

I thought of Jay's little screw-face, saying, "I ain't goin' to no camp. That stuff's for losers, man!" I could have convinced him if I had tried harder. Seeing the boys all excited, grabbing their bags, joking around with Damon, I felt bad. This would be good for him, show him that there's more to life than skipping school and hustling.

"Next time, man," I said, putting my arm around Misha. "Next time, yeah?"

Misha was quiet all the way to the end of the road. Then she turned to me and her face was all serious.

"Dee," she said, "what do you want to be when you grow up?"

I laughed, surprised by how serious she sounded. "What d'you mean, girl? Why you getting all serious on me all of a sudden?"

She bit her lip and looked away. Normally, I loved it when she did that – bit her lip – but I tried to stay focused. "It's just that..." She shook her fringe out of her eyes and, for the first time since I had known her,

183

I really thought she didn't know how to say what she wanted to say. I began to get nervous.

"Look," she tried again. "We're cool, right, you and I? You're into me, I'm into you, but I can't help feeling that we're on different paths, that we're going in different directions. I felt it when you came to my house, but then I thought it was just my family being difficult. But being here, seeing you in your community, listening to you talk about Islam and Malcolm X, I can't help thinking we come from totally different worlds. And that maybe those worlds will never fit, never make sense together. Do you understand where I'm coming from?"

I could feel my insides going cold. What was she saying? Was she for real? Or was she playing a game with me? Was she trying to break up with me? But I couldn't let her see how the thought of losing her made me feel.

I stepped back from her and turned away. "So what, you came all the way over here to tell me you want to end it?"

"No, Dwayne, of course not! I'm just telling you what I see..." She put her hand on my arm but I shrugged it off and put my hand up to her.

"Yeah, well, it sounds like you want to break up.

That's what it sounds like. And if that's what you want, just go ahead and say it." It cut me to say those words to her but I had to. I wasn't about to let myself get played, by Misha or by anyone else. Free that!

But then she started crying! Oh my days, I hadn't expected her to do that!

"Misha, stop, what you crying for?" I couldn't believe that I had made her cry proper tears – how could I do that to her when all I ever wanted to do was put a smile on her face? I reached out and tried to wipe away her tears but she brushed my hand to the side.

"How can you say that?" she sniffed. "I was just being honest with you and you go all cold and start talking about breaking up! I need you to reassure me, Dee, not push me away. Sometimes, I just feel that I don't know you at all..." And she blew her nose with a tissue she had found in her bag.

'What did you have to go and do that for, man?'

'What?'

'You made her cry, eediat!'

'I know, man, I know! But I didn't mean to! It just came out...'

'You switched on her, that's what you did. What's wrong with you anyway, why can't you just have an

honest conversation with her?'

LOL.

'What you laughing for?'

'There is no way I can be honest with her, blud. No way. There's too much about me she doesn't know. Too much I don't want her to know.'

'Why?'

'Coz I know that, if she knew, she wouldn't be able to handle it. And then I'd lose her for real.'

'And then?'

'And that would be like losing the one part of me that's good, that's worth something.'

'Well, you'd better make it up to her then, innit.'

I took her by the shoulders and turned her round to face me. "Misha, I'm sorry. I didn't mean to go all cold. I just thought you were saying..."

"You didn't even listen to me! You just jumped to your own conclusions and then became someone else, something else. Not the Dwayne I know at all."

"The Dwayne you know is the real Dwayne, Misha. I promise you that. Don't watch what anyone else says. You and me, we're the ones that matter, y'get me." Then I looked into her eyes. I wanted her to see how dead serious I was. Whatever other lies I was telling, whatever other secrets I had, this was the truth. "Misha, I don't want to waste my life, y'know. That ain't what I got planned. I'm gonna make you proud of me, you'll see." Then I took her hand and put it on my chest so she could feel my heart beating. "With you by my side, Misha, I feel I can do anything, achieve anything I want to, y'get me. The sky's the limit. Just stand by me, yeah, believe in me and I promise you I won't let you down. OK?"

She smiled and nodded. "OK, Dee."

"So we're cool, yeah?"

"Yeah, we're cool."

"Right, you better get to your dad's before your mum starts to wonder what's happened to you."

She began to walk off down the street, looking back at me over her shoulder. I ached to run after her, to take her back to my place, to have some time with her before my mum came home. But I knew she couldn't risk it. She had to go.

"Dream of me, yeah?" I called after her.

"Always, Dee, always." I loved it when she said that.

Daddy's Little Girl

MISHA

I couldn't wait to get to my dad's house. The whole experience in Saints Hill had left me drained and shaky.

Although Dwayne and I had parted on good terms, I was still shocked by the way he had turned on me. I felt like I was losing my grip on the situation and, not for the first time, it occurred to me that there was so much I still didn't know about Dwayne. Was he being deliberately evasive or was this just a normal part of a relationship, finding out about each other bit by bit? I didn't know for sure – but I knew that I wanted to be back on solid ground. I wanted to be with my dad.

Dad's flat always smelled of cooking and incense. Today was no different. Fading posters of reggae artists and dusty African art adorned the walls, books and records stacked against them. As soon as I stepped on to the landing, my gorgeous stepbrothers and sister ran to meet me, their gold-flecked dreadlocks bouncing, their faces bright with smiles. I had missed them so much!

"Misha!" cried Imani, jumping into my arms. "We thought you weren't coming!"

"Yeah," said Mark, the eldest, "you're well late, man." And he and I exchanged our special handshake: over, under, pull, click finger, pow-pow.

Little Joshua lifted up his arms and I scooped him up, unable to resist. "Did you bring me chocolates, Mishie?" he lisped.

I opened my mouth to speak, but then my stepmother Leona came out of the kitchen, wiping her hands on her purple kaftan, her cheeks pink.

"Misha, baby!" She smiled warmly when she saw me, like she always did, and came and hugged me.

"Now, now, Joshie," she said, poking his belly, "what did Mummy say about too many chocolates, eh? They're not good for you. They'll rot your teeth."

"Awww!" cried Josh. "But we haven't had chocolates forever!"

"Then another day won't kill you," retorted Leona. "Now let your sister come inside properly."

"Where's Dad?" I asked, kicking off my shoes.

"Oh, he's in the living room, listening to some old records. Go tell him that lunch is on the table. Kids, go and wash your hands, OK?"

I walked down the narrow corridor to the living room and pushed aside the beaded curtain. The afternoon sunlight shone through the bay windows, filling the room with golden light. I loved this room, especially at this time of day. Dad was lying on the faded green sofa, against the cushions he had brought back with him from Ethiopia a few years before. His eyes were closed and he sang along to the sounds of Peter Tosh.

I crept towards him on tiptoe and knelt down beside him, holding my breath. I had always done this since I was little, to test if he really could see with his eyes closed, as he always told me he could.

"You took your time," he growled, a smile curving his mouth. Then he opened one eye.

I smiled. He always knew when I was in the room, even when he seemed to be fast asleep. "Better late than never, eh?"

Dad sat up and patted the sofa next to him. I sat down beside him and he put his arm around me and hugged me. He smelled like he always did: smoky, spicy and familiar.

"How's my girl then?"

"I'm good, Dad, I'm good."

"Good."

That was Dad: a man of few words. I felt so comfortable, there in the crook of my dad's arm, that I could have stayed there all afternoon, even fallen asleep. But then we heard Leona's voice calling us to eat and I realised that I was starving. I hadn't eaten all day.

✧ ✧ ✧

Leona had laid on a real feast. There was a spicy lentil and sweet potato stew, made with coconut milk, tofu stir-fry, rice'n'peas and a carrot salad that smelled of oranges and cinnamon. She'd even made my favourite: 'ital stew': a thick, thyme-scented broth, heaving with yams, sweet potatoes, carrots and okra, fiery with Scotch bonnet peppers. As Rastas, Dad and Leona ate a strictly vegan diet, but they sure knew how to spice it up!

"Wow, Leona!" I grinned. "You've really outdone yourself!"

Leona patted her headwrap and smiled proudly, then put a hand on my stepbrother Mark's shoulder.

"Well, I did get some help from little Masterchef himself."

My amazing twelve-year-old brother, Mark, he of the sun-bleached dreadlocks reaching halfway down his back, grinned.

"I made the ital stew," he said, and I noticed with a jolt that his voice had just started to break. "Mum wrote the recipe down and I followed it – but, of course, I had to add a bit of the Mark magic, y' know what I'm saying!"

"OK, everyone, enough talking!" said Leona, sitting down. "Let's eat!"

"You'll see," said Mark, while we were all tucking into his ital stew. "In a few years' time, I'll have my own line of sauces and seasonings in Tesco, like that guy off Dragons' Den. Mark's Vital Ital – I can see it now!"

"Well," I smiled at him, "I know many people would pay a lot of money to be able to take home stew like this!" We all agreed that this was the way we were finally going to get the Reynolds name into the papers. Trust my little brother Mark to have it all figured out.

"Leona," growled Dad, with a lopsided smile on his face, "this is food for the mind, body and the soul!"

Leona smiled back at him and I noticed with

a pang how Dad's eyes went soft when he looked at my stepmother. They were just so compatible – it was clear that they were totally on the same wavelength. I found myself wondering whether he had ever looked at Mum like that but I pushed the thought away. It felt wrong to think like that, especially in Leona's house. He was still my dad: nothing could change that.

Imani was talking about her project for her weekend school for Afro-Caribbean kids and Joshua tried to sing us the song he had learned at nursery.

"After lunch, Josh," said Leona. "We're eating now."

After lunch, the kids went out into the garden to play. I helped Leona clear the table, then went to sit down in the front room with my dad for some father-daughter time.

"How's your mother?" asked Dad. "She's happy about the offer from the school?"

"Of course she is, Dad, what do you think?"

"She's worked hard to get you where you are today," he replied thoughtfully. "She expects a lot from you... sometimes too much, I think."

I frowned. I hated to hear either of my parents criticise the other.

"Dad..." I began, but he held up his hand.

"No, I'm not going to start, but I'm just saying: it can be dangerous to expect so much from your children. They are their own people and, one day, they may choose a different path, one you didn't plan for them. And then what will you do?"

I looked at Dad, his kind, intelligent green eyes behind his steel-rimmed glasses, his long face framed by a mane of silver-peppered dreadlocks, and wondered whether I should tell him about Dwayne. Would he approve? Would he be angry? He had never broached the subject of boys with me before, except to say that all boys were after one thing and none of them could be trusted.

I decided to give it a try. "Dad, how do you know whether you can trust a guy or not? Like, how do you know if they're being straight with you?"

He raised an eyebrow at me and said gruffly, "Hmm, you're sixteen now. I guess it's time to start asking those questions, eh?" He folded his arms, jutted out his chin and growled, "You are a queen, Misha. That is what I have always taught you. And you must insist that anyone who wants to be with you treats you like a queen, respects you, honours you. Without respect, no relationship can work. But I have to tell you, there's not many lickle boys nowadays that know how to treat a queen. So my advice to you is to leave all that foolishness and concentrate on your schooling. There'll be plenty of time for all that drama later, trust me."

"But what if you think you've found someone... and you like them but you're not sure whether he's the right one, or whether you have a future together. Look at you and Mum: you were both so different..."

"Yes, we were totally different... she was a student from a strict Christian house and I was a carefree Rastaman doing my music... we were crazy to think it could work. But then you came along and made it all worthwhile. So your mum may hate me, she may blame me for ruining her life and doing her wrong, but she can never deny the gift that our relationship left us with: you."

"Oh, I love you, Dad," I said, hugging him. He always knew just what to say. "Thank you."

He stroked my hair gently and murmured, "I love you too, baby love. And I always will, y'understand?"

"No, Dad," I smiled. "I don't understand, I *over*stand, seen?"

Dad laughed and gave me a push. "Go help Leona," he said, turning up the volume on the stereo.

"And make me a herbal tea while you're there, OK?"

"OK, Dad."

Just as I got up to go to the kitchen, I heard my mobile phone ring. Thinking it must be Dwayne, I picked my bag up. "I'll just take this call, Dad..."

Dad nodded and flicked on the TV. It was time for Match of the Day.

I answered the phone as soon as I had stepped into the dining room. "Dwayne?" I whispered, my heart fluttering in my chest.

There was a pause on the other end. A sharp intake of breath.

"Misha?"

It was Mum.

Moment Of Truth

MISHA

"Where have you been?" Mum's face was tight, her jaw set, her brown eyes blazing.

"I was at Dad's!" I opened my eyes wide, trying to look as innocent as possible.

"*Before* you got to your dad's, Misha! And don't try and tell me that you were with Effie because I have already spoken to her *and* her parents!"

For a split second, I considered insisting that I'd gone straight to Dad's but one look in Mum's eyes, and I knew I couldn't lie to her. Not again. She had always been able to see right through me. "I was with Dwayne."

I would have given anything not to have seen that look in Mum's eyes: a mixture of disappointment and disgust. It was almost unbearable and I felt shame and regret burn my insides like acid.

Mum kissed her teeth and turned away abruptly, growling, "Just get inside; you've got some serious explaining to do."

I stepped into the hallway after her and turned away to pull off my jacket. I tried to breathe normally, to steady my nerves, but inside I was trembling. I had never seen her so angry in all my life. But what would she do? What was the *worst* she could do?

I would soon find out.

"Sit down," said Mum curtly as I stepped into the living room. Everything about the room looked dark and menacing, nothing like the comfortable, welcoming space it usually was.

I sat down on the edge of the sofa, chewing my bottom lip. Mum took a deep breath. "OK, Misha, this is how it's going to work: I'm going to ask the questions, you're going to tell the truth. Do you understand, Misha? *The truth*. No more lies."

I nodded. What else could I do? There was nothing to say.

"Right. Firstly: have you been seeing that boy, Dwayne?"

"Yes."

"Even after I told you to end it with him?"

"Yes."

A pause. I decided it would be safer to avoid Mum's eyes and look at the floor. That way there was a chance I would be able to delay the tears that were already threatening to fall.

"So you've been sneaking out to see him behind my back?"

"Yes." What kind of tears were these? Unfamiliar as they were, I could name them: these were tears of shame mixed with regret.

Mum took a big, shuddering breath. "All right, Misha, I don't need to tell you what a terrible disappointment this is to me. I trusted you – and you betrayed my trust. Did you think I wouldn't find out? What kind of fool do you take me for? You think I don't know when my own daughter is lying to me?"

"Mum, I..."

"No, Misha, there can be no explanation for what you have done, no excuse. I invited that boy into my home and gave him a chance to prove himself. He failed miserably, on so many levels. And out of my love for you, I told you that it was best that you didn't see him again. Haven't I always done what is best for you? Haven't I always sacrificed everything for your happiness?"

"For *my* happiness?" I was incredulous. Mum didn't really expect me to agree with her – did she?

"Yes, Misha, for *your* happiness! Everything I have worked so hard for over the last few years has been for you..."

"Mum, all that has had nothing to *do* with my happiness! It's always been about what *you* want, not what I want!"

Mum kissed her teeth and shook her head in irritation. "Oh, Misha, grow up! I'm not talking about you being happy for a few weeks because some boy is sending you a thousand text messages! I'm talking about your future here, your life – what's best for you ..."

"But how would you know, Mum?" I felt anger build up inside me at last. "How would you know what is best for me? You've got no idea who I am, Mum! You may think you do but, really, the only Misha you know is the one you expect me to be..."

"Misha, I know you better than you know yourself, believe me."

"How can you say that?"

"Because I am your *mother*!" Mum's voice was high and she got up abruptly, pacing the floor in front of me. "Because I gave *birth* to you! Because nobody else in this world has sacrificed as much for you as I have..."

"Stop saying that!" I shouted suddenly, jumping up, my hands over my ears. I just couldn't stand to hear her say that one more time. "Stop beating me over the head with that every time I disappoint you, every time I don't live up to your expectations! It's like you're making me pay you back for giving birth to me, for you and Dad splitting up, for bringing me up on your own – I didn't bloody ask to be born!"

The slap came so hard and fast that it took me completely by surprise. The fire of Mum's hand spread across my cheek like a hot, red stain.

"Don't you *ever*," choked Mum, her chest heaving, "speak to me like that again. I am your *mother*. And I always will be. And don't ever go thinking that you will be able to pay me back for that because you never will, do you understand?"

All I could do was blink, as my cheek throbbed. I was stunned. She had never hit me before. "Why did you hit me?" I asked, my voice trembling.

I saw Mum falter and her eye flickered. Maybe she regretted it. Maybe she would apologise now.

But no.

"Misha, you need to come to your senses. This life

is not a game; you can't just go gambling your future on some lickle..."

"No!" Tears were streaming down my face now and I wouldn't let her finish, couldn't let her have the last word, not this time. "No – why did you hit me? Why did you *hit* me?"

Mum tried to ignore my tears, tried to keep talking, talking about my future, about the challenges I would face, how I couldn't allow anyone to hold me back. But I was way past listening to all that.

In my mind, memories were crowding together: our house on Coldharbour Lane, cosy afternoons spent at Gran's place, Rachel and other friends I had ditched because Mum said that they weren't good enough for me; taking Science instead of French because Mum said more black girls needed to excel in Maths and Science; growing my hair when I had wanted to keep it short, relaxing it because Mum said braids looked common; and Dwayne, of course. Years and years of doing what made Mum happy, what she approved of, rose up to choke me.

"How could you? How could you hit me for telling the truth? How could you *hit* me?"

She tried to reach out towards me but, just then, something inside me snapped.

"Don't you touch me," I shrieked. "Don't you come near me!"

"Misha!" barked Mum. "Get a hold of yourself!"

But it was too late for orders. I stumbled from the room, everything a watery blur in front of me. Escape, escape, escape. The word built up to a crescendo inside my head and, before I knew it, I had wrenched the front door open and was running down the path towards the gate, the early evening air cool against my burning cheeks.

"Misha!" Mum's furious voice echoed in the deathly quiet of the Sunday night street. "Come back! Come back right now!" And she rushed to stop me at the gate. But she stepped back when I whirled to face her. I wanted the neighbours to hear; I wanted her to be unable to face them the next morning.

"All my life," I shouted, "I've tried to live up to your expectations! I've been everything you've wanted me to be, tried to make you happy. And now that I've found a happiness of my own, a happiness you don't understand, you want to take it away from me..."

"Misha, love, it's got nothing to do with that..." Mum tried to take my arm, to lead me back inside where the neighbours couldn't see us, but I shook her hand off.

"No, Mum, I'm not coming back inside! Not until you can learn to listen to me, to what I think, what I want. You say Dwayne isn't good enough for me? Maybe the truth that you can't face is that I'm not good enough for *you*."

"*Misha*!"

But I was already running, running down the street, escape, escape, escape pounding its own rhythm inside me.

Retribution

DWAYNE

After Misha left, I went home to change. I had planned to stay home, maybe give Tony a call, play some Playstation, basically lay low.

I was about to call for pizza when my second phone – my 'work phone' – rang. It was Spoonz telling me that they had scored some top class weed and a bit of crack cocaine. He asked me if I wanted to come get some.

The deal was too sweet to resist. Avoiding Jukkie and Trigger, going to after-school maths class and spending time with Misha all meant that I was seriously broke. I needed to refill the coffee jar of cash I kept in the lining of the sofa in my room.

I knew that, in a couple of hours, the crackheads would be coming to the wheelie bins underneath

St Paul's to score their nightly fix. I reckoned I could make some quick dough without getting into beef with anyone, as long as I left the house tidy and was home before Mum got back.

Just as I left my room, I caught sight of Malcolm X's autobiography, lying face-down on my sofa next to my copy of the Qur'an. I bit my lip and thought for a minute.

'Do you really need to do this, blud?'

'What's that?'

'Go sell some crack to feed a junkie's nasty habit. I thought we were past that...'

'You may be past that, blud, but as for me, I've got to make my Ps, same way.'

'So you ain't gonna listen to nobody: not your mum, not Ms Walker, not Brother Malcom, not even your Lord? Let alone what Misha would think if she knew.'

'That's what I hate about you, man. You're so idealistic. You don't think practically. Yeah, I want to go straight, I want to sort my stuff out. But in the meantime, man has to eat. And if those crackheads don't get it from me, you know they're gonna get it from someone else, innit? I didn't create the market, blud, I just supply it.'

Silence.

'So what, now you ain't got nothing to say?'

'You make me sick, man.'
'Stay like that.'

✿ ✿ ✿

But by the time I had spent a few minutes standing around those stinking bins, I was regretting it. There were some other man there too, eyeing each other up. Someone said that they heard that the 5-0 would be patrolling so everyone was on high alert. I had just wanted to chill, score some easy money, and go home and eat pizza. But it didn't look like it was going to be that kind of night.

I was tense, listening out for any police sirens coming into the estate. It was Brixton so, true say, there were always sirens going off. What mattered was how far away they were. Did you have enough time to stash whatever you were holding and make a run for it before they came with their sniffer dogs and batons?

One by one, the crackheads starting appearing from the dark corners of the estate. I tried my best to be polite to them for the sake of business but, to tell the truth, most of them made me want to heave. How could they let themselves go like that? Matted, dreadlocked hair, funky clothes, teeth that hadn't seen toothpaste since before I was born. I tried to avoid touching them; I was sure they had lice and stuff like that.

But hey, these were the customers and you know what they say: the customer is always right. So I smiled and joked with them same way, happy that my bag was almost empty and that I would be going home soon.

When I had one bag left, I decided to call it a night. I was mash-up and proper hungry. I'd be ordering an extra large pizza when I got home.

"Yo, I'm out," I called to the others who were still standing around, hoping for more customers.

"Catch ya later, yeah?"

"Stay safe..."

As I squeezed through the narrow gap between the two bins that hid our spot from the rest of the estate, I bumped into a little kid, his hood over his head.

"You got some punk, bro?" he asked, trying to make his voice sound all manly. I frowned and pulled his hood back off his head. I knew that voice.

"Spaz!" I almost shouted. "What you doin' here, man?" It was Jay's best friend from school.

He seemed embarrassed to see me. "I just came to get some weed, innit. My brother's vex' with me coz I broke his iPod, now he won't get me any weed.

Told me I have to get it myself until I pay him back for the iPod."

"What you gonna do with weed, man? Ain't you still in nursery school or something?"

He stood up taller and said, "I sell it at school, innit. 'Nuff boys can't get it for themselves but, through my brother, I can get it for them. Make a little dough, y'get me..."

And I looked down at the bright white trainers he was wearing – the latest style. I didn't have to ask him how he was spending his money. I thought about the trainers I bought for Jay every couple of months. I never wanted him to go through what I went through: being teased because your mum bought your clothes from Primark, never having money to get the latest trainers. I made sure that my little brother had everything he needed – mainly so that he wouldn't have to be hanging around bins under St Paul's with a bunch of junkies and drug dealers.

I looked down at Spaz. He was just a little kid, man. He should have been home in bed, not out here on his own. I flipped his hood back over his head and pushed him away from the gap between the bins.

"Go home, man," I growled. "It ain't safe for you out here, y'get me."

But he wasn't having it. "What're you talking about, man? I can handle myself! I just need to get some food, that's it. Why don't you just sell me some, innit? I've got the money..." And he put his hand in his back pocket and pulled out a bunch of ten pound notes. He looked up at me and, in that moment, I saw Jay's face instead of his.

It was too much for me.

"Nah, I said go home, man! I ain't selling you nuffin'. Now go home before I mash you up, yeah?" And I gave him a shove to show him I wasn't joking.

He swore at me, then spat on the floor next to my shoe. But he still turned and walked away towards his flat on the other side of the estate.

"And don't let me catch you here again, y'undertand?" I shouted after him.

He gave me the finger.

Feisty.

By the time I got home, I didn't even feel like pizza any more. I felt sick. I just wanted to sleep, to block out everything that had happened that day.

That's one of the wonderful things about sleep: it's like a warm, dark tunnel where you can go to escape from everything and everyone. I counted myself lucky that I didn't dream and, if I did, I never remembered my dreams when I woke up.

I wondered why I hadn't heard from Misha, then remembered that I had put my 'non-work' phone on silent while I was out on road. I took it out of my pocket and checked it for messages. Two from Misha and five missed calls from Mum. Five missed calls? It must have been serious because Mum hardly ever rang my phone.

I rang her number.

"Dwayne?" Her voice sounded weak and tired and straight away I got scared. What had happened?

"Dwayne... it's Jay..."

"Jay? What, Mum? Has something happened to him?"

"Well, sort of... I need you to come, come now..."

"Mum, where are you? Just tell me, I'll be there."

"We're at the police station in Brixton, Dwayne. Your brother's been arrested."

Scapegoat

DWAYNE

Jay, Jay, what have you done, man? What have you done?

A million questions were buzzing around in my head as I ran all the way to the police station on Brixton Road. I had seen him just that afternoon! Where the hell did he go when he left the house? Who had he seen? I thought of his little face in the bright neon lights of the police station. He was only ten! He didn't belong there! Did they rough him up? 'Cuff him? Who did they put him in a cell with? A ten-year-old for God's sake!

I was jittery by the time I got to the station but I took a deep breath before going in. I had to hold it together, for Mum, and I didn't want the police to go asking any questions about me either. Although I had managed to keep myself out of trouble with the police so far, I knew that one false move, one stupid mistake, and you would be banged up in a cell with rapists and junkies, on your way to remand or jail somewhere mad far like Portsmouth, where your family couldn't even come see you on the regular.

I stuffed my hands into my pockets – and my heart nearly stopped beating.

I still had the bag of weed in my jacket pocket.

✧ ✧ ✧

I stood there, chewing my lip. What the hell was I going to do? My phone rang again. It was Mum.

"Yeah?"

"Dwayne, where are you?"

"I'm almost there, Mum. Just give me a minute..."

I looked around. If I did anything here, the CCTV was bound to pick it up. But I had to get rid of the bag. There was no way I was walking into the police station with it, not with the sniffer dogs. And anyway, the 5-0 could easily stop and search me for no reason other than that I was a black boy out on the street. I had to be smart about it.

Nice and easy, I backed away from the entrance and turned to walk up Gresham Road. I figured if I stashed it in one of the bins, I would be able to get it back again later. As I walked past the row of terrace houses, I looked across the road and saw that the lights were on in the mosque – Tony's mosque – and there was some sort of party going on. There were loads of brothers with beards, short thobes, puffa jackets and Timberland boots standing around outside, talking, laughing, sitting on the curb. It looked like they were having a barbecue or something and I could smell the jerk chicken from where I stood, on the other side of the street. My mouth watered and I heard my stomach growl – man, I *still* hadn't eaten!

'Boy, man would love to just step there and grab some jerk chicken, y'know.'

'Yo, rudeboy! Focus! How're you going to go to the mosque with a pocketful of weed and eat chicken while your kid brother's sitting in a police cell? Dash the ting and let's go, blud!'

'Yeah, you're right, man. You're right.'

'KMT. You know I'm right – I'm **always** right. Now just drop the bag in this bin here and let's get back to Jay and Mum. Forget your belly for once.'

In a few minutes, I had put the bag in one of the bins further up the road, being careful not to touch it with my bare hands, and sprinted back to the station. Usain Bolt couldn't have got there any faster.

When I stepped in, I saw Mum sitting on the bench. I looked around – Jay was nowhere to be seen. Were they planning on keeping him overnight? I began to walk up to Mum but she saw me coming.

"What took you so long?" Her voice was harsh but her eyes were red and raw and tired-looking. She must have been crying for ages.

"I'm sorry, Mum. I just had to deal with some stuff, y'get me. Where's Jay?"

"They've finished with him now. They've taken his fingerprints and everything already..."

"But what happened, Mum? What did Jay do?"

"They say he was caught trying to rob an old lady on the street. Said that he pushed her over and ran off with her bag but someone on the street catch him before he could get away. That's what *they* say."

"Jay? *Robbing*?" I shook my head. It didn't make no sense, no sense at all. Jay didn't need to go robbing nobody – I made sure he had everything he needed. What was he thinking? "Will they be keeping him overnight?" I turned to glare at the officer behind the desk.

She'd been listening to us, of course. "No, he's too young to be kept in custody," she said with a shrug.

I wanted to give her one across the face. It sounded

like she *wanted* to throw my little brother in jail.

When Jay came out into the waiting room, escorted by a female officer, I jumped to my feet.

"Jay..." I said, wanting more than anything to hug him and strangle him at the same time. What had the little nutter been thinking?

But Jay avoided my eyes and, instead, looked towards Mum, who took him firmly by the hand.

"We'll see you again tomorrow then, shall we, when the Youth Offending Team will meet with you both?"

Mum nodded, her lips pressed together. "Let's go," she said shortly.

Mum didn't say anything on the way home; she walked two steps in front of me, her pace getting faster and more determined the nearer we got to the house. Jay was practically running to keep up with her. I was glad to see that her strength was coming back but her silence was making me didgy.

When we got inside, I wanted to have a go at Jay, even give him a beat down. But Mum pushed Jay down the corridor. "Get in your room and don't come out, y'hear me, boy?"

"You go and sit down, Mum. Just relax." I went into the kitchen, thinking she would be needing a cup of tea. But when I turned around, she was standing in the kitchen doorway, still wearing her coat, looking right at me. Her eyes were dry now, but hard, harder than I had ever seen in my life.

"*You...*" she said in this hoarse, grating voice I didn't recognise. "You did this."

Her voice and the way she was looking at me proper freaked me out.

"What are you on about, Mum?"

"This is all happening because of you. Your little brother Jerome has had his fingerprints taken and seen the inside of a police station because of you."

"What?"

"You heard me, Dwayne Kingston! I blame you for this!"

"Mum, I had nothing to do with this, I swear down! I didn't even know Jay had gone out! How was I supposed to know that he was robbing old ladies?" I tried to go up to her and hug her, take her arm and make her sit down or something. It was the shock, for sure. That was why she was acting so crazy.

But instead of letting me hold her, she reached up and slapped me across the face.

"Shut up, Dwayne!" she shrieked, her face screwed up, her eyes blazing. "What kind of fool do you take me for? You think I don't know what's been going on

217

these last few years? You think I don't know what you get up to when you're out with your boys? You think I don't know about the drugs, the stealing, the money you've got hidden in your sofa?"

Total shock.

"You think I'm blind? That I don't see the trainers, the sound systems, the clothes? You think I don't know where you got the money for all that?"

I couldn't say anything. I was still reeling from the slap and the force of her words. And the way she was looking at me, like she proper hated me, cut deeper than any of Jukkie's knives ever could.

"You brought all that madness into my house! And the worst thing is, Jay *idolises* you, wants to be just like his big brother when he grows up – and now look where it's got him!"

"Nah, Mum, don't even go there, yeah! I love Jay! There is nothing I wouldn't do for that kid and he knows it!"

"Jay doesn't need that kind of love, Dwayne! He doesn't need you as a guide to life. There is nothing that you can give my son, Dwayne, nothing! And you know why?" Then she leaned in real close and poked me in my chest. "Because you're wort'less. You're wort'less, just like your father!"

I swallowed hard to gulp back the tears. What was it about the way she said it that cut so deep? I wished I knew. If I knew, maybe I would have been able to protect myself or something. But I couldn't. All I could say was, "So, what, I'm not your son now? It's all about Jay now?"

But she carried on talking as if I hadn't said anything. "You know, Dwayne, that day we were in the headteacher's office, I thought there was hope for you. I thought that you were going to change, to stop your badness and be the son that I always hoped you would be. But you've let me down again and again, and now your actions have hurt the most precious thing in my life." She took a deep breath.

"I want you out, Dwayne, *out* of my house."

"*What*?"

"Pack your tings, take your lickle stash of money from your sofa and *leave this house*. I don't want you here when Jay wakes up in the morning."

"Mum! I'm sixteen, I've got my exams coming up – where am I supposed to go?"

"You think I care? No, Dwayne, it's way too late for that. Go to one of your boys; I'm sure one of them will take you. As for me, I'm finished with you."

And she turned on her heel and marched out of

the kitchen. It was all I could do not to start bawling right there.

Now what was I going to do?

❖ ❖ ❖

It was well late when I knocked on Tony's door in Camberwell. I had spent most of the night walking the streets in a daze, not knowing where to go, who to turn to. My mind turned from Misha to Jukkie to the other boys to Ms Walker – none of them could help me now.

"Oh, God," I found myself praying. "Help me." Then I thought of Tony and I knew that he would have my back, just like the old days. I didn't expect him to answer his door but when he did, I almost cried with relief.

"Hey, what's up, man?" he yawned, rubbing his eyes.

"Long story, bro... can I cotch with you for a few days?"

"Beef at home, huh?"

I nodded. I still couldn't talk about it.

"Of course, man." Tony smiled, punching me on the shoulder. "Any time. Come in."

Give And Take

MISHA

"Misha? Yes, she's here..." Leona looked over at me, her eyebrows raised. "You'd like to speak to her?"

I shook my head vigorously. I had just spent the last hour crying into one of Dad's Ethiopian cushions. I certainly did not want to speak to my mother.

"Well..." Leona was visibly uncomfortable. "Misha's a bit tied up right now. Can I get her to call you back? No? You want to speak to Isaiah? OK, hold on..." Leona called out to my dad. "Isaiah, Dina wants to speak to you. Maybe you'd better take it on the other line..."

Leona put the phone down carefully and came to sit next to me on the sofa. She didn't say anything and I was grateful for that. I had done more than enough crying for one day. If she said anything, I knew

221

I would burst into tears all over again. She just rubbed my back and started singing under her breath. It was really comforting. So comforting that I forgot to be nervous about what Mum was telling Dad.

Big mistake.

When Dad had finished on the phone, he came out of his bedroom. His face was red. He asked Leona to excuse us. Then he sat down and gave it to me, really gave it to me. He was shocked about Dwayne. He couldn't believe that I had been lying to Mum and him all this time. He was furious with me for fighting with Mum – a cardinal sin as far as he was concerned. But worse than anything, he was disappointed in me.

"You've betrayed our trust, Misha," he kept saying. "This is not what I expect from you."

Then, just before he got up to go, he added, "Your mother said that some kid tried to rob your gran today. She took a fall but she's OK. They caught the kid who did it. She said you should call her."

Of course I called Gran straight away. She sounded all right, just angry. "I don't know what the world is coming to," she kept saying. "Right there, on Coldharbour Lane. Lawd a' mercy."

"Don't worry, Gran," I said, trying to sound reassuring. "I'm sure the police will deal with him, whoever he is. He was probably just doing it for a dare or something, you know what kids are like."

I promised to go and see her in the week. Then I went to bed, Dad's words echoing in my head. They kept me up all night, crying over everything that had gone so horribly wrong.

Where was Dwayne? I didn't know – and Mum had made Dad take away my phone until they could decide what to do with me. I couldn't even call him to hear his voice, to remind myself of why I was putting myself through all this trauma. I felt exhausted and utterly alone. Sleep couldn't come fast enough.

✿ ✿ ✿

Dad took the kids to school the next day. Leona had taken a day off and it was clear that they had decided that I needed some time to get myself together. Leona was very kind to me and called the school and told them that I was feeling under the weather.

"She should be in tomorrow," she said. "Just let her get back on her feet."

"Dad's really good with the kids, isn't he?" I remarked, after watching Dad get all the kids ready for school and out the door. "Mum always said that Dad never helped her at all when I was young."

"Well," said Leona, shaking the clothes out before putting them in the washing machine. "People change, you know? When we got together, he was a very traditional Rastaman, absolutely useless around the house, never wanted to get his hands dirty. But I soon let him know that that wasn't happening, not with me working and all that. So he got the picture and started helping out a lot more – and now he loves it!"

I got up to help Leona fold the dry clothes that had come out of the dryer.

"Do you really believe that people can change? Mum always says that a leopard never changes his spots..."

"I suppose it depends on whether they want to change. I believe that anyone can change if they put their mind to it. Where there's a will, there's a way, that's what I say."

"But what if the odds are stacked against you?" I asked, avoiding looking Leona in the eye. "What if everyone is telling you that you'll never amount to anything and they won't even give you a chance? What then?"

"Are you talking about your fella, Dwayne?"

I didn't say anything. Everything was very still. Leona had stopped folding clothes, the street outside was empty – even Josh's constant chatter had ceased. I felt heat rise to my face and I faltered. I looked into Leona's calm green eyes to see whether I could trust her. Leona stood quietly, her hands on the pile of clothes in front of her, a serious yet tender look on her face.

"Don't you think it's time to trust us, Misha?" she asked softly, reaching out to touch my fringe. "Don't you think it's time to let us in?"

I closed my eyes. How did she know that all I wanted was someone to talk to, someone I could trust to listen without judging and going crazy on me?

"Oh, Leona!" I cried, my chin quivering. "I just don't know where to start!"

"Come," said Leona, leading me away from the ironing board towards the kitchen table. "Let's start with a cup of green tea."

While Leona put the kettle on, I cleaned Josh's cornflakes-covered face with a flannel. But my mind was elsewhere. Was I really ready to tell Leona everything? Although I had always liked Leona – partly because she never tried to force our relationship or take Mum's place – I had always harboured a tiny spot of resentment towards her. She had Dad, after all, and Mum had no one. And although I liked Leona, confiding in her was not something I had ever thought to do. I sensed that Mum would feel slighted, that I had chosen my stepmother over her. And yet there was something about her tone, that look in Leona's eyes, that told me to trust her.

Leona took Josh out of his high chair and sat him down with some books and toys in front of the TV. When she came back into the kitchen, she smiled cheerily and sat down across the table from me.

"Right," she said. "Let's begin at the beginning. How did you two meet?"

But before we got to that, I had to get one thing straight: "Umm, Leona," I looked at her earnestly, "before I say anything, please promise that you won't go telling Mum and Dad. Please? I want to tell you what's been going on, I need advice, but I don't want to get into any more trouble with either of them."

Leona looked at me steadily as she sipped her steaming hot tea. "I won't tell if you don't want me to, Misha. Now go on, tell me how it all began."

So I went for it, I told her everything: about the party where we first met, about Dwayne's poetry, about his eyes. I told her about the afternoon in Battersea Park, about reading Golding under the oak trees.

"That must have been really special, Misha," smiled

Leona, a soft look in her eyes. "Not many boys know how to romance a girl like that these days."

"That's the funny thing, Leona, it didn't feel like he was trying to sweeten me up or 'chirps' me or anything. Even he said that he'd never done anything like that before – but it just felt right somehow..." I smiled and blushed as I remembered how Dwayne had looked when he made up those lines about chocolate-fudge sweetness, a supermodel smile and a mean left hook.

He had looked so open that day, open and unafraid, as if he knew instinctively that he could trust me, that I had his back, that I was on his side. And I was, I realised, even now. Because the belief that I'd had then, the certainty that he was different somehow – special – hadn't changed, even after everything that had happened. The only thing I wondered about now was whether it meant anything: was I just one of those gullible girls, blinded by 'lurve' – or was this real?

Leona's face changed when I told her about Dwayne meeting Mum and Auntie Loretta and Auntie Dionne. "That must have been tough..."

"It was awful!" I cried. "And Mum basically shut it down after that, told me I wasn't allowed to see him again."

"So why did you disobey her?"

"I didn't, not straight away. I told him we couldn't see each other any more but then..."

"Then what?"

"Dwayne said it didn't matter what she thought. That what mattered was what I thought, what I felt about him. And no one had ever told me that before." I bit my lip. "And I realised that all my life I've been living by Mum's rules: what she likes, what she doesn't like, who she approves of. And I thought, no, this time I have to do what I want... That's what the fight was about last night..."

"I see..." Leona took another sip of her tea and rested her chin on her hand, gazing at me steadily. "And Dwayne said it would all be all right?"

"Yes, he did..."

"Well, of course he would," said Leona, leaning back in her chair and smiling. "What boy wouldn't? You're a lovely girl, Misha. He should consider himself blessed to have a girl like you believing in him, willing to risk so much." Then she frowned again. "And that is where I have a problem with this whole thing."

I was taken aback. "What do you mean?"

Leona got up and went over to the kettle to refill her cup. "Correct me if I'm wrong, Misha, but it seems to me that you are doing all the sacrificing here. Your schoolwork, your friends, your family – all these are things that you are ready to risk for him. But what has he had to sacrifice? Anything? Or are you just neatly fitting into his plans somehow?"

My face clouded over – I hadn't expected this. "You... you sound just like Mum." I felt tears prick my eyes and I blinked, willing myself not to cry. I had been stupid to expect Leona to understand. After all, she didn't even know Dwayne.

"Do you know why I sound like your mum, Misha?" asked Leona, her hand on her hip, her head to one side. "Because I care about you, just like she does. We may not see eye to eye on a lot of things but where you're concerned, we are totally on the same page."

"So you think he's just some useless gangbanger too, do you?" I sniffed.

"No, Misha, that is not what I am saying, not at all. Dwayne sounds like a lovely boy, someone I would like to meet and get to know better. But what I don't like is you selling yourself short."

"Selling myself short ... why, because he's not rich, or posh?"

"Misha, please!" Leona laughed. "Which side of

this Rasta woman looks posh to you? No, love, I'm as down-to-earth as they come so I'm going to give you down-to-earth advice. Let me ask you something."

"Yes?"

"Does Dwayne know that your mum doesn't like him?"

"It was kind of obvious, to be honest..."

"OK, does he know that she told you that you couldn't see him any more?"

"Yeah, he does..."

"And so he knows that when you are going out with him, you are going behind your mum's back?"

"Yeah, I guess so – but there wasn't any other way..."

"See, this is where my problem begins. The fact is, Misha, that you've given this boy everything without him having to fight for it!"

"And how did I do that then?"

"By lying, Misha! By sneaking around! By letting him off the hook with those who matter to you. Treating yourself, your family, your values, as something cheap, something you're willing to trade at the drop of a hat! When things didn't go well with your mum and her family, why didn't you come to us? We're your family too!" She took hold of my hand and looked into my eyes. "Misha, let me tell you something: your heart, your body is your sacred space. No one, and I mean no one, should be able to enter that space without showing you the respect that you deserve."

Had Dwayne disrespected me? Not by his standards, not at all. But what about by mine? My mind whirled with questions. Had I been too easy on him? Too hard on Mum? Too quick to agree to his way of seeing things, of dealing with things?

Leona continued. "What you did was wrong, Misha. You shouldn't have lied to your mum; she loves you and, after everything she's done for you, she deserves more than that. By deceiving her, by deceiving us all, you've shattered the trust we had in you – and that is a terrible thing. But what is worse is that you allowed this boy, Dwayne, to think that it's OK; that, in your book, it's all right to lie in order to get what you want, or avoid facing tough choices or difficult situations. That is the lesson you have been teaching him all this time."

Tears pricked at my eyelids and I blinked and turned away. Leona had touched a raw nerve: *had* I sold myself short? How many times had I felt disappointed in Dwayne – how he'd responded to my mum and everyone, what he'd done to that teacher's car, how he'd switched on me when I tried to bring these issues up. And not once had he acknowledged my feelings or accepted that my point of view was valid. He hadn't even stopped using the 'n' word, for Goodness' sake!

What was stopping me from making him take me seriously – was I afraid that he would walk away and never come back? Did I need him that badly? Badly enough to settle? The questions ripped at my heart because I knew that I didn't have the answers, not yet. Crying was the easy option.

Leona put her arms around me, smelling of patchouli and peppermint. "There, there," she soothed. "Don't cry, love. Don't cry. All is not lost. We can fix this. We can."

"How?" I sniffed, my face buried in my hands. "How can we sort this mess out?"

Leona knelt down next to me. "Tell Dwayne to come and meet your father."

I let out a ragged breath. "Meet *Dad*?"

Leona nodded emphatically. "Yes, Misha, tell him to come and meet your dad. It's the only way. You can't keep covering for him. He's going to have to man up and face what he's dealing with here. We're a package deal, Misha, he can't have all of the smooth and none of the rough." Then she looked searchingly into my eyes. "If he's everything you believe he is, he'll be fine. But you've got to let go and let him sink or swim. For his sake and for yours."

She held me close for a long moment then turned and got up heavily. "Come on now, Josh must be bored silly. Let's bake some bread. Joshie!"

I sat at the table for a little while longer. Dwayne? Meet Dad? But I knew that it made complete sense. Dad was more perceptive than Mum, less prejudiced. And he could smell bull a mile away. If Dad liked him, we had a chance. If he failed to impress, there was little hope for us.

Oh, Dwayne, you've got to come through for me this time. You've just got to.

Commitment

DWAYNE

Mum wouldn't even let me come by the next morning to accompany Jay to the station. She said she didn't want me anywhere near him. But I had to see him.

I went down to Brixton High Road and waited inside the Favourite Fried Chicken. I sipped at my Coke nice and slow until the owner said, "You gonna order anything to eat, mate? This place not a park, y'know."

I scowled and kissed my teeth at him – but I ordered a box of chicken and chips anyway. But as soon as I had told him what I wanted – two legs, *not* a thigh – I hurried back to the window, just in time to see Mum and Jay coming out of the station. I pulled my hood up and ducked out of the door.

"Hey, where you goin'? You haven't paid,

234

you bastard!"

I kept a safe distance away from them. I didn't need Mum seeing me and making a scene in front of Jay. He looked all right, a bit pale and lost, but all right. He kept looking behind him, as if he was looking for someone, someone who should have been there with him. Someone who should have been there for him.

His wort'less older brother.

That was when I fell back and let them walk on towards Coldharbour Lane without me. Maybe Mum was right. Maybe Jay was better off without me around.

'What you sayin', blud?'

'Maybe Mum's got a point, innit? If it weren't for me and the whole RDS ting, Jay wouldn't be robbing no old ladies.'

'Jay is reading the lines he sees in front of him, y'get me. Look at Spaz, his best mate. Look at all the bredders he looks up to: you, Jukkie, Trigger, Spoonz. Jay ain't no different to how you were at that age, when you first started shotting with Jukkie. He sees the lifestyle, he wants a piece. Ain't no one showed him any different.'

'I wanted to show him different.'

'It ain't too late, Dee. But you have to man up and be strong. Fight the temptations of the road, y'get me, concentrate on school, clean yourself inside and out.

Then maybe Mum might give you a second chance. You best stick with Tony, blud. He's always been solid – and that Islam stuff he's chattin' sounds solid too...'

'Ya dun know!'

❖ ❖ ❖

I'd only been cotching with Tony for a day but I could already see the effect Islam was having on him. I heard him wake up proper early the next morning, while it was still dark, to go to the bathroom, wash and pray. I saw him whisper 'Bismillah – in the name of God' before he ate. He'd started eating with his right hand too, even though he was left-handed.

"In Islam, the left hand is considered unclean," he explained. "We use our right hand to eat and drink and ting."

I just nodded. It was a lot to take in, the Islamic lifestyle, the changes in Tony. The dress, the way of speaking, not to mention the wife and college courses. But I noticed other changes too, ones I could appreciate, especially with everything else that was going on. He was more chilled than before, thinking about things more deeply. He talked about doing the right thing, sticking to the straight path, even when everyone is against you. He talked about our duty to God.

"'Nuff man living like they'll never have to answer for what they do. It makes them reckless, y'get me. Robbin', sellin' drugs, stabbin' up man, ready to shoot man over foolishness. You know how we stay, innit, you don't expect to live long so you might as well raise hell while you're here, get high, sleep with 'nuff girls, make money any way you can – because you don't care. Get rich or die tryin', innit?"

We laughed. What he had described was exactly the way I had come to think: the hustler's creed. Tony had been on that too. So had 'nuff of the brothers at the mosque.

"But as Muslims we know that we'll have to answer to Allah on Judgement Day. And that day's gonna be a terrible day, blud, if you've lived your life on badness."

Now these former pimps, hustlers and gangbangers were on Islam, trying to live righteous lives, trying to get straight. I thought of Malcolm X and thought, 'I could do that.'

Tony gave me some books to read. He played CDs of the Qur'an being recited in Arabic. It was proper nice, soothing. I didn't understand a single word but there was just something about it that touched me somewhere deep.

But I kept quiet. I didn't want Tony to know I was that interested because, true say, I really didn't think I was ready to commit to such a huge change, to make such an important decision.

So I played it cool, real cool.

All that day, I thought about Jay. It was like an ocean between us. I had tried to sneak up to see him but Mum had had the locks changed. I rang for him but Mum picked up the phone.

"Who is it?"

I hung up, of course.

I thought about Misha too. I hadn't been able to reach her on her phone and, by evening, I was starting to get worried. We usually spoke to each other at least twice a day, standard. At about eight o'clock, my phone finally rang. It was a landline, looked like a Tottenham number.

I picked up.

"Dwayne! Where've you been?"

Misha's voice sounded so far away that I felt a physical ache. I wanted to be near her, to hold her, to...

"I was worried about you, girl! Where have you been? Why is your phone off?"

"Oh, that. Long story."

"I've got time..."

"Mum found out about us."

"*What?*"

"Yeah, we had a big fight about it and I'm at my dad's, but he's got my phone."

"Raah, that must have been bait, babe. So you're at your dad's now?"

"Yeah, for the time being..."

"Safe..." I lost my train of thought. I was thinking about Jay and how much I would have loved to tell Misha what had happened with him, and between me and my mum. I knew that she would understand how I felt, that she would be able to comfort me.

But it was too close to home. Telling Misha that Jay had been arrested would basically blow the door to my life in the hood right open – and I didn't want her knowing anything about that. Nothing at all. And I didn't want her judging Jay – just like I didn't want her judging me.

But, man, I needed her right then. Just to hold her, to feel her beside me.

"Misha, I need you here with me. I'm falling apart here, man. So much stuff has happened... I just need to hold you, y'get me. I need you, Misha. Can't you come over, just for a little bit?"

I heard her take in a sharp breath. I knew how that

kind of talk made her melt inside. I could feel myself grow warm, thinking of how much it meant to me for her to be there with me.

But she surprised me.

"No, Dwayne, I can't. I can't. I'm at my dad's and he's upset with me over everything..." Her voice shook a little. "I need you to do something for me, Dwayne."

"What is it, babe?" I couldn't help feeling a bit irritated, still. Why was she asking me to do something for her now? I needed *her*, didn't she get it?

"Come and meet my dad."

"*What?*" Something inside me snapped. What was she on about?

"Come and meet my dad, Dee." She was talking really fast, like she was nervous or something. " That way we can keep seeing each other and it will be legit. This is the address..."

I hardly heard the house number and road name. "No way!" I didn't mean to shout but I did – and I heard her gasp.

"*What?*"

"I said allow dat, man! No way man is putting himself through that again, no way!"

She didn't say anything for a few seconds. I guess

she was trying to process what I had just said. "A-are you serious? Dee?"

"I am, Misha! Sorry, I ain't going through that again, not for you, your dad or anyone! No way, blud, no way..."

"What the...?" That was the first time I had ever heard Misha swear. The word sounded like a shotgun and I reeled from the impact. "You've got a nerve, Dwayne Kingston, a bloody nerve! How can you talk about what you will and won't go through? I put everything on the line for us, *everything*! I've fallen behind at school, I've had a fight with my mum, left home, my dad's vex' with me, my mum's vex' with me, all because I'm standing up for your lame arse!"

Man, she was really tripping. I tried to get her to calm down. "Yo, Misha, easy, man, easy..."

But she wasn't having it. "So, it's OK for me to go through crap for you, is it? Huh? Doesn't matter what I want, what my family think of me, of us, as long as you're still a badman, is that it?"

"Yo, baby..."

She kissed her teeth. "Don't 'Yo baby' me! I've had it with you, Dwayne, you hear me? I've had it up to here with your selfishness and your stupid pride! You don't want to come and meet my dad and be

241

a man, fine! But don't expect ever to see me again."

"Misha, wait, don't be like that... it ain't like that, it's just that..."

"What have I asked you for, Dwayne? Huh?"

The pain in her voice came across loud and clear – and it cut me deep.

"*Nothing*! All I've done in this relationship is give, give, give – and now, when I ask you to give, when I ask you to step out of your comfort zone, you refuse point blank! Well, I don't know what they call that where you come from, but where I'm from there's a word for that – and it isn't 'love'!"

"Misha, OK, I'm sorry, all right? I'm sorry..."

"You know what? You *are* sorry – a sorry punk-ass waste of space! I never want to see you again, *ever*!"

The phone went dead. I realised that I was shaking. I was fuming, man. I threw the phone against the wall but it didn't smash into a million pieces like I wanted it to.

What had gotten into Misha? Just when I needed her most – what was she playing at?

'She's just woken up, that's all. It was bound to happen sooner or later, you knew that. Now it's time for you to make a choice, blud.'

'Free dat! I can think of nuff gyal that can come keep

a man company, y'get me.'

I picked up my phone and began scrolling through the names: Lachelle, Ṣhannon, Mariah, Chantelle, Rachel ... Then I flung the phone against the wall again and threw myself onto the bed. I was proper vex'. I didn't want any of those girls. I wanted Misha.

'Time to make a choice, blud. Ya dun know!'

❖ ❖ ❖

It was Tony who finally talked some sense into me. He had heard me shouting down the phone so he asked me, straight out, what the problem was.

I told him all about Misha. About her mum, her lifestyle, how she made me feel. And this fight we had just had about coming to meet her dad.

He laughed. "Looks like you're just gonna have to man up, innit. What are you worried about? Just be yourself and let them see that you're not a wasteman, that you've got plans, and that you want to treat their daughter well. They can't ask for more than that."

"True dat."

"Remember the verse from the Qur'an? Allah doesn't change the condition of a people until they change what is in themselves. If you want good to come to you, you have to do good. And pray, man, pray for whatever you want."

I nodded. It made sense. So much of it made sense.

Then Tony laughed again. "You never know, the two of you could both become Muslim – then you could just marry her and make the whole ting halal, innit?"

I smiled but I was kinda shocked by the idea of marriage, still. But then I thought about having Misha with me all the time, not having to sneak around: waking up next to her, seeing her face first thing in the morning and last thing at night, telling her everything, letting my guard down... It was like a fantasy, a dream.

Of course, I didn't think about school or money or where we would live or even whether Misha wanted to become a Muslim. Hell, *I* wasn't even a Muslim yet! But I was just feeling the idea of the two of us on a path together, something to unite us, to keep us strong. Why not Islam?

Man, I was starting to lose my mind for sure.

The Prodigal Boyfriend

MISHA

Mum wasn't happy about me staying at Dad's in Tottenham. She wanted me to come home.

"Misha, darling, this is just silly," she said on the phone. "You're making life difficult for your dad and his family. It really is too far to travel on your own – and what are the chances of you getting to school on time? And you've got your exams to think about, love. Please, be sensible. Just come home."

I pressed my lips together and tried not to scream. Mum refused point-blank to talk about what had happened the day I left home. And now, here she was, trying to convince me to come back so I could get to school on time!

"Mum," I said, trying to control my voice, "I love you and I miss you. But I'll come home when we have had a chance to talk things through. I'm not coming back until you agree to start listening to me. Until you can respect that I have a mind of my own, that I have my own views..."

"Oh, darling, if this is about that boy..."

"No, Mum, it's got nothing to do with Dwayne; this is about you and me. This is about me growing up... I'll be at Dad's until you're ready to talk, all right? I've got to go now."

"Misha!"

"Bye, Mum. I love you."

The mention of Dwayne's name put me in a bad mood all over again. Just as I was starting to adjust to the withdrawal symptoms. Of course, I had cut him off totally. I had a new number anyway, since Dad had taken the other phone and, now that I was in North London, I didn't have to think about running into him around Brixton, near Gran's.

It hurt. Of course it did. It hurt so much that I had to force myself to get out of bed in the mornings, to bother to brush my hair, to read my Biology notes. But I forced myself all the same. Misha Reynolds did not do 'lovesick teenager', remember? And exams were fast approaching – a fact I had conveniently ignored since our relationship took off.

Dad and Leona had become used to me moping around. Every time Leona saw me with a long face, she patted my arm.

"This too shall pass," she would say. "Now, don't you have some studying to do?"

Dad had laid down the law. Obviously, I was grounded and had to apologise to Mum for disrespecting her. I was to concentrate on my books from now on.

"As for this boy – Dwayne – I will make my own judgement of him. I've heard some things from your mother, of course, but, as we don't see eye-to-eye on this type of thing, I'm going to make my own mind up about this young man when he is ready to meet the family properly. Until then I don't want you to see him."

"We've broken up anyway," I mumbled.

Dad just grunted and shook the pages of his newspaper.

A whole week passed and I was getting ready to eat another Sunday lunch at Dad's. But just as we sat down to eat, we heard the doorbell ring. Mark, Mr Running Man himself, leapt up to go and see who was at the door. When he came back from the door, he was grinning from ear to ear.

"It's someone for you, sis," he smiled, winking at me.

"For me?" I frowned. I looked over at Dad, who nodded his approval of me leaving the table.

I got up and walked towards the front door, hugging my jumper around myself, trying to still my jangling nerves. Who could it be?

When I got to the door, I saw a young boy with a hoodie and bright yellow trainers standing on the step in front of the door.

"Jerome!" I exclaimed. "What are you doing here? Are you on your own?" But before I could look around to see how on earth Jerome Kingston had made his way to my father's flat in North London, an older boy stepped out in front of me, his hood down, his hands behind his back.

It was Dwayne.

I jumped when I saw him, stifling a gasp with my hand. He was the last person I had expected to see – and here he was with his little brother, standing on my dad's doorstep.

"Dwayne?" I whispered. "What are you doing here?"

But instead of answering me, Dwayne shook his head and gave Jerome a nudge. Jerome looked up at me and said, "Dwayne said he's sorry." Then he glanced up at his older brother and, with a mischievous glint in his eye, continued: "Dwayne said he's sorry for being a total wasteman, a loser, a waste of space, a eediaat..." He struggled while Dwayne held his hand over his mouth, trying to keep a straight face. When at last Jerome had finished struggling, Dwayne let go of him and motioned for him to start again.

Jerome readjusted his clothes, then said in a very important voice, "Dwayne said he's sorry for the way he went on bad. He would like you to forgive him and he would like you two to get back together. And he's come to meet your family."

Dwayne interrupted. "If you'll let me, Misha," he said. "Only if you want me to meet them. I know I've hurt you and I've taken you for granted but I'm gonna change, I swear down. Just give me a chance... please?"

And although I felt like crying and flinging my arms around him, I held myself back. I nodded and stepped aside to let them in.

"Come in then," I said quietly. "You're just in time for lunch."

Dwayne looked up at all the posters on the walls and the African masks on the shelves and let out

249

a low whistle. "This is proper old skool, innit," he said softly.

When we reached the dining room, Dwayne finally came face to face with Dad, sitting at the head of the table, looked dignified and serious, his silver dreadlocks like a lion's mane about his shoulders and down his back. He was looking at him with a neutral expression: neither welcoming nor hostile, just expectant. Unlike Dad, Leona had a welcoming look on her face, a small smile playing on her lips. Mark had already run off to the kitchen to fetch two extra chairs.

Dwayne swallowed and said, "Good afternoon, Mr Reynolds, Mrs Reynolds, I'm sorry to disturb you during lunch... I...I wanted to come over and apologise for..."

Dad held up his hand. "Later, son," he said, gesturing towards the chairs that Mark had just dragged in from the kitchen. "For now, sit. You and your little brother will eat with us."

Leona smiled and said graciously, "Welcome to our home, Dwayne. Please, sit down."

"These are for you, Mrs Reynolds," said Dwayne, handing a slender bunch of lilies to Leona. I was seriously impressed!

Leona's face lit up and she beamed with pleasure. "Oh, thank you, Dwayne, that is so sweet of you. Look at these, Isaiah, my favourites!" She turned to Jerome. "And what's your name, little man?"

"J-Jerome, Miss," stammered Jerome, apparently caught off balance by her school-teacher voice.

Imani laughed. "She's not Miss, she's Mum!"

"Well, you can call me Mrs Reynolds, or Leona – though most of the children call me Auntie Lee."

"OK, then... Auntie Lee." Jerome grinned sheepishly and sat down.

DWAYNE

I was well proud of the way Jay was handling himself. After a week, Mum had calmed down and let me see him again, even though she wouldn't let me move back in.

"Jay needs space, Dwayne," she said.

But I didn't mind – as long as I got to see my little bro, y'get me. I had slapped him around a few times about the robbery. He'd been lucky – the judge let him off with a warning.

"But if you try pulling any stunts like that again, I'll bang you, y'understand?"

Jay looked scared out of his mind but he nodded. He knew I wasn't playing. I think Mum knew I wasn't messing around either. I sat her down and we had a real heart-to-heart: I told her that I was off the badness, that I was thinking of becoming Muslim, that I wanted to be a good role model for Jay.

I could see in her eyes that she really wanted to believe me. Which is why she finally agreed to let me take Jay with me to North London, to see Misha's dad.

"Don't go showing me up, y'know!" I'd said to him while I got ready. "I'm trying to make a good impression, y'get me, so any foolishness from you and I'll bang you, y'understand?"

"Don't worry, Dee, I won't let you down," Jay replied. He looked chuffed that I was trusting him with this, telling him about my business, something I never did.

"Yeah, I know you won't, man, I know. Now, how do I look?"

"Like a badman!"

"*What?* No, seriously, do I look decent, y'know, proper?"

Jay put his head to one side and looked me up and down: the big diamond earring was gone, I didn't have a cap, just my favourite leather jacket and a pair of jeans. Jay frowned and peered at the jeans again.

"Yo, Dee, your boxers aren't showing!" he cried, before laughing out loud.

I hitched up my jeans. "Man has to come correct, y'get me," I muttered, swiping at his head. "Shut up, man! Shut up before I mash you up!"

He ducked and ran off to his room to finish getting dressed. "You must really love this girl," he shouted from his room. "Man is going all the way to *North London* – with a belt on! That's love for you, man. That's love."

✿ ✿ ✿

I watched Jay as he stared at the plate of vegetable stew and dumplings in front of him.

'*Eat!*' I willed him with my mind.

I knew that Jay was a well fussy eater, mainly living on pizza and chicken nuggets – and rice and peas on a Sunday – but I had already told him to make sure he didn't show me up. He took a small bite, and then another, then another. And before I was halfway through mine, he was done.

He looked up, all surprised.

Everyone was staring at him.

"Well," chuckled Misha's stepmum, "your little brother certainly likes Mark's stew! I've never seen food disappear so fast! Here, give me your plate, there's more in the pot."

I turned to Mark. "You made this? Raah... you can cook, huh?" I was well impressed.

"Any chance I get," grinned Mark. "When Mum will let me in the kitchen..." And he made a face at his mum as she came back in from the kitchen.

"Now, what's this boy been telling you, eh? Slandering his mother, is he?"

"Nah, Mum, never, never," Mark laughed, helping himself to more dumpling. Then he leaned over to me and whispered, "Actually, she's jealous of my skills, y'know. One time, I made this wicked soup and Mum's friends came round and when they tasted it, they were all like, 'Oh Lawd, Leona, this is some fine soup yuh cook 'ere!' and Mum just smiled and said nothing – all the time it was me who made that soup, y'know!"

We all laughed and, just like that, the tension disappeared. It was amazing: we became just a regular family, eating dinner together on a Sunday afternoon.

I felt myself relax and, when Misha smiled at me across the table, I knew deep inside that everything was going to be all right.

Man Talk

The chat with Misha's dad wasn't that bad. He rolled up a joint and offered me some but I said no. It didn't feel right to be smoking a spliff with your girl's father, even if he was a Rasta.

He asked me about myself, my family. I was as honest as I could be: no dad, hardworking mum, best little brother in the world.

He asked me about my interests, what I liked doing. I told him about my music, how I had been approached by some DJ crews to spit for them, how I had won 'nuff MC battles. I told him about maths, about the Higher Tier exams and tutoring the little kids after school.

"To tell you the truth, sir, I really didn't think much about exams and school until... until I met Misha..."

"Really? Why is that?"

"None of us did, y'get me. Where I'm from, school is just a place, a place your parents send you to get you out of their hair for a few hours. Hardly anyone takes it serious. They're like, 'What's the point? Ain't no good jobs for black boys anyway'. Plus everyone's making money out on road. No one ain't talking about going college or university or anything like that. And then I meet Misha and she's like talking about studying Latin and wanting to take Spanish for 'A' Level, going university to become a linguist. Man, I had to go Google that one coz I didn't even know what a linguist was, y'get me! And she's talking to me, yeah, telling me about stuff I've never heard of, ideas I've never thought of, and I'm like, raah, this girl is something else, something special. Making man see the world differently, y'understand. So I start to fix up. Start to get serious about school, start thinking about my future, where I wanna be in five years' time. Coz I wanna live up to who she thinks I can be. Coz no one ain't believed in me like that before, ever..."

I stopped talking then and looked up at Misha's dad. I was afraid that he would be vex' with me or think I was crazy. But he actually had a little smile on his face!

"I feel like I know you, Dwayne Kingston," he

said. "Like I see a small part of myself in you. You have a good heart, I can see that. But let me tell you something," he growled. "My daughter is a queen, y'understand? My daughter is a queen and deserves only honour and respect. Do you know how to respect a woman? I go tell you. To respect a woman is to love her, to trust her, to be honest and upfront with her, to protect her and to elevate her. Can you do all of this for my daughter? Can you? Because if you are playing a game with her, I advise you to leave my house right now." His eyes blazed as he glared at me.

I shook my head.

"No, sir," I squeaked. "I... I'm not playing games, sir. I... I love her... I love your daughter, sir."

Mr Reynolds sat back in his seat. "So it looks like I will have to be having a word with Misha's mother. But I'll be keeping a close eye on you two. You are both still very young and foolish. So we'll have to see where this whole thing goes. Now go 'long! Tell Misha I said to come here with my cup of herbal tea. You can go and join the rest of the family now." And he put his head back against the sofa and closed his eyes.

I left as quickly as I could. I was sweating!

When I gave Misha her dad's message, her eyes were full of questions. "It was fine, babes, we're sorted.

It's gonna be fine."

Misha squealed with delight and jumped up and held on to my neck.

"I'm sorry, Misha," I whispered. "I'm sorry for being such a eediat. Will you forgive me?"

"Of course I will, Dwayne," she smiled. That was what I wanted to do: put a smile on her face every day.

Misha's little sister, Imani, tugged my hand.

"Come, Dwayne," she said in her high little voice. "I want to show you the African dance I learned this weekend."

When Misha came in from seeing her dad, she found us all in the lounge: Mark and Jay on the cowhide drums, Imani dancing away in the middle and me spitting some freestyle over the beats. Leona was ad-libbing with snatches of a chorus she had made up. "Come dance with us, Mishie!" called Josh and, soon, Misha was in the centre of the lounge, copying Imani's moves, moving to the beat of the drums and my voice flowing over all of them.

✧ ✧ ✧

Jay fell asleep on the train on the way home. I had to carry him back to the flat on my back. When we left

Misha's dad's place, I messaged Mum to tell her that we were on our way back so that she wouldn't stay up worrying. I knew she had the early shift at work and needed to get to sleep early.

I got us into the flat and kicked open the door to Jay's room. I laid him on his bed and slipped off his favourite yellow trainers. The ones I had bought him for his birthday. Jay shifted and opened one eye. He smiled a crooked smile.

Joker. He'd been awake all along!

"That was nice, Dee," he said sleepily. "Misha's family's really nice..." Then he closed his eye and his head flopped to one side.

I stayed there for a few moments, looking at his little chest rise and fall. "Thank you, Jay," I said softly, pulling the covers over him. "You were a star tonight. You smashed it."

When I got to my room, I sat down on the bed, thinking about Misha and her family. Thinking about how it felt to know that Misha was still into me, that we were back together, that her dad had my back. I grinned. I couldn't have hoped for better. Times like this, man just had to show a bit of gratitude.

"Thank you, God... Allah... Thank you...for everything."

Reconciliation

MISHA

I spent two weeks at Dad's before finally going home
to Mum. We spoke on the phone most days but, often,
those conversations ended in an argument or either
one of us putting the phone down. On Thursday night,
we had a particularly bitter argument and I refused to
speak to Mum when she called back.

"Looks like we need to have a family meeting,"
said Dad gravely.

Leona's eyebrows shot up. "Are you sure, Isaiah?
You know what Dina can be like..."

"I can't be having all this dissent and upheaval in
my family," Dad said. "We must sort it out once and
for all."

Early the next morning, Dad rang Mum while she
was on her way to work. "Dina, I want you to come to

the house tonight."

"What? Why?" She was on speaker-phone, so I could hear everything she said.

"Because you and Misha must sort this thing out."

"Well, Isaiah, if you think I'm coming up to your place so that you and Leona can have a go at me, you've got another think coming. I am perfectly capable of speaking to my own daughter – but at home, in private."

"Enough with your foolish pride, Dina!" Dad raised his voice. "No one is saying you aren't capable – we know that you are. But this thing here needs a family discussion, where we can all share our views and come to the best decision. Please, Dina, just put your pride to one side for once."

"I don't want Leona there," Mum said stiffly. "She's not really family, is she?"

"Dina, Leona *is* family," Dad growled. "She is family because she loves Misha, like we all do. And to be honest, she's really been there for Misha through all of this, giving her some real good advice, listening to her. Don't try and shut her out now. For Misha's sake."

It was strange to meet Mum at the door of Dad's place. We had never even spent more than two nights apart, ever. She looked different somehow, older. At first I didn't know what to say, what to do or where to look. So much had happened. But then I saw a shadow cross her face and I knew that she was just as unsure as I was.

"Mum," I whispered, stepping forward.

"Oh, Misha," she breathed and held her arms out to me, her only daughter. "My baby, come here..."

I stepped into her arms willingly and held her hard, suddenly hit by the realisation that I had missed her, missed her a lot. We stood there for a long time, Mum rubbing my back, stroking my hair. We were both sniffling by the time we separated.

"Come on then, Mum," I said, my voice hoarse, "everyone's waiting for you."

And, for the first time in living memory, Mum stepped over the threshold of Dad and Leona's house in North London.

It didn't go as badly as I had feared. Mum was civil to Leona, even quite warm with Mark and Imani, letting Joshie play with her keys. It was when we all moved to the dining room that things got a little heated.

"Misha, please, how many times do I have to tell you," Mum cried out at one point, "I'm not trying to ruin your life! I'm just trying to protect you from the things that could destroy your future."

"Yes, Mum, I know that but I have to have a say in my future too!" I responded with feeling. "It's my life!"

Then Dad's soothing voice: "Dina, you have done a fantastic job with Misha. You've given her direction, you've taught her, you've passed on the values we all hold dear. You've done your job well. But now Misha needs space to put it all into practice, to make the right choices instead of you making all her choices for her."

"That's right, Dina," added Leona gently. "Can't you see that all you are doing is weakening the very strength of character you tried so hard to build? We need to be empowering Misha, getting her ready for the big bad world, not trying to hide her from it."

Mum pressed her lips together and said nothing for a while. She blew her nose and wiped her eyes, then held her head up. "Misha," she said carefully, turning to face me. "Do you want to come home?"

"Of course I do, Mum!" How could she even ask me that?

"All right, well I suppose that's a start, isn't it? Now, let's talk about how we are going make this work."

And so we did, everyone contributing to the discussion, everyone sharing their view – it was great, like something out of *Supernanny*! In the end, it was decided that I would go home with Mum on Sunday, after spending some more time with Dad and the rest of the family. Mum agreed to let me take languages for 'A' Level instead of Maths and Sciences. I promised not to lie about where I was any more – and to accept 'no' for an answer when I got it.

There were more discussions, more battles to be won and lost, but I knew that we had won the war when Mum agreed, however reluctantly, to allow me to continue seeing Dwayne.

"I talked to the boy, Dina," said Dad. "I like him. He has a good heart, I know it. You know I can sense these things. Let them see each other in the open where we can make sure that they are safe, y'understand?" And he looked at her meaningfully. That was exactly what Gran had failed to do when Mum had *her* unsuitable boyfriend – Dad.

Mum swallowed hard, then turned to me. "The two of you will have to use your time together to study," she said, wagging a finger at me. "You both have exams around the corner – and while you may not need the help, I'm sure Dwayne could use some encouragement and support. And let me tell you this, young lady: I'll be keeping a very close eye on him. He'd better be on the straight and narrow because if I find out that he's up to anything, *anything*, he'll be out of your life so fast his head will bounce."

No one knew what to say to that but at last Leona said, "Well, the two of them are welcome here anytime. We had a lovely evening with Dwayne and his little brother on Tuesday and I am sure that Misha would like to have him over again. And I'm certain that he will not disappoint us, not now that he knows what is expected of him."

I smiled to myself secretly, because I saw Mum look away, a pained expression on her face. Her experience with Dwayne hadn't been nearly as lovely. Still, for the first time, I began to see how things could work for us. I wasn't sure what was going to happen about him and Mum but I didn't want to think about that. Mum was here, I had spoken, she had listened and we had made a decision as a family. I couldn't ask for more. It was like the dawn of a new era for our family, a new era for me.

Life Changes

DWAYNE

I was well happy when Misha told me she was back at her Mum's place. And I couldn't believe it when she said her mum had agreed that we could see each other! What a turnaround!

"But we have to be responsible, Dee," Misha warned. "We've both got coursework due and exams coming up so we need to focus."

I was feeling that. I had already started on my English coursework and Maths was a breeze now that I had extra tuition at school. But I was still struggling with the other subjects, mainly because I hadn't paid attention in class for the whole of last year. But I was determined to do my best.

I got rid of my work phone and put the word out that I was out of the game. Some of the mandem took the mick out of me a bit, but they knew that I was rolling with Tony now and they knew what he was on.

"You're gonna do the Muslim ting, yeah?" they said. "Safe."

Only Jukkie and Trigger and some of the hardcore Youngers were unimpressed. They thought I'd gone soft.

"Just coz you're on that Islam stuff don't mean you have to quit the game, man!" Jukkie said. "'Nuff man down Myattsfield are Muslim now – but they're still badmen at the end of the day. Ain't you heard about dem 'Muslim Boys' that are all over the papers? They're keeping it real, man, not this fake-arse holy mosque crap!"

In a way, Jukkie was right: there were a lot of gangsters that had become Muslim. But they were still on badness – they said that the Qur'an said it was OK to rob from non-Muslims – and their role models were Al-Qa'eda, the ultimate enemies of the system.

"Watch out for that lot," Tony warned me. "They got a twisted understanding of Islam. Islam ain't about dealin' drugs, robbin', shootin' and killin' – then going mosque to pray. It's a whole lifestyle, y'understand? And you can't be messing with it. If you're gonna be a gangster and a thug, go do it. But if you're gonna be Muslim, you have to come correct."

"Ya dun know."

"But what you sayin', man? We've been talking about Islam for weeks now and, so far, you seem to agree with everything I'm telling you. So what's stopping you from taking your *shahadah*?"

I took a deep breath. This was the moment of truth. "Well, I've read everything you've given me about Islam and it all sounds good, y'get me."

Tony started grinning like crazy then. "Masha Allah, bro..."

"But I don't know whether I'm ready to come correct, like you say. I don't know whether I'm ready to pray five times a day and grow a beard and all that. I don't really care about the booze and the bacon any more – but what about my music, and my girl, Misha..?"

"Don't worry about all that now, Dee," Tony said. "That's just Shaitaan whispering to you, trying to make you doubt what you know is the truth. At the end of the day, if you believe in the fundamentals, in the basics, you should take your *shahadah*, innit. You can work on the rest later..."

"What do you mean, 'the basics'?"

"I mean, if you believe in Allah and you believe that the Prophet Muhammad was his prophet, you should take your *shahadah*. That way, if you die tomorrow, you will die as a Muslim."

I laughed. "Woah, I ain't plannin' on dyin' any time soon!"

But Tony was dead serious. "Bro, no one plans on dyin'. You know that. Think of that kid who was shot down in Streatham – do you think he was planning on dying that day? No way! Allah decrees when our time is up, bro."

And I suddenly realised that this ting was deadly serious. This was a commitment I was making to obey God – Allah – and to live a righteous life. This was not some joke ting. This was about my life now – and the one after death, the Afterlife.

I agreed to go down to the mosque with Tony. I could feel this fizzing inside me, this excitement that was building up and making me jittery. The other brothers were hyped up, happy to witness a new *shahadah*.

There were all races there – black, white, Asian, Somali, even a Chinese-looking bredder. 'Nuff of them shook my hand, hugged me, asking me all sorts of questions.

"Where are you from, bro?"

"This your first time in a *masjid*?"

"You thinking about becoming Muslim?"

Tony laughed and told them to take it easy. "He's ready to take his *shahadah, alhamdulillah*, not play 20 questions!"

The leader of the mosque, Imam Abdullah, sat down with me on the carpeted floor. He asked me what I knew about Islam, whether I believed in Allah, in all the messengers, in all the holy scriptures – the Torah, the Bible, the Qur'an. Whether I believed in the angels, and the divine decree, and the Last Day, Judgement Day. I said yes to it all even though I hadn't read up on everything in that much detail. What I knew for sure was that I believed in God – Allah – and that the Prophet Muhammad had been sent with a message to guide mankind to righteousness. And for the first time, I wanted that, more than I'd ever wanted anything in my life.

"OK then, repeat after me: Ash-hadu ..."

I stumbled over the unfamiliar Arabic words as I repeated the testimony of faith: "*Ash-hadu an laa ilaah illAllah wa ash-hadu ana Muhammadan 'abduhu wa rasulu.* I believe that there is no god worthy of worship except Allah, and I believe that Muhammad is His slave

270

and messenger."

"*Masha Allah*, brother, welcome to Islam!" The imam beamed and gave me a huge bear hug, clapping me on the back. Tony was grinning too and had to hide his face when he came to shake my hand and embrace me.

"Bro," he said, all choked up, "I'm so happy, man. I'm so happy for you. *Allahu akbar*. God is great."

"*Allahu akbar!*" All the other brothers were buzzing too. Everyone wanted to meet me, shake my hand, say '*Asalaamu alaikum*' and welcome me to Islam. We decided to go get something to eat with a friend of Tony's, a big brother called Rashid.

By the time we were sitting down in the fried chicken shop on the corner, I knew 'nuff tings about Rashid. I knew that he had grown up in a foster home and had been in and out of prison and remand centres since he was 11 years old. He had been part of the PDC and been busted for armed robbery. He accepted Islam in prison. Since then, he'd tried to steer clear of the gang life and get involved in youth work.

"What was it like for you inside, man?" I wanted to know.

"You know, at night, when I was lying in that cell, all on my own, I used to look up at the ceiling and think, 'why did this happen to me? Why me? 'Nuff man out there on badness, why was I the one who got caught?'"

"True dat," I said, thinking of all the stuff Tony had managed to get away with.

"It's the little things that you miss when you're inside, y'know. It's the freedom to go where you like, to see who you like, or not see anyone. Being in jail wears you down, man. Unless you have something to hold onto, something to believe in. You know what I used to think about? I used to repeat this little verse from the Qur'an: 'Allah does not change the condition of a people until they change what is in themselves.' That was when I decided that I was going to come out of jail a better person. That I was gonna change my life..."

"But it can't be that easy though," I interrupted. "When you try to make a change, bare man wanna drag you down, innit."

"Yeah, boy, and what they're saying sounds good still," Tony agreed. "'Come with us,' they say, 'we know where to get some food, just one last time, just to get yourself on your feet. Ain't you tired of going college? Don't you need some money? How can a man live on £100 a week? Come on, man, don't be a chief, we'll hook you up, we know where the best stuff is...' On and on they keep chattin', like devils, trying to drag man down."

"Bro, how do you manage? How do you resist all that?" I couldn't imagine the kind of pressure Tony had been under since he started practising. Tony was *known*, y'get me, by 'nuff people. He was Mr BigMan, the playa, the party man, the man with the cash, spraying champagne everywhere and stuffing bank notes down girls' bras. That was how everyone knew Tony. I shook my head. What a comedown it must have felt like to him.

Rashid answered the question:

"I fear Allah, man. I know that He brought me out of jail to give me another chance, y'get me. 'Nuff man go jail and come out worse than before. But Allah protected me from that. He blessed me with some good brothers and we studied the Qur'an together, stayed out of all the madness. And now I'm out, I have to make it work. I've got to show some gratitude still and come correct for my wife and my kids."

"That's safe, man. It really is." I was chuffed, y'get me, proud to be a Muslim on the righteous path, like Tony and Rashid.

"Now go have a shower, bro, get clean. All your

sins have been forgiven; it's time to meet your new life!"

❖ ❖ ❖

That shower, the *ghusl* that I made in my mum's house the day I took my *shahadah*, was one I will never forget. I felt like all my feelings of hopelessness and fear, all the badness I'd ever done, was dissolving in the soapy water and washing away, away, away down the drain. When I stepped out of the bathroom, I literally felt myself glowing: it was as if I could feel hope and newness shining out of my skin.

Jay came running past and stopped dead when he saw me standing outside the bathroom with a towel around my waist. "Yo, Dee, what's up? You look different."

"I'm a Muslim now, Jay."

"Yeah? Safe!" And he ran off to ride his bike with his friend who was waiting at the door.

And no lie, when I looked in the mirror, I could almost *see* the difference. It was something in my eyes, something about the skin across my forehead. I looked cleansed, like after a baptism, ready for a new chapter of my life to unfold.

'I'm proud of you, bro.'
'Thanks. Allahu akbar.'

I was a Muslim. Now all I had to do was live up to the name.

And try to convince Misha.

❖ ❖ ❖

Convincing Misha about Islam was way harder than I thought it would be. I tried everything: dropping it in conversation, giving her books, sending her links, even inviting her to come down to the mosque when they were having a bazaar. But that had been a disaster and she just wasn't having it.

"Look, Dwayne," she said one day, "I'm not going to become a Muslim, OK? I'm a Christian. I was born in the church, raised in the church and I will die in the church. And there is nothing you can tell me that will convince me otherwise."

"But Misha, you haven't even given it a chance! At least read the books I'm giving you, innit!" I looked over to the coffee table next to the bookshelf. The pile of books looked exactly the same as it had the last time I was there.

Misha threw her hands in the air and pushed past me towards the front door. "Dwayne, if you're on a quest to discover the truth, that's fine, but count me out! I'm perfectly happy as I am and I don't need someone who only just started reading the Bible to tell me about the true religion!" She opened the door. "I think you'd better go."

I walked slowly to the door. I was proper disappointed. Why wouldn't she give Islam a chance? Why was she shutting mans down like this? I leaned over to kiss her goodbye but she turned her head and I ended up kissing air.

"Are you sure Muslims are allowed to kiss?" she said coldly as I walked past her. I turned to say goodbye, to tell her that I would come by tomorrow to study Shakespeare but I didn't get the chance. She had closed the door in my face.

Feisty, man. Out of order.

When I got back to Saints Hill, I was still bubbling. I never knew Misha could be so hard-headed. She wouldn't even read a book!

'She's afraid, blud.'

'Afraid of what though, man?'

'Afraid that it will actually make sense to her – and that she'll have to rethink some of her ideas. You're OK because you're still searching, but Misha? Misha thinks she knows who she is. She's secure in her identity, y'get me. Learning

about Islam is a threat to that. And it's a threat to the two of you.'

'Don't I know that! I never thought Misha could go on so ignorant!

'Have some faith, innit. Best start hitting the prayer mat in some sujood, asking Allah to guide her or you're gonna be facing some tough times ahead.'

'True dat.'

"Hey, Dwayne! *Salaam alaikum!"*

I spun round to see a girl walking up to me. She was wearing a short puffa jacket with a little scarf on her head, covering her hair. I squinted, trying to work out where I had seen her before.

"Y'alright, Dwayne?" she said in a little girl voice. And straight away I remembered who she was.

"Rachel!" I said, smiling. "Where've you been? Haven't seen you around for time!" Oh, yeah. I remembered Rachel. We'd had a fling in Year 10. She had been proper wild back then.

"I've been around, y'know. It's you who's been keeping a low profile. I heard that you were seeing some posh girl from down Dulwich sides."

"But who's been telling you my business though?" I said, giving her a crooked smile.

'Easy, Dwayne, easy. You just got asked about your

*status and you didn't confirm it or say Misha's name and,
in fact, you changed the subject. And now you're giving her
that smile. Fall back, soldier, fall back. I don't like this.'*

'I beg you shut up, blud.'

Rachel shrugged her slim little shoulders. "Word
gets around, innit."

"So where's your man then?"

Rachel laughed and popped her gum. "I ain't on
that no more. I'm on deen now. I'm a Muslim. You
know Sean from school? He was giving me *da'wah*
for time." She touched her little scarf. "We just took
shahadah last week, me and my girl, Natalie."

"Really?" I was impressed. "But are you proper on
it though? Do you pray?"

"Of course I pray, man! Do *you* pray?"

"I'm trying my best, innit. It's hard to remember all
the actions and what to say. But my bredren Tony, he's
teaching me. *Insha Allah*, I'll get there."

"Ain't that Jukkie's big brother?"

I nodded.

"Safe. Heard he's proper on it. Anyway, I've got to
go; I promised my mum I'd babysit. She's going out on
the razz – these *kufars*, they're something else, innit?"

She laughed then, that tinkly laugh of hers, and I
began to feel light-headed. "And listen, if you need

any help with your prayers, let me know. I'll come over and help you." And then she looked me in the eye and something flashed between us.

*'What the hell was that? Did she just give you **the look**?'*

'I don't know, blud, swear down! Phew! That was tough! It took all my willpower not to ask her for her number, man!'

'Astaghfirullah! Chirpsing girls on deen – while you've got a girl yourself? Disgusting! You're a tramp, Dwayne Kingston, a total ho.'

'Ah, but I didn't actually ask for the digits, did I?'

'But you wanted to!'

'But I didn't and that's what counts – what you do with your limbs.'

"Oh, Dwayne, I forgot." Rachel was back, fishing around in her little shoulder bag. "Here." She handed me a piece of paper. "My number in case you need me. *Salaam alaikum!*"

"Thanks, Rachel."

"Oh, and you can call me Ruqayyah now, OK?"

"OK, Ruqayyah... see you around. *Salaam alaikum...*"

'Eediat!'

Larkside Games

DWAYNE

Over the next few weeks, I hardly saw Jukkie. I knew that he was rolling with Trigger on the regular now and didn't have time to come and check me. The two of them had 'gone country' – out to rob and push drugs in the suburbs where there was less competition.

A part of me missed Jukkie – he was my bredren at the end of the day – but another part of me was glad that he was staying away. I didn't need his influence around, not while I was trying to go straight.

But one day, while I was on my way back from after-school maths tuition, I heard a car beep.

I turned to see who it was: it was Jukkie, in a brand new convertible. My man looked proper pleased with himself.

"Yo, Dee," he called. "Come and roll with your boy, innit!"

I looked at the other seats: empty. I could handle Jukkie when he was on his own, so I nodded and jogged across the road to the car.

Once we were in the car, it was like old days. Jukkie was playing his favourite tune, *Me against the world* by Tupac. Jukkie was crazy for Tupac. Even after other rappers had come on the scene, even when everyone else started listening to grime, Jukkie stayed loyal to Tupac.

"Tupac understands my life, y'get me," he would say. "He's like the father I never had."

We chewed the fat for a while, chattin' about this and that. It was nice, man, just like old times.

"Let's go for a drive," he said, as he swung the car up towards Thornton Heath. "I need to burn some rubber in this baby!"

It was all good until Jukkie's phone went off. He had received a message. He kissed his teeth and picked up the phone to look at the screen. It was a video message. It sounded nasty.

I could see Jukkie's face grow darker as he tried to figure out what was going on on the screen. Then he swore loudly and slammed the brakes on the car.

The car screeched and stopped and the car behind us beeped long and loud.

"Maniacs!" called the man as he sped past us, giving us the finger.

Jukkie ignored him and put the car in reverse. Faster and faster he went backwards down the one-way street. I looked in my sideview mirror, praying no cars would appear behind us.

"Easy, Jukkie, easy!"

With a squeal of tyres and the stink of hot rubber, Jukkie swung the car back towards Stockwell.

"What's going on, man?" I was panting as I ran up the stairs behind him. This was where one of his girlfriends lived. I had been there before, for a house party. But Jukkie didn't say a word.

When we got to the house, he banged on the door.

"Open up, Lachelle!"

Jukkie's girl, Lachelle, opened the door and he barged in, pushing her inside. To my surprise, I saw that she was at least six months pregnant. So, Jukkie had a pickney on the way...

Jukkie didn't say a word, just gave her a slap that sent her spinning.

I stepped forward. "Yo, Jukkie, easy, man. The baby..."

"What's up with you, man?" she squealed, holding her cheek.

"You're a dirty sket, that's what!" Jukkie yelled, his face all twisted with rage and disgust. "I can't believe I ever trusted you."

"Why, Jukkie, why? What have I done? I ain't done nothin'!" The girl was crying now, trying to grab on to his arm, trying to make him look her in the face.

"Yeah? Well then how do you explain this?" With bared teeth, Jukkie shoved his mobile phone in her face. I saw her flinch and look away from what was obviously some nasty video, a video of her.

"By now, every man on the estate will have seen it!" Jukkie spat full in her face. "You must be mad if you think I want anything to do with you!"

"Please, Jukkie, don't go..."

"Move from me, bitch!" And he barged past me. "Let's dust, man."

He paused at the door to look back one last time. "And you can get rid of that baby an' all. Probably wasn't even mine."

Before the door slammed shut, I saw Lachelle collapse against the kitchen counter, her fists jammed against her mouth to keep from crying out.

That was heavy.

Without Jukkie saying a word, I knew what had happened. A couple of weeks before, Lockjaw and the Larkside crew had started a new craze down their endz: they went after girls who already had boyfriends and drugged them up – sometimes with their consent, sometimes without – and made them do all kinds of nastiness, and every member of the crew got a piece. Then they would film everything and send the videos to each other, to the girls' boyfriends, post them on the Internet.

After something like that, a girl's name was dirt. She was known as a sket by the whole estate and then Larkside mandem could get her to do practically anything: drugs – using, pushing, carrying – videos, turning tricks.

They had got one of Jukkie's girls this time.

Jukkie was so wound up, I asked him to drop me on the high road. I knew that he was going to go and get high now and I didn't want to be with him when he was like that.

But I passed by Tony's place to tell him what had happened.

Tony shook his head. "Dem mans are gettin' worse and worse. In my day, none of this stuff used to go down." Then he looked at me straight in the eye.

"Don't forget that you're a Muslim now, Dee. You need to keep good company or you'll end up off the rails again. Come with me to the mosque this Friday and chill with the brothers. There's a talk on and a barbecue afterwards."

"You know what, Tony, I'd love to, but this Friday ain't gonna happen. I'm performing at Club Loco – and Misha's coming to see me rock the mic there."

I was so chuffed that I hardly noticed the disappointment in Tony's face. "You're going raving, Dee? And taking Misha with you? I thought you were leaving all that..."

"Yeah, but man has to take things one step at a time, innit. I'm praying now, *masha Allah*. I've quit smoking – and I ain't gonna drink any alcohol while I'm there..."

Tony's face looked pained. "It's wrong, Dee," he said. "You shouldn't be there, not with all that haram around you. Can't you take Misha somewhere else? Why not bring her to the mosque for the barbecue?"

I kissed my teeth then, growing impatient with Tony for the first time. "Nah, man, Misha ain't interested in coming to the mosque. We asked her mum and dad if she could come to see me spit and they agreed – so we're legit. And this could be my big chance, my one shot at the big time. Do you have any idea who's gonna be there?" And I started listing the DJ crews and producers that the organiser had invited. "This could be it for me!"

But Tony went all quiet. "I'm worried about you, Dee. I don't think you're thinking straight. If you decide to change your mind, you're welcome to join us at the *masjid*. You and Misha."

It was like he hadn't even heard a word I said.

Night On The Town

MISHA

"Does your mum know where you're going tonight?" Effie eyed me in the mirror as she carefully blended foundation over her cheekbones.

"Yes, she does, actually. Both Mum and Dad agreed to let me see Dwayne perform – but Mum needed a bit of convincing, of course!"

"Well, you are sixteen, aren't you?" called Victoria from the bathroom. "That has to count for something."

"Yes, well, she said she's trusting us this once – so let's hope nothing happens, eh?"

"Yeah, I meant to ask you about that: this place we're going to tonight, is it safe? I mean, I'm all for street art and underground music and all that cool, edgy stuff but I don't want to get caught up in some drive-by shooting or anything!"

"Dwayne said it would be fine – I trust him."

"OK, ladies, let's not forget it's the weekend," said Victoria. "I don't want to have to think about anything but having a good time." And she brought out a small packet of white powder and a credit card and flashed a brilliant smile. "Daddy's gold card, ladies – who's in?"

❖ ❖ ❖

The taxi ride from Ladbroke Grove to North London was long but made longer by Victoria's too-loud voice, singing along to the silent sound of her iPod earphones. She was always a handful when she got high. She thought it made her cute and carefree but I found her loud and over-excited, difficult to get through to.

Besides, I wasn't really in a party mood. I'd agreed to come because I really wanted to see this side of Dwayne, his creative, artistic side, his public persona – but I had a bad feeling. I couldn't explain it. Things had been so wonderful once Mum and Dad had agreed to give me some space – but now they had become complicated again.

Why did Dwayne have to go and accept Islam –

and why did he expect me to follow him? I thought we had dealt with the street stuff, with the lack of ambition, with his insensitivity towards my feelings and points of view. We worked through all that, and now this!

Deep down I knew, like I had always known, that Dee was a really great guy. But I couldn't help feeling that his choices were dragging him down, away from me, away from achieving his full potential, away from where I wanted him to be – where I needed him to be.

"What makes Dwayne think I have the remotest interest in becoming a Muslim?" I had raged at Aalia that day at school. "If he thinks he's going to get me hiding behind a scarf, chained to the kitchen sink with ten children, he's got another think coming!"

Aalia's eyes showed hurt and confusion. "Is that what you think Islam is all about, Misha?"

I mentally kicked myself – Aalia was Muslim too, wasn't she? Talk about insensitivity!

I backtracked. "Well, no, not really. I mean, I don't know. To be honest, he's given me loads of books but I haven't opened even one of them."

"Maybe you should, Misha. You might learn something..." She sighed. "Anyway, you have to choose, Misha. You either take him as he is, accept whatever flaws he has, however he is growing and changing, or leave him for someone more like you, on your social level."

"But I don't want anyone else, Aalia!" I wailed. "I want Dwayne."

"Well," was Aalia's response, "you'd better deal with everything that comes with that. At the end of the day, are you prepared to rethink your dreams and future plans to take into account where he is coming from? Are you prepared for the fact that he just might not get his GCSEs, may never go to uni? This is the reality, Misha, and you're going to have to face up to it if you're in it for the long term."

"I'm not a snob, Aalia, I can still respect someone who hasn't gone to uni – I'm not like my mum..."

"It's not about being a snob, though, is it? It's about having different aspirations, different outlooks on life. Look at my parents: with them, it's easy. Our religion and culture are their priority. After that, education is the most important thing to them, as far as we kids are concerned. It's yet another thing they have in common, it unites them. It may make them really tough to please but at least that is one area you know they aren't going to budge. Imagine how Dwayne will feel when you go off to uni and leave him on his council estate. Don't you think he's going to feel a little jealous, a little out of his depth? What about when he meets your university-educated friends? It's going to be awful for him!"

"I'm so afraid that you're right..."

"I am right, Misha, and you know it. You know what I'm like: I don't do sugar-coating! If you want that, go speak to Victoria, she'll give you plenty of the romantic dreamer stuff. Me? I'll tell you straight because I care about you... and I don't want to see you get hurt."

"You don't think there is a future for us, do you?" I asked sullenly.

Effie appeared, eager to hear the latest episode of the soap opera that my life had become.

"You're sixteen, Misha, what's all this talk about futures?" She laughed. "I say enjoy it while it lasts. He's hot; he's totally into you – just enjoy the moment! You're still young; you don't need to be compatible like that. Trust me, in a year or so, you will have moved on and so will he – you never know, Leon Grant might have you back!"

"Oh no, I'd rather die!"

"The thing that worries me, Misha," Aalia said,

"is that you're living this Romeo-and-Juliet fantasy – but just look at how they ended up!"

"Don't you believe in love, Aalia?"

"I do, Misha, I really do. I just don't know how much you can love someone at sixteen – or how real that love can be, seeing as you're still getting to know yourself. Do you see where I'm coming from?"

And I hadn't said any more about it. Maybe I was just being silly. Maybe Aalia, Effie, Victoria, Mum and my aunties were right: Dwayne was just a passing phase, best enjoyed before it was over.

I tried to tell myself that several times that day but, every time, my heart whispered back to me: 'Liar'.

✪ ✪ ✪

I peered out of the window as we drove down the high street. This side of town was a jumbled mass of kebab shops, cheap outlet stores and off-licences. Torn posters flapped against the worn brick walls and rubbish nestled in the gutters. Not somewhere I would ever have considered coming, had it not been for Dwayne's invitation. I looked down at the 'A to Z' on my lap. I always followed our route in the A to Z, even when we took cabs, just to be safe.

"I think this is the road coming up, Effie," I said.

"Right at these traffic lights."

The cabbie turned into a dingy street and Effie raised an eyebrow. "This place looks like it could use a little gentrification..." she mused. We both looked out of the window, trying to spot the name of the club. "Vee, keep it down, girl! We're trying to find this place."

Victoria, who had been singing along to Mariah Carey at the top of her voice, stopped suddenly and began to giggle uncontrollably.

"Girls, girls," she laughed, "tonight is going to be fabulous, darlings, absolutely fabulous!"

Just then, I saw the line of people snaking along the pavement and the flashing neon sign above them: Club Loco. "Look, Effie, there it is!"

Effie took one look at the people in the line and burst out laughing, almost choking herself in the process. "You can't be serious, Misha! Just look at these people!"

I peeped out of the cab window and stared at the people who were queuing up to get into Club Loco. I felt a shiver of uncertainty, of fear, run through me. Caps, braids, giant puffa jackets, baggy jeans that revealed patterned boxer shorts, Timberland boots and diamond earrings adorned the guys who stood around, looking hard, screw-face. The girls, decked out in the latest choppy hairstyles and short skirts, fake nails and huge gold hoop earrings, surveyed us as we parked up, their mouths set, arms crossed in front of them.

Not a happy crowd.

"You girls sure you're going to be all right?" asked the cab driver, eyeing the kids in the line.

"Yeah, we'll be fine. We're meeting someone... but... do you mind waiting?"

The cabbie shrugged and pointed at the meter that was still ticking away.

"Where's Dwayne?" Effie asked, looking sceptically at the huddle of people crowded around the door. "If he doesn't come for us, we're finished. This lot look like they eat posh West London girls for breakfast."

I laughed nervously. "Dwayne wouldn't ask us to come anywhere dangerous, Effie. He's got more sense than that. He wouldn't let anything happen to us."

But, if I was honest, I would admit that I felt self-conscious, embarrassed for myself and my friends – and for Dwayne. I had known that his crowd was different to mine, but this? This seemed like a totally different world, a world we didn't belong to, could never fit into, with our Karen Millen outfits and clutch bags. These were straight-up, raw ghetto people, the kind Mum despised, the kind she had always warned me about. Perhaps it had been a mistake to come here. Maybe we were better off just going home now. The taxi was still here; it wouldn't be a problem to simply jump back in and head for home.

Then my phone rang.

"Hey, babe," came the familiar voice. "Where are you?"

"Oh, Dwayne! We're here, we're just parking up. Where are you?"

"Right behind you," came the voice from outside the window.

I looked out to find Dwayne standing there, the essence of fineness, a lazy smile on his face. All my fears melted away. Dwayne was here: everything would be all right.

"Thought you were gonna stand me up," he said, taking my hand. Then he nodded towards Effie and Victoria. "Hey, Effie, Vee, wha' gwan'? You ready for the show tonight?"

Effie put her head to one side and raised her eyebrow at Dwayne. "As long as you can guarantee that there won't be any drive-bys or anything like that, we should be cool."

"Nah, man, it's all love. These peeps have come for a show, to have a good time, y' get me. They ain't looking for no beef."

Victoria emerged from the taxi and gave a little squeal of excitement when she saw Dwayne. "Ah, here you are at last, Dwayne, darling! Now the show can begin!"

Dwayne looked over at me. "I ain't never seen her like this before. Is she all right?"

I nodded and made a sniffing sound with my hand against my nostrils.

Dwayne's eyes opened wide and he said, "Yeah?"

"Yeah..."

He chuckled. "Vee's ready to party then, innit?" And he put out his hand to steady her as she careened towards us, almost twisting her ankle as she stumbled in her leopard-print platform heels. "Easy, girl, easy!" he called, laughing. "Let's get you inside, shall we?" He grabbed me by my waist with his other arm and pulled me close. "I'm the luckiest man here tonight," he whispered in my ear and I giggled, butterflies dancing in the pit of my stomach.

Then he was guiding us through the intimidating crowd of b-boys and b-girls hanging around outside the door, stopping to greet some of them, being stopped by others, pumping hands, being slapped on the back.

"Yo, Boy Wonder! Wha' blow?"

"Waiting for your slot, man!"

"You're gonna light up the spot, bro!"

"We came all the way down from Bristol, dog!"

"Hope you've got some surprises for us, innit!"

DWAYNE

I was on top of the world, bubbling with pride and excitement. Here I was, walking with my arm around my girl, feeling the love from the fans I had gained over the past year. I had worked hard for this. Tonight was my night, my big chance to impress the headline act and the other MCs and producers that were bound to be there.

The main act was a local boy who had made it big on the charts, taking grime – urban street music – to the mainstream. Although the venue was tired, it was an honour to be supporting him.

And Misha was here to see it. My heart grew soft when I thought of her, felt her, smelt her perfume, right next to me, in this place. She was here for me,

297

just for me, to see me shine, and that made me feel big, bigger than I had ever felt in my life.

'You love her, innit?'

Silence.

'Just admit it, man! It's me you're talking to here.'

'Y' know what? I think I do. I think I love her. Oh God.'

'Scary innit?'

'Swear down, bruv!'

'LOL.'

When I walked up to the door, one of the bouncers smiled at me and hugged me – a huge man hug.

"This is my girl, Misha, and her friends, Effie and Victoria. Girls, this is my cousin, Darren."

"Pleasure to meet you, ladies, come in. Have a good time."

And we were in.

Spittin' Light

MISHA

In spite of my initial misgivings, I found myself caught up in the mood of the crowd and excitement bubbled up inside me. After all, why shouldn't I enjoy myself? I was going to see Dwayne at his best, in his comfort zone at last.

The underground club was packed. People lined the staircase going down into the main room, the walls and floor vibrating to the bass of the music. The main area was a sea of people, the same intimidating figures from outside, with hard-looking faces, eyeing each other up.

"Dwayne," I shouted into Dwayne's ear, "how come they all look so angry? Aren't they here to have a good time?"

And Dwayne laughed: "That's just the way de

mandem are, innit. Don't worry, once the tunes start up, you'll see them start to grin teeth..."

"That's the trouble with you hiphop heads!" Effie laughed to cover her nervousness. "You're just not happy people, are you?"

"You sure you can handle this lot, Dee? They look like they may get violent if you don't come correct..."

"Hey, this is Boy Wonder you're talking to – of course I'm gonna come correct! Trust me, I've played for worse crowds than this one."

We finally found some empty stools, at the far end of the bar.

"Make mine a Mojito!" hooted Victoria, shaking her shoulders to the throbbing bassline, swinging the ends of her feather boa in the air in front of Dwayne's face.

He laughed and swatted at her, ducking out of the way as she spun round, her skirt flying up. "Easy, Vee!" he called. "Watch yourself!"

Effie and I exchanged a look.

"We'd better keep an eye on her," Effie whispered in my ear. "She's as high as a kite!"

Remembering that Dwayne didn't drink any more, I squeezed his arm and said, "I think I'll have an orange juice, Dee."

Dwayne laughed. "Orange juice, yeah? You're too much, girl." And he turned away and called out to the barman who was busy with some other customers at the other end of the bar.

Victoria's dancing caused a stir and brought several admirers over to where we were standing, like bees around a pot of honey. One of them, a tall bald-headed man with skin like polished ebony and a red satin shirt, came up to her from behind and began dancing with her, his arms round her waist.

Victoria tossed her head back and laughed, raising her slim arms in the air, waving her feather boa, moving her hips from side to side.

The baldhead was delighted with her response. "Mmmmm, shake it, girl! That's right!"

Soon the two of them were on the dance floor, under the flashing, glittering lights.

Just then, there was a minor commotion at the door – the main act had arrived. He came in, surrounded by his entourage, his red cap to one side, his white t-shirt glowing blue in the ultraviolet light. Beneath the cap, his hair was cropped close and a huge diamond glittered in his ear, a simple – but thick – gold chain around his neck. Everyone craned to have a look, even the hardest of the badboys, although they tried to hide their curiosity and excitement.

Effie looked over at the members of his entourage and licked her lips. "Ooh," she purred, "there's some talent in here *tonight*! A bit rough around the edges, I'll admit, but talent all the same."

I gave her a sideways look. "You're spoken for, remember?"

"Oh, come on!" teased Effie. "A cat can look at a king, right?"

"True..." And we both watched as the star of the show made his way to the VIP area, trailed by admirers, hangers-on and hopefuls.

Dwayne handed us our drinks and, before long, the club manager was walking up to us and shaking Dwayne's hand, thanking him for coming down, telling him he would be on in ten minutes.

"You ready, babe?" I asked, brushing an imaginary speck of dust off his shoulder.

"Yeah, I'm ready, man, I'm ready..." Then he squeezed my hand and murmured, "My sweetness ... I want you in the front where I can see you, OK?"

"Of course, babe, I'm there. Now off you go – and don't be nervous! You're going to be great, I know it."

He kissed my hand and winked up at me. "Thanks, babe."

And he turned and was soon swallowed up by the crowd just as the DJ was calling on the crowd to show the Boy Wonder some love.

One Chance

DWAYNE

As the DJ played the intro to my tune, the beats drummed in my head, thrummed in my fingers, pumped through my veins all the way to my heart. Fresh beats. Wild, life-giving beats. Almost immediately, they lifted me up and took me to another level. They got inside me, right up inside me, under my skin, wrapped around my insides. And then the words came out, flying, spitting, sparking, setting the mic on fire.

Words tripped over words, slipping into phrases, staccato. They had come from inside my head, from all that I had seen, everything I had heard, from the electricity in the air around me, and I had worked them into something potent, something explosive.

The crowd went wild, whistling, hooting:

'Braap braap!'

I could see Misha looking up at me, mesmerised. I held the mic to my lips with one hand while my other hand flew around in front of me, touching the outstretched hands of the people in front of the stage. I was good that night, man, really good, better than I had ever been.

I was on top of the world.

✪ ✪ ✪

Misha and her friends were totally impressed.

"You were sensational!" Misha grinned and I ducked my head. Girl was making man blush!

Just then, a tall, big guy in a sharp black suit and black silk shirt came up to me.

"Hey, Dwayne!" he smiled, his gold teeth glittering almost as much as the diamond in his ear. "What you saying, bro? I didn't know you was gonna reach tonight! You was dynamite up there!"

It was DJ Risquee, from the Karnage Krew, one of the hottest DJ crews around.

I put my arm round Misha and turned to Risquee. "This is my girl, Misha, and her friend, Effie..."

"Yeah? Sweet! Well, you ladies make sure you have a good time. I wanna see you on the dance floor later, yeah?"

Both girls smiled and nodded.

'Damn, this girl is beautiful, man!'

'Innit!'

Then Risquee turned to me and slung his arm over my shoulder. "So Dwayne, listen, yeah. My partner and I, we was talking about you after your show in Tottenham... we want you to come down, lay down some lyrics and ting, something we've got in the pipeline."

I was buzzing. The Karnage Krew already had a string of underground hits and their latest track had just hit the singles charts. They were red-hot.

"Yeah, man, of course! Just name the place, innit!"

"Safe, bro, we'll hook it up. But listen, why don't you come and meet him? I know that tonight's gonna be a mad one – de gyal dem already queuing up! – but I can introduce man still, y' get me?"

I nodded, grinning. "Sounds sweet, blud." Then I turned to Misha. "You don't mind, do you, babes? I won't be long, I promise."

"Of course, Dee, I'll be fine. Effie and I will just wait for you by the bar."

MISHA

After Dwayne and the DJ disappeared into the crowd, we made our way back to the bar and stood there, sipped our drinks, moving to the throbbing beat of the music. We were so busy enjoying the fizzing energy, the vibe created by Dwayne's performance, the spell being woven by the DJ, that we didn't notice a group of guys with green bandannas enter the club. Not until one of them came up behind Effie and put a rough hand on her arm.

"Yo, Effie! What're you doin' here?"

Effie gasped and whipped round at the sound of the voice.

"Lawrence! I–I came with my friend, Misha," she stammered. "Her boyfriend got us in..." She winced slightly – was he hurting her?

"Yeah?" Lawrence's eyes narrowed. "How comes I didn't know nuffin' about it?"

"I didn't think..."

"Nah, ya didn't, did ya?"

Effie tried to pull her arm away and smile but he wasn't letting go. "Hey, babe, what's the big deal? We're here now, aren't we? Why can't you just relax and have a good time?"

"I don't like stuff happening that I don't know about..." But he relaxed his hold on her arm.

"But you never told me *you* were coming here either, did you?" Effie seemed relieved that he had started to calm down. "And now you're here, the party can really start, right?"

Lawrence looked her up and down, then smiled a crooked smile. "Yeah, I guess it can, innit? Yo, man, where's the champagne?"

Victoria, who had danced her way back to the bar, leaned over and giggled. "Did I hear someone mention champagne? Girl, your man sure knows how to party!"

Effie smiled and raised her glass in a toast. But I could see her hands trembling, just a little.

Lawrence winked at me as he handed me a fluted glass of sparkling champagne. I felt the tiny bubbles pop on my fingers as I took it from him. His fingers brushed mine, just for a moment or two longer than necessary.

"And what's your name?" he asked in a low, husky voice. His tone and the way his eyes burned into mine sent a warning shiver down my spine.

I faltered and tried to smile. "Er... I'm Misha... Effie's friend..."

"Ah, safe..." he said, leaning back, looking me up and down. "Nice..."

My cheeks burned with embarrassment and I looked desperately over at Effie – but she was busy filling Victoria's glass with more champagne and she didn't see anything.

"Yo, Flint!" Lawrence called out to one of his friends, a tall, thin, light-skinned guy whose lopsided green bandanna revealed a tattoo-like pattern shaved into the side of his head. He squeezed in next to me and jerked his chin towards me.

"So, who's this 'tick piece, then?"

Lawrence smirked. "One of Effie's friends, innit?"

"Hmmm, sweetness! Where have *you* been hiding?" He was so close to me that I could smell the leather of his jacket and the Jack Daniels on his breath.

The two of them leered at me and I tried to move away but Lawrence grabbed my hand and pulled me towards him.

"What's the matter?" he rasped. "Why you goin' on all stoosh? You frigid or something? Don't you like my boy, Flint?"

"Yeah, don't be like that," smiled Flint. "I won't hurt you – unless you want me to..."

What?

"Oi!" I shouted, finally coming to my senses and pushing Flint aside. "Look, just get lost, yeah? I'm not interested!"

"What, you got a man or something?"

"Yes, I have, actually."

"Yeah? So where is he, then?"

"Right there!" My heart leapt when I saw Dwayne on the other side of the room, about to make his way back to me, and relief flooded my body.

Lawrence turned to look – and his eyes narrowed. He definitely seemed to recognise Dwayne.

But then he turned to me and smiled slyly. "You should dash him, y'know, come and hang with my boy, Flint. He knows how to treat the ladies, y'get me?"

"And just what are you trying to do to Misha, Lawrence? Scare the living daylights out of her?" It was Effie, trying to diffuse the situation with her wide smile and tinkly laugh. She grabbed my hand and pulled me out from between the two men.

"I can't believe you left me alone with those two!" I hissed, my heart still hammering in my chest.

Effie looked back to where Lawrence was standing with his friend. "Those two?" she laughed. "They come off all hard but they're harmless really!"

"Harmless?" I was incredulous. "You could have fooled me! I felt like I was about to be gangbanged or something!"

Effie rolled her eyes. "You and your crazy stereotypes! You definitely need to get out more. Now, where's that Romeo of yours?"

We both peered into the crowd, our backs turned to Lawrence and his friend.

"Effie!"

We both turned round.

"Don't your friend drink champagne?"

Effie took the glass and handed it to me. I brought it slowly to my lips and sipped, aware of the two men's eyes on me, aware of the dark shadow of foreboding that had begun to creep over me.

"Cheers!"

Payback

MISHA

After finishing my glass of champagne, I escaped to the dance floor.

As soon as I stepped beneath the strobe lights, I was swept up by the electric vibe that flowed through the club and I moved effortlessly to the insistent, driving beat. My mind emptied and I surrendered to the music, to the pulse of the crowd, to the rhythm that flowed through my veins.

I didn't care about the heat or the sweat that had begun to trickle down my neck, down my back. I just wanted to dance and blot out everything except the good feelings, except thoughts of Dwayne as I had seen him up on stage. I didn't want anything to spoil this night. I was at one with the music and nothing, nothing, nothing else mattered.

'This is what I want,' I thought to myself. 'To dance all night long, as if I have no worries, no worries at all – no school, no exams, no Islam, no pressure, no doubts. No talking, no thinking, no stressing – just the music.'

Dwayne made his way to me and we danced together for a while, then Effie and Victoria joined us. When they left us to go and get another drink, Dwayne told me he was going to go to the toilet.

"Don't worry!" I laughed. "I'll be here!" And I waved at him as he was swallowed up by the crowd.

Then something strange started happening.

One minute, I was fizzing with the energy of the music, the people and the alcohol in my system, the next, the room started to sway. The people around me moved in and out of focus. I put out my hands to steady myself, confused. What was happening to me?

All of a sudden, my feet wouldn't do what I wanted them to. My tongue felt thick and clumsy in my mouth and I heard myself slurring as I tried to speak, to call out to Dwayne, to tell him that I was tired, so tired, that I needed to sit down, to stop the crashing in my head, to stop the room spinning round and round.

DWAYNE

I was grinning to myself as I made my way back to the dance floor from the toilet. Recording with Risquee was every young MC's dream – the night was turning out even better than I had hoped. I craned my neck to see where Misha was, trying to spot her red dress in the crowd.

Then I heard a voice I hadn't expected to hear that night of all nights.

"What you sayin', blud?"

It was Trigger.

I turned to find Trigger's face inches away from mine, his mouth twisted to one side. "Seems like you've been on a bit of a solo ting lately, eh? Is it your girl? She got you on lock down? Or is it coz you been rollin' with that wasteman, Tony?"

I swallowed hard and shook my head. "Nah, man, not at all. Just been a bit busy, that's all." I thought to mention the Islam ting but it felt kinda hypocritical, still. A Muslim had no business in a club surrounded by alcohol and people grinding up on each other. Then I looked over Trigger's shoulder and saw several RDS mans, looking screw-face. "What's up anyway? What're you mans doing here?"

"You never heard what went down?"

"Went down? Where? With who?"

Trigger laughed: "Jeez, man, sometimes I swear it's like you live on another planet! Larkside man – they broke into Jukkie's yard, bruck it up bad; armsed up his mum..."

"What?" I couldn't believe what Trigger was telling me. Half of me hoped I had misheard him, that the thumping bass had mashed up his words. I thought of Jukkie and Tony's mum, so small and fragile, and my throat went tight. How could man do that?

But then, there was Jukkie, his eyes blazing, his face like stone. "See what happens now," he snarled. "See what happens now. Man have fi dead fi dat!"

"Of course, man, that's just plain disrespect..."

But my words dried up as soon as Jukkie opened his jacket. I recognised the 12-inch blade Jukkie had tucked into his waistband. It was Jukkie's favourite: stainless steel, Japanese-made.

"No man comes into my yard..." mutttered Jukkie, and his blazing eyes floated away from me to rest on Lockjaw, who was still standing by the bar. I did a double take when I saw who he was standing with: Effie, Misha's friend.

'What the hell's Effie doing with Lockjaw, man?'

'*I don't know!*'

'*She don't know who she's messing with!*'

'*I know... oh God...*'

I swallowed hard. In my heart, I could feel a premonition stirring, a dream that had played itself over and over in my head; a dream about me, Jukkie and a sharp, sharp knife.

I reached out to grab Jukkie's arm and hissed, "Not here, man!"

But Jukkie turned on me, a twisted scowl on his face. "What you afraid of, bruv? I jukk dem man live – live, in front of *everyone*, y' get me? I don't care if I go down for that!"

He kissed his teeth and shook my hand off. "And I ain't your girl, yeah, so don't touch me! Move from me before I jukk you too!"

And he strode off into the crowd of people. I was shaking. I had never seen Jukkie this crazy. The wildness in his eyes was new, much worse than anything I had seen, in all the time we had been friends. I looked over at Trigger, who had been watching the exchange between us without saying a word.

"Tonight," Trigger said, "Larkside man are gonna get what's coming to them, seen? And none of us

316

is gonna be able to stay out of it; ain't no one gonna be able to keep their hands clean – not even you Muslims. You know how these things go, blud. It don't stop until mans come out on top, until mans have proved that we can't be messed with, that we run tings. Just make sure you're ready when the time comes..."

Trigger smiled his crooked smile and his gold teeth winked in the strobe lights. "So I reckon you chose the right night to come spit some bars, innit?"

When Trigger said those words, my heart just dropped to my stomach. He was looking to cause more beef – tonight!

I frowned as I saw the RDS mans spread out on one side of the club, eyeing up the Larkside boys on the other end of the room. This was not going to be pretty. But they couldn't be planning a beat-down here, could they? It wasn't possible. There had to be another plan. I looked up at Trigger who winked at me and put his finger to his lips.

'Watch this,' he said, before stepping away into the crowd of dancers.

I felt the room begin to spin, the lights whizzing around and around. From where I stood, I could see Lockjaw, Effie and some other Larkside mans at the bar on my left. I could see Trigger and the RDS boys dotted around in the crowd to my right – they weren't wearing their bandannas tonight. That was when I knew that they weren't playing for show tonight. They were playing for keeps.

Suddenly, there was a scuffle on the other side of the dance floor, on the opposite side of the club to the bar. I peered over the heads of the dancers and saw that Trigger had tipped over the drink of one of the Larkside man who had been lounging on a seat, squeezed between two chicks.

The guy was screwing, embarrassed in front of the girls, ready to take Trigger out there and then. He was shouting at Trigger, pushing him in the chest, all up in his face. Trigger stayed calm though and stood his ground, looking down at him, daring him to do his worst.

I saw the other Larkside man begin to reach, pushing through the crowd, getting ready for a fight. The bouncers noticed too and walked quickly towards them, speaking into their walkie-talkies.

This was it.

My heart began to beat in time to the music and I felt the storm clouds gathering behind my eyes. I thought of Jukkie's mother. I still remembered her as she had been years ago, when we were boys running around the estate: her smile, her shining, clean flat, her delicious roast dinner. And, as I thought of how frightened she must have been when those green bandanna-wearing goons broke into her home, my blood boiled.

Larkside man had gone too far this time. There are some things you just don't do. And Larkside man had done them, again and again and again. Messing with kids, with man's girl, with man's family.

I took a deep breath and stepped forward, flexing my fingers, cracking my knuckles.

But then, out of the corner of my eye, I saw a flash of red, like a flame flickering on the edge of the dancehall.

It was Misha.

But something was up with her.

She was swerving, tottering, staggering almost, reaching out for Effie. My eyes narrowed when I saw the look on Lockjaw's face, the smile that slid across his crooked lips, the way he grabbed Misha by the waist and pulled her towards him. She swayed against him, her eyes half shut.

'Yo, what's up with Misha, man? Is she drunk?'

'I don't know, man, I don't know!'

I started to step to them – but then I saw Jukkie,

silent as a thief in the night, come up behind Lockjaw, and I froze, unable to move.

While Misha tried to get herself away from Lockjaw, Effie shouted at her, trying to make her focus, trying to get through to her. Lockjaw was laughing – he looked like he was telling Effie to calm down, to take it easy.

I could imagine him saying, "She probably just had too much to drink, innit?"

It was all a joke to him.

Until Jukkie stepped up behind him and, with a motion as smooth as silk, drove his knife into his side.

'Who's laughing now?'

It was over in seconds and, when I blinked, Jukkie had disappeared, melted into the crowd, leaving Lockjaw holding his side with a look of shock and surprise on his face. The blood from the knife wound spread like a poppy on his white suit jacket and he slumped forward on to Effie and Misha.

Then Effie started screaming.

I finally found that I could move my feet. I pushed past the dancers that swirled around me on the dance floor and made for the bar.

But then, in seconds, there was Jukkie, right in front

of me, breathing hard, his face hidden by his hood.

The next thing I knew, Jukkie had pushed the bloody knife deep into my jacket pocket. I felt the stainless steel edge tear the inner lining and my stomach clenched.

"Hold it, hold it!" Jukkie's voice was hoarse in my ear and I nodded, numb, unthinking.

Then he was gone.

Blood Sport

MISHA

"Dwayne!"

I struggled to raise my voice and cut through the sound of the music, the crowd and Effie's screams.

Through the fog, I could see Lawrence on the floor, an awful patch of red spreading across his jacket. My stomach lurched and I turned and retched.

The music was so loud and the club so packed that, for several minutes, hardly anyone realised that someone had been stabbed: that a man lay on the floor of the club, bleeding into his white Armani suit. It was like a nightmare.

The people standing at the bar were the first to realise. Alerted by Effie's screams, the barman and the people around him looked over and saw Lawrence, his eyes rolled back in his head, his blood spreading over the floor.

I became aware of shouts, curses, bodies moving, some away from me, some towards me, and again and again, louder and louder, Effie's strangled cries.

"He's been stabbed!" Effie was screaming. "Oh my God, he's bleeding! Help! Someone help! *Please*!"

I tried to reach out for Effie but my arms felt like lead, my head as if it was stuffed with cotton wool.

'Tired, so tired...'

The room tipped and swayed as flashes of green bandannas swam in and out of focus... there was Victoria, a horrified look on her face... Effie, her face streaked with tears... the sound of angry voices, accusations, swirled around me. I cowered from the commotion of the crowd, swaying, pressing my hands over my ears as I struggled, struggled to find my footing, to remember how I got there, what was happening, where I had left my bag.

But it was too much for me. I just couldn't do it.

Someone bumped into me and I felt myself falling, as if from a great height. It took so long for me to reach the floor that I thought I could be falling forever, down, down, down, away from the noise, from the stench of alcohol and sweaty bodies, from the man on the floor, his blood so very red against the bright white of his jacket.

Falling, falling away... until Dwayne caught me.

"It's OK, babes, I've got you..."

That was when I began to cry, great big tears of relief. Dwayne was here. Everything would be all right. I was safe.

DWAYNE

Things in Club Loco had begun to kick off.

One by one, Larkside man began to realise that one of them had been taken down, that Lockjaw had been taken down – and that RDS man were in the place. It was obvious what had happened and they started scanning the club, looking for anyone from RDS, to take their revenge. I knew exactly what man were feeling, had felt it myself many times: your blood boils and your heart swells with the hunger to draw blood, to take lives.

I didn't need anyone to tell me how lethal the situation had become. This was standard: the escalation, the upward spiral, the racing headlong toward the climax, the final scene, the endgame.

My pride made me strong; I wasn't afraid to fight. An old feeling stirred inside me, from deep inside me, ingrained since boyhood: just then, I was not afraid to die for my boys, to lose my life to protect the rep of our crew, to have Jukkie's back. This was it, the true test of everything the street had taught me. Now I would know the true meaning of loyalty, the true price of respect.

I would stand firm.

'Eediat! What the hell are you thinking, man?'

'What?'

'Stop that blasted stupidness and get the hell out of there – or this beef ain't never gonna end. It ain't worth it. And Misha needs you!'

'I don't know, blud, what about..?'

'Listen, yeah, you're carrying a knife with next man's blood on it. Listen! You hear that siren? It's the 5-O, coming to arrest mans over yet another stabbing. You ain't stupid; you know how they're going on with knives and that these days. Where's Jukkie? You see him hanging around? Nah, mate! What you need to do is get Misha and her girls and get the hell out of there before the 5-0 reach!"

That was just what I needed to hear: a wake-up call. This wasn't my scene any more. This wasn't my war. Man had to get the hell out of there.

Bare people started shouting, cursing, pushing. I squeezed myself against the wall and watched as Trigger and the other RDS mans began brawling with the Larkside boys, just as the bouncers arrived with their walkie-talkies.

All of a sudden, a gunshot went off, then another. The girls all screamed and dived for cover and everyone starting stampeding, rushing for any exit they could find. I grabbed Effie and Victoria, lifted Misha up and charged for the emergency exit that stood at the end of the bar.

The crowd of people that surged behind us made it hard to get the door open but we did and in seconds, we were outside. Victoria and Effie stood gasping for air but I knew that there was no time for that. We had to find a cab and get out of there.

Back Home

DWAYNE

Effie's teeth started chattering on the taxi ride home. Her breath came in short, shallow puffs and, when I touched her hand, it was cold and clammy.

"Effie," said Victoria, shaking her by the shoulder. "Effie, are you all right?"

But Effie didn't say anything. She was just staring, staring, her head lolling against the car seat, her eyes glazed over, her breath puffing, puffing.

"Oh my God, do you think she's in shock? She's not responding to me, Dwayne! Dwayne?"

"You're just gonna make things worse, man! Jam your hype! Calm down... try and talk to her, innit, rub her back an' ting... Oh, yeah, and put her legs up..."

"OK... Thank God we're almost there!"

I stared at the posh houses that lined Victoria's

street. "Which one is your yard?"

"Number 49, the one with the red door."

Next to me, Misha moaned and turned in her seat, bumping her head against the window.

I reached out for her and settled her head against my shoulder, away from the window. I was proper anxious. She had slept all the way home.

"What happened to *her*?" wondered Victoria. "One minute, she's fine and, the next, she's staggering around like a prizewinning drunk... I didn't think anyone could react that badly to champagne..."

I turned to stare at Victoria. What had she just said?

"Wait, when did you lot have champagne? I ordered orange juice for Misha..."

"It was Lawrence... he bought it for us. I remember I saw him handing Effie Misha's glass to give to her."

I felt my nostrils flare as I breathed in deeply, trying to control the rage that was building up inside me. I could feel the pressure building up at the back of my head as it all became clear.

Lockjaw.

Lockjaw had spiked Misha's drink.

He must have known that she was with me.

The psycho bastard.

I looked down at Misha.

'Thank God,' I thought, my blood running cold. 'Thank God what happened happened – or it would have been me taking Lockjaw's life.' I shook my head. No way. I had to stop myself from thinking about it in case I started mashing things up. The taxi stopped.

"OK, Dwayne," said Victoria, "let's get them inside."

Effie stumbled to the front door with Victoria and I carried Misha up the stairs to Vee's room.

"Listen, Vee, call me later, yeah, as soon as Misha wakes up. I need to know that she's OK."

"Sure, no problem..." Then Victoria shivered and wrapped her arms around herself. "Do you think they'll find whoever stabbed Lawrence?"

I looked away. "I don't know, man, depends, innit? No one ain't gonna talk to the police so it could be kinda hard, still... I'm just sorry you guys had to be there when it all happened."

"Well, it's always interesting to see how the other side lives..."

"Nah, I don't want Misha thinking that this is what it's always like, that this is all it's about. I just wanted to share something, my music, with her... but I guess it flopped, innit..."

"Yeah, I guess it did."

We were both quiet.

"You'd better get going. Will you be OK to get home, all the way back to South London?"

"Yeah, I'll just catch the night bus, innit."

"OK, well, watch your back..."

"Yeah, you too. And listen, Vee, look after Misha for me, yeah? And don't send her home until she's feeling better."

"Of course I won't, what do you take me for?" Victoria laughed. "The last thing I want is Counsellor Dina Reynolds looking into my drink and drug habit!"

✿ ✿ ✿

The night air was cold around my ears as I ran down the steps outside Victoria's house. With each step, I could feel the knife banging against my body, heavy inside my jacket pocket. Heavy, stained with blood. A silent witness against me.

I knew what I had to do.

As I walked past the black wheelie bin outside Victoria's house, I carefully pulled out the knife and threw it into the bin.

Gone.

Disappeared.

In a few hours, the rubbish men would come and dump all the black bin bags, full up with all kinds of posh leftovers, into their smelly trucks and drive them away, never to be seen again.

There was no need to tell anyone, no need to bring any trouble home. Jukkie would thank me for getting rid of the evidence.

It was gone now.

My heart lifted as I walked back towards Ladbroke Grove.

But when I turned back to look at the house one last time, I saw the curtains in one of the upstairs windows twitch.

I turned and walked quickly away from that house. I didn't look back again.

The Morning After

MISHA

"Victoria!"

We were woken by a fierce pounding at the door to Victoria's bedroom.

"What the..." Victoria sat bolt upright, her weave sticking out around her face, her eyes smudged black with stale mascara.

But before she could get out of bed, Paul, her elder brother, had crashed her bedroom door open and charged in, wearing just a pair of tracksuit bottoms.

"Get out, Paul!" Victoria screamed. "Or I'm telling Mummy!"

Paul ignored her and pointed his finger in her face. "What have you done with my Nintendo DS?"

"I'm not telling you."

"What?" He grabbed her wrist and dragged her

off her bed and on to the floor. "Oh yes you are! Where is it?"

"I'm not telling you, all right? I told you I'd get you back for breaking my iPod and I did! Now get the hell out of my room!"

"Arghh! You little..!" Paul roared, twisting Victoria's arm. "You'd better get me my DS back, in one piece, in the next hour, d'you hear me? Or you'll regret the day you were born, I swear!"

He shoved her away from him onto the floor and slammed the door behind him, leaving Victoria heaving on the floor and Effie and I staring, hearts beating, mouths dry.

It was a rude awakening.

I let out a shuddering sigh. "Your brothers, Vee, wow..."

"Tell me about it."

"Makes me glad I've only got sisters..." Effie rubbed her eyes and turned over, wincing.

"Ughhh..." Victoria fell back onto her pillows, her hands over her eyes. "Well, that was the night from Hell."

"Oh, God, don't," I giggled, covering my face with the duvet cover. "Don't even go there – I can hardly remember anything. I must have been off my head!

Did I throw up? Make a complete fool of myself? I seriously can't remember anything that happened after Dwayne's performance!" I shook my head, smiling, wondering at my bout of minor amnesia.

The other two looked at me, eyes wide, not saying anything. Then they looked at each other and shifted under the bedclothes.

"What?" I saw the look that passed between them and frowned. "What? Was I really that bad?"

Effie looked away, tears welling in her eyes. Victoria looked searchingly into my face. "Lawrence was stabbed last night, Misha."

"What?" I gasped, gazing at Victoria, uncomprehending. "Vee, what are you talking about?"

"For God's sake, Misha, you can't tell me you don't remember!"

"I don't, Vee, honestly!" I shook my head, my mind clouding, crowded with sounds, feelings, emotions, images that didn't make any sense. "Lawrence... stabbed? By whom? Is he OK? Effie?" I put my hand out to touch Effie's arm. "Did you see it? Was he with you?"

Effie did not look my way. "Yeah," she said shortly, wiping her face. "Yeah, he was with me... Listen,

Vee, I'd really like to get home. I need to be in my own space, clear my head – and find out what happened to Lawrence. We left in such a hurry last night..." She faltered then, twisting the covers between her fingers. "I don't even know whether he's dead or alive."

"Oh my God, Effie, I'm so sorry..." I was distraught. I reached out to hug Effie but she was already up and out of bed, searching through the piles of clothes on the floor for her jeans, looking for her bag.

"Do you think your driver will be able to take me home?"

"Of course, darling, of course. I'll just go and tell Mummy. Why don't you stay and take a shower, have some breakfast?"

But Effie just shook her head. "I just really want to get home, Vee. Sorry..."

"Of course, Effie, it's not a problem – after what you've been through, who can blame you?"

"I'll go home with Effie then, if that's all right." I looked worriedly over at Effie as she got off the bed and started picking her clothes up off the floor.

"Fine," Victoria shrugged, tying the sash of her white silk dressing gown. "I'll go and let him know."

We began to get our things together. But I was

puzzled. The silence between us was so thick, you could have cut it with a knife. I kept glancing at Effie. I expected her to be shocked, scared, traumatised – I mean, how often do you see your boyfriend get stabbed right in front of you? But what I didn't understand was this, the cold shoulder. It was as if Effie couldn't even bear to look at me.

"Effie," I said tentatively, "have I done something wrong? Did something happen last night, while I was out of it?"

Effie sighed as she turned away and pulled on her leather jacket. "No, Misha," she said pointedly, "*you* did nothing wrong. Let's just say that some people are not what they seem..."

"Some people? Who, Effie? What are you talking about?" I reached out to grab Effie by her sleeve. "Effie, tell me what's going on!"

Effie jerked her arm away and spun round to look me in the eye. "It was Dwayne, Misha!" she said, her lip curling, tears standing in her eyes. "Dwayne was the one who stabbed Lawrence."

I stepped backwards, reeling, as if she had slapped me in the face. "No, Effie..." I breathed. "Y-you you've got it wrong," I stammered, shaking my head. "D-Dwayne, he would never..."

"He would never *what*, Misha?" Effie's voice had a hardened edge to it and she glared at me with a new fierceness. "He would never what? You don't honestly think you know anything about him, do you? After what we saw last night?"

"So he's from a rough side of town... fair enough. That doesn't mean that he would ever stab anyone, or hurt anyone!"

Then Effie came up close to me, so close that I could see the tiny hairs of her eyebrows beginning to grow back, the clumps of dried mascara that still clung to her lashes, the red lines that criss-crossed her eyeballs.

"I saw him, Misha," she hissed. "I saw him with the knife!"

I froze.

"Yes, that's right, your Romeo was carrying a knife when we left the club and, after he dropped us home, I saw him throw it into the bin outside this house!"

"I don't believe you..." I whispered. "No... no way."

"I'm telling you, I saw him with my own eyes, Misha! Wake up! This isn't some fantasy! Lawrence was stabbed last night. He was bleeding all over the place. Look!" And she snatched my red dress from the floor and held up the bloodstain for me to see.

"That is Lawrence's *blood*! He could be dead right now, for all we know!"

Shock seeped through my brain, rendering me speechless, unseeing. I sank to a crouch on the floor and my eyes glazed over with tears as I stared at the red dress with the dark patch of blood on the left side. Lawrence's blood. Dwayne? No, it was too hard to get to grips with. There had to have been some mistake.

"Let's find the knife then," I whispered suddenly, looking up at Effie. "You said he put it in the bin outside? Well, let's go and get it."

In moments, I was downstairs, outside the front door, down the stone steps, looking around for the wheelie bin. I saw it facing the pavement and dashed towards it, wrenching the lid open.

Empty.

I groaned. The rubbish collectors had been and gone.

Now there was only one way to find out the truth.

"Come on, Effie," I muttered as I started up the stairs again. "Let's get our stuff and see where that driver is; I've got to pay someone a visit."

Judgement Day

DWAYNE

I was proper cussing myself all the way home.

'I should have listened to Tony, man. I should have stayed away. What kind of a Muslim goes raving anyway? I should never have taken Misha there – just look at what almost happened to her! After I promised to look after her and ting.' I shook my head. 'Now the whole situation is mash-up. Larkside man will be on our case again – and they saw me! They saw me with Trigger and Jukkie! Ain't no way I'm going to be able to stay out of the beef now. And what about Lockjaw? What if he doesn't make it? And who was behind the curtain at Vic's house? What did they see?'

Too many questions. Just too many questions.

I stayed off school and cotched at Tony's. I couldn't risk bumping into Leon or any of those boys. The truth was, I didn't know how the hell I was going to leave my estate again, not without packing. Not without something to protect myself. I had never been one of dem Youngers who liked to shoot people up, just for the fun of it, just to make a point. For me, it was about the Ps at the end of the day. And if I could make money without stepping on any toes, I was happy.

Tony had offered me a gun ages ago but times had changed. No way Tony would give me a piece now. He'd moved past that mentality, big time.

"You need to pray, bro," he kept saying. "You did wrong. You need to pray for forgiveness and start again. While you're still alive, there's always a way to start again."

I looked at him like he was crazy. Did he really think that praying was going to solve my problems? I needed a solution. I needed a miracle.

'Ain't that what God does?'

'What's that?'

'Work miracles?'

'Yeah, I guess so...'

'Then you best start praying for a miracle then, innit?'

✧ ✧ ✧

I went outside that afternoon. I wore an old hoodie

that I hadn't worn for time and pulled the hood right up. I wore a pair of old trainers and took a bag with me, just in case. I needed to buy some credit from the shop coz I needed to speak to Misha. Victoria had already told me that she had woken up feeling better but I still hadn't had the chance to call her and hear her voice.

It had started raining a short while before and the estate was deserted. I looked this way and that, trying to spot a car driving past too slowly, a guy on a bike, anything suspicious.

But it all seemed clear.

"Yo, rudeboy!"

I jumped and instinctively whirled round, my guard up, in case of any trouble. Then I relaxed.

It was Jukkie.

Jukkie looked proper mash-up, like he hadn't slept for days. His clothes were crumpled and his skin was ashy. And his eyes were red raw, as if he'd been smoking too much skunk.

"Jukkie, man!" My heart began to knock violently against my ribcage. "You tryin' to give man a heart attack or somethin'?" My mind flooded with images of the stabbing on Friday night, the feel of the bloodied knife, heavy, on the inside of my jacket. "What's goin' on? Where've you been? I kept tryin' to call you..."

"Yeah, I know, I had to keep my head down, innit. Lay low for a while." He slung his arm over my shoulder and began bopping away from the main road, his head low, his eyes flicking from side to side.

"Where did you go, man?" I let Jukkie steer me past the row of bins, down a narrow alleyway between the flats.

"After I left the club, I came home to check on my mum, tidy up and that." Jukkie's voice was hoarse. "Then I went up to Stonebridge to stay over at Candice's place. Thought it'd be better to stay out of the area."

We were almost at Jukkie's building, via the back route we'd always used as kids. We had shared the loot from our first shoplifting trip here. I had smoked my first joint beside these bins. But today there was no one here. The tower blocks that rose on either side blocked out the sun and the shadows were chilly.

"Why d'you come back, blud? Don't you think it'd better if you stayed up in North-West?" I tried to keep my tone light although my teeth were chattering.

"Yeah, yeah, I'm going back, innit; I just need to check on my mum. You know she's in a bad way. Plus I wanted to chat to you, bruv..." Jukkie stopped

342

walking, glanced over his shoulder then turned to look me in the face.

"Yeah? What about?"

"My knife, man. I need it back, to get rid of it, y'get me?"

"Nah, man, I took care of it, don't worry."

Jukkie eyed me up. "What d'you mean? Where is it?"

"I got rid of it, innit? Don't worry, the police will never find it."

"You sure?" Jukkie sounded doubtful. "Did you throw it in the canal or something?"

'That's what you should have done, man, not put it in the dustbin!'

"Nah, man, I got rid of it – don't worry! I took care of it, yeah?"

"All right, safe, man." At last, I could see him start to relax. He sounded relieved. "Thanks, bro. I owe you one."

"Nah, don't worry about it, blud. That's what we do, standard."

"Yeah, you're my bredren still, even though you've been going on like a bloodclart with this Islam ting."

We reached the entrance to Jukkie's building.

"Listen, yeah," said Jukkie, punching in the code

that opened the heavy steel door to the main entrance. "I need you to look after my mum while I'm in North West. Tony's planning to move in with his girl – his wife – but I may not be able to keep comin' down like this. I heard that Lockjaw's peeps know it was me who shanked him..." Jukkie chewed his lower lip and his eyes darted around as we waited for the lift to come down from the fifth floor. His voice dropped: "Spoonz said he heard that Loc's in intensive care, that he might not make it..."

And I caught the flicker of fear in Jukkie's eyes. For all his big-man talk, even Jukkie wasn't ready to be a murderer at seventeen. But the flicker disappeared when Jukkie scowled and his face closed up. "Serve him right, still!" he whispered fiercely. When we got into the lift, Jukkie screwed up his face and spat into the corner. "This lift stinks, man!"

I didn't say nothing but looked up at the flickering light on the ceiling of the lift. Something wasn't right. I felt proper didgy – there was something strange in the air of that lift, a bad feeling I couldn't name. Something was wrong, I could feel it.

When at last the lift reached the fifth floor, Jukkie flipped his hood back and stepped towards the doors as they slid open. But just as he was about to step out,

I reached over and grabbed his arm with a grip like iron. Jukkie frowned at me and was about to shake my hand off when I put my finger up and made a sign for Jukkie to stop and listen.

There were voices down the corridor.

White people's voices.

"Good afternoon, ma'am. We're here to see Marvin Johnson... we have a few questions we'd like to ask him..."

5-0.

"Oh, sh..."

Jukkie swore under his breath and I turned to press the keys to close the door of the lift, to get to the ground floor, to get the hell out of there, as silently as possible. My fingers pressed the sticky buttons and the door began to close, scraping as it went.

"Oi!" we could hear the officers shout out just as the doors were closing. "Who's there?"

In a panic, Jukkie began to press the button that closed the doors, again and again, trying to make them close faster, pure terror in his eyes.

I felt sweat spring up on my forehead, as cold and slick as the fear that gripped my insides. What had happened? How had they known to come looking for Jukkie?

'Oh my days, don't tell me they found the knife!'

The lift doors had almost shut when we saw the end of a police baton poke through the gap, banging, banging, from side to side, trying to wedge the door open. Instinctively, we both began to kick at the baton, trying to push it back out again, shouting, the sweat trickling down our backs.

But we were too late. With the baton wedging the doors apart, the policewoman who was holding it was able to get the doors to slide open again. When the doors opened, we both flew out, ready to battle. Jukkie swung his fist and caught the stocky policewoman on the side of her jaw. Then I pushed her and she crashed back against the railings and crumpled to the floor.

It took the other officers a couple of moments to realise what was happening – "That's him there!" – and they began to run towards us down the corridor, their hands to their sides. I ran toward the fire escape.

'Just get out of the building, man! Once you're out of here, you're laughing – the estate's too big and there are 'nuff places to hide and ting. And, even if someone sees you, ain't no one gonna tell the police nuffin'!'

'What about Jukkie?'

'Jukkie's coming, man! He's a big boy; he can handle himself!'

But Jukkie couldn't, not this time. The police got him before he could reach the door and, when I looked back to see whether he was behind me, I saw my childhood friend, the badman, the protector, the avenger, on his belly, his face pressed into the grimy floor, a red-faced policeman straddling his back, putting cuffs on him. His eyes were squeezed shut and I knew, like I knew my own brother, like I knew my own *name*, that he was struggling not to cry.

✧ ✧ ✧

It took them a bit longer to catch me. I made it out of the building and was about to gap it through the alleyway when I saw her.

She had just gotten off the bus. She raised her hand to wave at me – then I heard the police siren and the car swung up on to the grass verge in front of me. I dodged madly, turning to run the other way, but I caught my foot in a hole on the lawn and went down.

A couple of seconds later, they had the dogs on me, cuffs, everything.

"Misha!" I shouted out to her as they pushed me to the police car. "Don't worry! It's all a mistake! I'll bell you, yeah?"

But she didn't say anything.

We drove back out of the estate in a madness of police sirens. But I hardly noticed. All I could see was Misha's face, all crumpled, her hand over her mouth, crying as she saw Dwayne Kingston, her badboy lover, get arrested for the first time.

'Damn, you made her cry again.'

'I beg you SHUT UP, blud.'

'I'm just sayin'...'

Retribution

MISHA

Every time I closed my eyes, I saw Dwayne on the floor, the police dogs slobbering all over him, the officers slapping the handcuffs on his wrists. And his voice, his voice, calling to me: 'It's not what it looks like! I'm innocent! Please, Misha, please believe me!'

I left the Saints Hill estate in tears. I wandered blindly, numb, not knowing where to go, what to think, what to feel. The only possible explanation for what I had seen was that Effie was right.

Dwayne had stabbed Lawrence, and the police had caught him.

But, at the same time, it just didn't make any sense at all. Why? How? Was Dwayne really capable of that? Didn't I know him at all?

I found myself walking in a daze to Gran's house.

When she saw me at the door, my eyes red, my face wet with tears, shivering, she started asking a million questions. But I shook my head – "Later, Gran, please. I just need a moment... just a moment. Can I come in?"

So she opened the door and let me through to lie on her bed while she made me a cup of tea.

"I have a friend visiting, Misha," she said gently. "You don't have to come through until you feel up to it." Gran left me alone with my thoughts, thoughts that swirled in and out of the confused fog of my mind.

How could I have misjudged Dwayne so badly? How could he have fooled me all this time? I had suspected that there was more to him than he let on, but I would never have pictured him as someone capable of attempting to take a life, never. If he *had* been capable of such heartlessness, hadn't he changed? Hadn't he grown beyond that in the time we had been together? Was his new religion just a label? What was the point of all that talk about Islam if he was still the same as Jukkie and the other boys on his estate: violent, mindless, heartless?

Eventually, I found that I had no more tears. My heart was wrung dry. I came out of Gran's room just as her guest was leaving. The visitor, a middle-aged

Jamaican woman wearing a neat headwrap, was speaking on her mobile phone, worry written all over her face.

"Dwayne?" she said, frowning. "Are you sure about that, Mrs Kingston?" The person on the other end of the line was shrieking and Gran's visitor tried to calm her down. "There must be an explanation, love, just calm down, please. I am in Brixton, I'll be right over..." She turned to say goodbye to Gran and saw me standing there, my face full of questions.

"D-do you know Dwayne?" I asked, my voice scraping against my throat.

"Yes," she replied. "Yes, I do. He's a student at my school. Seems to have gotten himself into some trouble. His mother is in a bad way – I'm going over there now. And you are...?"

"A-a friend of his..." My voice faltered and I blinked away the tears that were threatening to fall.

She looked at me sympathetically. "You're Lorna's granddaughter Misha, aren't you? She's told me so much about you... and Dwayne. You sound like a smart girl, one who's going places. Dwayne is a lovely boy – bright in so many ways – but... don't let him come between you and your future. That's my sincere advice to you, woman to woman."

She smiled sadly and stepped out of the front door.

I didn't even try to stop the tears this time.

DWAYNE

They took us to Brixton Police Station to book us. The knife that had been turned in 'by a member of the public' had Jukkie's prints all over it.

"You're going down, sonny," said the officer in charge, sounding well pleased with himself. "We don't even need no witnesses now."

There had been a second set of prints on the knife and, when the police took my fingerprints, they realised that they were mine.

So, not only had I been arrested for the first time but, after years of being careful, I was being charged too.

And it wasn't grievous bodily harm, like I expected it to be. It was first degree murder.

Lockjaw had died while in hospital.

In the eyes of the law, Marvin 'Jukkie' Johnson was a murderer. And I was an accessory.

I almost cried, right there in front of the police officers. Jukkie, on the other hand, just scowled at them all and said, 'No comment' to everything they asked. I couldn't believe he could be so calm. Didn't he care that he was about to be sent down, possibly for a very long time?

Alone in the cell with him, I could hardly look at him. This was his fault, y'get me. I had no business here. But man didn't seem to care. He never said sorry or nothing. He was just lying on that filthy prison bed where a thousand murderers, rapists and junkies had been before him, his feet against the wall, spitting some bars about jukking the police.

"Yo, I beg you shut up, man!" I couldn't stand to hear his voice. I needed time to think, to get my head together. I needed to wash myself, I needed to pray.

"What's the matter with you, man?" he asked, turning to scowl at me. "You look proper scared, bruv!" And he threw the pillow at me.

I ducked and swore at him, disgusted by the musty smell of the prison pillowcase. "Leave off, man, before I bang you!" He couldn't fool me – I had seen his face when the 5-0 had him on the floor. But if there was one thing Jukkie could do well, it was put on a front.

Jukkie just smirked and walked over to the little window and began rapping that gangster anthem, Tupac's *'Me against the world'*. I wanted to smash his face in. Man thought he was some kind of hero!

The officer banged on the door with his baton. "All right, keep it down in there!"

But Jukkie just carried on, daring the officer to do something about it.

I'd had enough. I jumped up and ran at him and, with all my strength, slammed him up against the wall. He struggled, but I kept my arm against his throat.

"I said 'shut up'!"

He choked and wheezed, trying to move my arm, but I held it there until I could feel that his blood was flowing a little cooler. Then I grabbed him by the collar and threw him crashing against the bed. He looked up at me, all wounded, feeling the side of his mouth, tasting blood.

"What's up with you, man?" he hissed, his eyes narrow. "You're acting like a chief! So what if we go jail? So what? 'Nuff things we can learn in jail, innit? It's like school for thugs like us. By the time we come out, we'll be older, harder, smarter and everyone will know our names. We'll be so well-connected we'll be ready to go out there and make some *real* dough, y'get me! We'll be legends, bruv, *trust*!"

I looked down at him and shook my head. For the first time, I could honestly say that I pitied Jukkie. I really did.

"Is that what you're so hyped about, Jukkie? Goin' jail and coming out a legend? To go back out on road again?"

"Of course, man! What else would I be thinking about? Dem Larkside man know that we don't mess – I took out their main nigga, in front of everyone, blud! People are gonna be talking about that, Dee, ya dun know!"

I wiped my face with my hand. I was sweating. Jukkie really didn't get it, did he?

"Jukkie, you *killed* a man, blud. You took his life. And you're gonna go jail somewhere mad far like Wales or something where they'll tell you when to eat, sleep, go to the toilet. How do you know Larkside ain't gonna send someone to merk you in jail, huh? You've got no idea, blud. Prison ain't no joke ting."

"But we'll be together, innit? We're bredren. You got my back, I got yours. We're gonna run whatever place they send us cos we're RDS mans and we roll like that: thugs for life, innit?"

I kept quiet for a minute, thinking about what Jukkie was saying, how he thought this was gonna end. I had to break it to him. I had to tell him the truth, no matter how much it hurt him, no matter how much he cussed me. I had to let him know.

"I ain't on that no more, Jukkie. Allow the crew, allow the drugs, allow the money, allow the thug life. I'm out."

"What you sayin', blud?"

"You heard me, Juks. I'm out for good. I've got my Islam to keep me straight, y'get me. And I've got my future. I can't be messing around with this crap no more. It's time mans wised up."

Jukkie sneered at me: "I knew you'd gone soft, bro. I just knew it. From when you started seein' that posh gash and then hangin' with Tony, I could see you was turnin' into a punk."

"It ain't called goin' soft, Jukkie, it's called growin' up. It's called wakin' up. This life ain't no joke, Jukkie, it's the real deal. The one chance you get before you're judged with everyone else. D'you really think that there ain't nothin' more to life than this?" I looked around the cell, my face all twist-up. "Than *this*?"

"But it ain't forever, man! We'll be out of here in no time..."

"Jukkie! Don't you get it? A few years of my life is too long! I don't want the street life! I want to grow, y'get me, I want to see new things, I want to to be able to hold my head up, *be somebody*." My thoughts turned to Brother Malcolm. "I wanna rewrite the

script, Jukkie. I want more than this, so much more..."
And tears stung my eyes as I thought of Misha and
the sight of her face as she watched me being dragged
to the police car. My sweetness. True say, for all the
sweetness she had given me, I had only given her
bitterness in return.

Jukkie stared at me. I had never spoken to him like
that before. I know he wanted to sneer, to cuss me
out, to make me feel small – but there was no Trigger
around to impress, just him and me in a stinking
jail cell.

When he finally spoke, he wasn't high like before.
I could even hear fear in his voice when he said, "But
you'll cover for me with the knife, innit? If I say you
did it, and you say I did it, they won't be able to pin
either of us down. We'll both walk free after a few
years inside..."

A few years inside? Was he serious? But then
I knew that he was serious. This life was all he knew,
all he wanted to know. It made me even sadder to say
what I knew I had to say.

"I ain't lyin' to them, Jukkie." The cell was suddenly
as silent as a morgue. "I'm done with all that. I ain't
takin' the fall for you."

MISHA

Of course, Gran told Mum who told Dad who told Leona. They could have had a go – they had every reason to say 'I told you so' but, mercifully, they didn't. They gave me space to grieve and come to terms with what had happened.

Those days after the arrest were days of tears, nightmares and waiting, waiting for some relief. I blamed myself; I pitied myself; I tried to undo the knot of love that I still held in my heart, heavy as a stone. But, try as I might, I couldn't. I wanted to hate him, I really did. But I just couldn't. Which made my tears all the more bitter. For what is the use in loving someone you don't even really know?

Then, one day, out of the blue, Dwayne's Muslim friend Tony turned up outside my school. I was shocked to see him standing there, a strange figure in his beard and Muslim clothing, standing by the side of the leafy street in Dulwich. I hardly recognised him from that night at the party where I first met Dwayne, all those months ago, when he'd been surrounded by girls, pouring champagne for everyone. He said he needed to talk to me, to explain what had happened at Club Loco.

"I don't want to hear any more lies," I said coldly, walking away from him. "I'm done with the lies."

"Please, Misha, I've known Dwayne since he was in nursery school – he's like a little brother to me. I – I know how he feels about you and I think you deserve to hear the truth, still..."

I stopped walking and listened, my arms crossed over my chest.

"Misha, there are some things you need to know about Dwayne, some things he ain't told you. He grew up on the streets, like we all did, addicted to the hustle. He was part of my crew, Rule Da Streets, RDS... he had been since he was 11 years old."

"He was part of a *gang*?"

"We were all part of a gang, Misha, that's just how it works where we come from. Everyone is in a crew – or wants to be in one. The crew is your family, your protection, your identity. RDS was Dwayne's family and I was his big brother."

"And what exactly did you do with your 'crew'?"

Tony bowed his head and looked away for a minute. When he spoke, his voice was low. "'Nuff stuff, Misha, stuff you wouldn't want to know about. Dwayne never wanted you to know. He wanted to keep you away from that side of his life. He knew that you wouldn't have it..."

"You're damn right I wouldn't..." I said through gritted teeth. Cheated. That was how I felt. Betrayed. How come Dwayne had never told me about any of this? But I already knew the answer: if I had known that he was really one of those people, I would never have given him the time of day. Mum had done her job well with me.

"Dwayne will probably kill me for telling you all this – he would have wanted to tell you himself. But I figured you probably wouldn't give him the chance – unless you knew how much he's changed because of you..."

"What do you mean, 'because of me'?"

"He started changing when he met you, Misha. You made him start to see things differently, y'understand? You opened his eyes to how things could be different. He started making an effort with school, for a start. Then, *alhamdulillah*, he became interested in Islam. To tell you the truth, I always loved Dee – he felt like my real younger brother. To have him taste some of what I experienced when I became Muslim – the peace, the security, the sense of purpose – was like a dream come true."

I started fidgeting. I didn't want Tony to think

he could start lecturing me on the benefits of Islam –
if Islam was so great, why was Dwayne in a jail cell
with a prison sentence hanging over him? "So you're
to blame for him becoming Muslim, are you?"

"Misha, I schooled Dwayne in the ways of the
streets. How could I not show him the way out that
I had found?"

"But why such a drastic move? Why change your
religion? Why let this new craze come between *us*?
I was there from the beginning – I would have helped
him..." I felt the ache in my heart start to throb and I
realised something I had not wanted to admit: I was
jealous of Dwayne's Muslim faith. I saw it as a rival,
an obstacle, something I couldn't share.

"Misha, sometimes man just needs that extra
support, that extra guidance. Yeah, true say you
showed him a new way to think about life, new goals
and that. But how was he supposed to reach them?
He never had what you had..." And he looked up at
the school gates and beyond them – to the world of
privilege and opportunity that I had long taken for
granted.

"Anyway, when Dwayne became Muslim, he
found an anchor. The deen was what gave him the
strength to get clean, to stop rolling with the mans.

Well, Jukkie didn't like that. He blamed you and me for taking Dwayne away from the RDS, away from him. But I want you to know what happened this weekend. You need to know the truth. It all kicked off when Jukkie found out that Lockjaw and his crew had drugged his girlfriend and raped her – and made some mad video and put it out on the Internet."

I shuddered with revulsion, thinking of my encounter with Jukkie on Dwayne's estate.

"But it didn't end there: the Larkside mans came into my yard and roughed up my mum. Jukkie couldn't take it. He lost his mind, wanted to smash everyone up. He'd stopped listening to me long ago – but Trigger, who took over as head of the RDS, told him how he could pay Lockjaw – Lawrence – back. That's how he ended up at Club Loco with a knife. He'd intended to do Lockjaw, right there in front of his crew. But once he'd stabbed him, he gave the knife to Dwayne to hold. The poor guy didn't know what to do – you know how he hates knives, innit. So he dashed the knife after he dropped you at your friend's house in West London. But someone found it and took it into the police station. Their prints were on it – the rest, you know..."

I took a deep shuddering breath. It all made

362

so much sense. But did I dare believe it?

"He asked you to come and see him at Feltham. What should I tell him?"

I gave Tony the only answer I could. "I don't know, Tony," I said. "I just don't know."

✧ ✧ ✧

But the next weekend, I rode the bus to Brixton and took a cab up to Feltham. My insides shrank when I thought about Dwayne in that awful place. Ever since the arrest, I had had nightmares of him in jail, the police beating him, being assaulted by the other inmates. I hoped that they were keeping him with other young offenders. At least that way, he would be safe from the influence of the older prisoners.

DWAYNE

When I saw Misha walk into the visitor's room, it felt like the first time I had breathed since they took me into custody. She just looked so beautiful to me, it was as if someone had opened the curtains and flung open the window: a breath of fresh air, y'get me. My heart, my mind, my whole body ached to be with her again. But then I saw the pain and confusion in her eyes and stopped myself.

'Fall back, blud. You know what you have to do.'

I got up to hug her but the officer rapped his baton on the table and barked, "No contact!"

We sat down and, for a while, we didn't know what to say to each other. There was too much to say, too much that had been left unsaid.

I was the first to speak. "Did Tony come and see you?" I wanted to know.

Misha nodded.

"So you know the full story?" I looked into her eyes for a sign that she believed what Tony had told her, that she forgave me, that she still... that she still cared.

She nodded again. "Are they treating you all right in here, Dee?" she asked, keeping her voice low. "What are the charges?"

I took a deep breath. "Well, you know Lockjaw's dead, innit. So they've got Jukkie up for first degree murder. They wanted to charge me as an accessory but my lawyers are arguing that I'm a minor – and that I don't have a previous record."

"So you might get off?"

"Yeah, maybe with a few months in a detention centre or something. Depends on the judge, innit." I wanted to sound positive, upbeat, but true say, I felt shame. To see my beautiful Misha, my sweetness, in this awful place, because of me, it just broke my heart all over again. All I had ever wanted to do was put a smile on her face. Damn. I'd flopped it. Big time.

I could see that she was trying hard to be brave, not to stare at the other kids in there, with their hoodies and tattooes and hard, hard faces.

'She's afraid you're going to become like them, Dee. That you already are like them...'

I took a deep breath. I had to get it over with before I bottled it completely. "Listen, Misha, I need to tell you something."

She looked up at me then, as if to say, 'Tell me something good, Dee, anything to make all this go away.'

"Misha, the first thing I want to say is that I love you, girl. I know I ain't said it before, not properly, but I have loved you since that first day in Battersea Park. You are the most amazing girl I have ever met in my life, Misha, I swear down. I don't even know how I ever got lucky enough to be with you...." Tears welled up in my eyes then. I couldn't even stop them. I swallowed hard. "I know I hurt you, Misha. I know I let you down. And I know I betrayed your trust. And I'm sorry. It breaks my heart to see you in this place. You shouldn't be here – you deserve better than this. Better than me..."

Tears were falling down her cheeks as I reached out to hold her hand. At that stage, I didn't even care what the officer said or did. I squeezed her hand, blinking back tears, trying to keep my voice from shaking.

"I've thought about this every day since I came here. I've prayed on it, five times a day, and in the middle of the night. So I know this is the right thing to do. Misha, baby, I want you to leave this place and forget all about me. "

For a moment, she just stared at me, totally speechless.

"That's right, girl," I whispered. "Just turn around and walk away."

Then she found her voice. "What are you saying, Dwayne?"

"You deserve the future you've always wanted for yourself, Misha. You don't need a loser like me holdin' you back. So, even though it's tearin' me up inside, I know I have to let you go. I can't keep goin' on selfish, y'get me. I have to think about what's best for you, innit."

I wiped my eyes and smiled. "Just know that, wherever you go in life, there's a badman who loves you more than you'll ever know." And I busted a few of the lines I had made up, just for her, a lifetime ago in Battersea Park: the lines about the chocolate-fudge-coloured sweetness and the mean left hook.

Then she really started crying, burying her face in her hands. I knew what she was feeling, coz I was feeling it myself.

MISHA

I hid my face in my hands and sobbed. How could a heart break so many times? Why did it feel like the whole world was pressing down on me, squeezing the life out of me? Would I keep quiet and accept the open door, the way out he had offered me? Or would I stay and fight it out, against all the odds? Who did I love more: him or me? And what did that love mean? I had always heard that love hurt, that true love requires sacrifice – but did that mean sacrificing myself, my family, my future, too?

I thought of everything that had happened since the first day I met Dwayne Kingston: the incredible highs, the awful lows, the tears, the laughter. What did it all mean? What was the purpose of it all?

And then, as if he had been reading my mind,

Dwayne answered my question. "It was all written, Misha: meant to be. Without you, I wouldn't have found this path I'm on now. I would never have seen what I was capable of. You believed in me from the start, even when you had no reason to. Now I believe in me too. And I believe in you. So I want you to fly, Misha-girl, fly like a butterfly away from anythin' that could hold you back. Some bredder – I bet you know his name – once said, 'If you love someone, set them free. If they return, they were always yours. If they don't they were never yours to begin with.' I feel that. I do."

I didn't try to hide the tears.

And then he stood up, a soft, soft look on his face. And I knew then that he really did love me, possibly more than he had ever loved anyone in his life. And he was letting me go.

He touched his fingers to his lips and whispered, "A Muslim man will only ever kiss the woman he's married to. So this will have to do for now, y'get me." And he blew that kiss towards me, blinking to hold back the tears that had welled up in his eyes.

And then he walked away.

DWAYNE

How can I explain how I felt, walking away from Misha on that cloudy day in Feltham? I felt like the world's biggest loser – and the biggest winner at the same time. I felt empty but full, so full that I wanted to put my head to the ground, right there. Finally, man had come correct. I had done the right thing. And even though it burned me up inside, I knew that the verse was true: 'With hardship comes ease, with every hardship comes ease.'

I thought of that verse again, weeks later, after the court hearings, the detention, the warnings, when I went with Ms Walker to the small patch of green near Angell Town estate. The railings that surrounded it were rusty. Mash-up bunches of flowers were tied to the bars. We had bought fresh flowers from the Tesco Express down the road.

"This is where he was killed," whispered Ms Walker, pointing to the spot where the flowers and cards clung to the iron bars. "Right here."

I knelt down with Ms Walker as she tied our flowers to the railings, carefully taking down some of the older, more raggedy ones. There were so many of these shrines, dotted all around South London and anywhere else where there were angry mans with chips on their shoulders and knives and guns in their back pockets. I looked up at the yellow brick of the Angell Town estate where the Peel Dem Crew had run tings for as long as I could remember.

They had changed their name now. They weren't the Peel Dem Crew anymore – now the PDC stood for Pray Days Change. They were trying to straighten up: some of them had become Muslim, others were trying to make money from music instead of drugs.

"Pray days change, Miss," I said, looking over at the legendary estate. "Pray days change."

The wind blew some rain towards us. Ms Walker opened her umbrella. Some leaves were blown against the railings and stuck there for a few moments.

Then another gust of wind blew and the leaves escaped the railings and were flying free, swirling further and further away from the iron bars, from the estate, from the shrines to dead boys and girls killed for no good reason.

Free at last, y'get me.

Just like Misha.

And just like me.

Acknowledgements

My sincere thanks to all who helped shape this book:
my husband, the ex-badman; Aaminah, Rahma,
Humayrah, Jannah and Yaseen of Deeper Readers;
Eesa Walker, Ismael Lea South,
Abu Bakr of Roadside2Islam,
Rachel Lewis, Ngozi Fulani and Indigo Williams.
And Harry Hasek and Gail Lynch.

Na'ima B. Robert was born in Leeds, grew up
in Zimbabwe and attended Queen Mary & Westfield
College in London, where she was introduced to
Black British culture and served as African Caribbean
Society president. She began writing children's books
when her first child was a toddler.

Black Sheep was inspired by her experiences of
living in Brixton as a new Muslim in the early 2000s.
Her other novels for teenagers include
From Somalia, with love, *Boy vs. Girl*
and *Far from Home*.

Naima was a finalist for Published Writer of the Year
at the Brit Writers Awards 2012

from
Somalia,
with love

Na'ima B. Robert

My name is Safia Dirie. My family has always been
my mum, Hoyo, and my two older brothers, Ahmed
and Abdullahi. I don't really remember Somalia –
I'm an East London girl. But now Abo, my father,
is coming to live with us, after twelve long years.
How am I going to cope?

Safia knows that there will be changes ahead
but nothing has prepared her for the reality of
dealing with Abo's cultural expectations,
her favourite brother Ahmed's wild ways, and the
temptation of her cousin Firdous' party-girl lifestyle.
Safia must come to terms with who she is – as a
Muslim, as a teenager, as a poet, as a friend, but most
of all, as a daughter to a father she has never known.
Safia must find her own place in the world,
so both father and daughter can start to build
the relationship they long for.

From Somalia, with Love is one girl's quest to
discover who she is – a story rooted in Somali
and Muslim life that will strike a chord with
young people everywhere.

"Warm, engaging and intensely thought-provoking"
Carousel

Boy vs. Girl

Can a sister
save her brother,
or will he draw them
both into danger?

Na'ima B. Robert

Farhana swallowed and reached for the hijab. But then she saw with absolute clarity the weird looks from the other girls at school, and the smirks from the guys. Did she dare? And then there was Malik... What should she do about him?

Faraz was thinking about Skrooz and the lads. Soon, he would finally have the respect of the other kids at school. But at what price? He heard Skrooz's voice, as sharp as a switchblade: "This thing is powerful, blud. But y'know, you have to earn it, see? Just a few more little errands for me..."

They're twins, born 6 minutes apart Both are in turmoil and both have life-changing choices to make, against the peaceful backdrop of Ramadan.

Do Farhana and Faraz have enough courage to do the right thing? And can they help each other – or will one of them draw the other towards catastrophe?

"A fantastic read" – MsLexia

FAR FROM HOME

HOME

Torn apart
by war,
thrown together
by fate

———

Na'ima B
Robert

Katie and Tariro are worlds apart but their lives are linked by a terrible secret, gradually revealed in this compelling story of two girls grappling with the complexities of adolescence, family and a painful colonial legacy.

14-year-old Tariro loves her ancestral home, the baobab tree she was born beneath, her loving family – and brave, handsome Nhamo. She couldn't be happier. But then the white settlers arrive and everything changes – suddenly, violently and tragically.

Forty years later, 14-year-old Katie loves her doting father, her exclusive boarding school and her farm with its baobab tree in rural Zimbabwe. Life is great. Until the family are forced to leave everything and escape to cold, rainy London

Atmospheric, gripping and epic in scope, *Far From Home* brings the turbulent history of Zimbabwe to vivid, tangible life.

Winner of the Muslim Writers Awards 2011: Published Children's Book
"A beautifully written, emotionally powerful story" – School Librarian